Wreck My Plans

By Jillian Meadows

Wreck My Plans
Give Me Butterflies

Wreck My Plans

Plans

A Novel

JILLIAN MEADOWS

AVON

An Imprint of HarperCollins*Publishers*

WRECK MY PLANS. Copyright © 2023 by Jillian Meadows. Excerpt from GIVE ME BUTTERFLIES © 2023 by Jillian Meadows. Bonus epilogue copyright © 2024 by Jillian Meadows. All rights reserved. Printed in the United States of America. No part of this book may be used or reproduced in any manner whatsoever without written permission except in the case of brief quotations embodied in critical articles and reviews. For information, address HarperCollins Publishers, 195 Broadway, New York, NY 10007.

HarperCollins books may be purchased for educational, business, or sales promotional use. For information, please email the Special Markets Department at SPsales@harpercollins.com.

Originally published as *Wreck My Plans* in the United States by Jillian Meadows in 2023.

FIRST AVON TRADE EDITION PUBLISHED 2024.

Interior text design by Diahann Sturge-Campbell
Christmas ornaments © Katy's Dream/Stock.Adobe.com

Library of Congress Cataloging-in-Publication Data has been applied for.

ISBN 978-0-06-341612-3

24 25 26 27 28 LBC 5 4 3 2 1

To the ones who are still finding themselves.
It's okay to not have a plan yet, I promise.

Dear Reader

Wreck My Plans is intended for adult readers (18 & older), as it contains explicit language and on-page sexual content.

While I wrote this book intending to make you smile, there are a few subjects addressed in it that may be upsetting for some readers.

- Brief mentions of parental abandonment and life in foster care
- Reference to past depression and thoughts of self-harm
- Brief mentions of alcohol and drugs

If any of these topics are difficult for you to read about, please protect your heart. I hope I have portrayed them with the care they deserve, but your mental health is important to me, and I completely understand if you cannot read about these subjects.

Wreck My Plans

Chapter 1

Lena

*C*leaning puke off my new Christmas pajamas just isn't a part of my journey this year," I inform Millie as my tires screech on the pavement, trying to gain traction on the hill up to my mom's house.

"But if you come back here, we could be sick in a blanket fort together." My best friend's voice is laced with disappointment as it echoes through the car speakers. "We can hide in there and rewatch *Bridgerton* while Finn plays nurse for us."

"Mmm, being waited on by your boyfriend does sound tempting. Is he going to dress up? I might be willing to risk a stomach bug for that."

This was going to be the first year I spent the week of Christmas away from my family. *Ever.* But my plan to stay in Wilhelmina with Millie and her new family imploded this morning when Finn's niece, Eloise, threw up all over their game of Uno.

"I'll get online right now and order a costume as a last-minute gift," Millie says. "Think they make sexy nurse outfits big enough to fit him?"

Our combined laughter fills the car as I reach my mom's two-story cabin and park behind her SUV. "He's going to hate me for giving you this idea. I'll be subjected to even more of his scowls and eye rolls. It's a wonder he's not sick of me yet."

"If he was, we'd have to seriously reconsider our arrangements over here," she says. "He'd be sleeping in Pepper's dog bed from then on."

I snort a laugh as I unbuckle my seat belt. "I'm about to become an even clingier best friend just so I can see that." Pulling my keys from the ignition, I twist them in my grip. "I'm here, Mills."

A whoosh of breath crackles over the line as she sighs, the sound dousing me with the urge to hug her. "Okay. Everything is going to be great. They'll be so excited you ended up coming, and at least you don't have to spend your week with a stomach virus."

"I will pray to Santa and Mrs. Claus that everyone feels better soon," I promise.

"Thanks," she sighs. "Love you. Try to forget all the job stuff for a week. It can wait until you get back."

"Love you too, and I'll try. Kiss your girls for me. And sneak a picture if you get Finn in that costume."

When the call ends, I blow out a long breath, letting my gaze trace over the white Christmas lights trimming the house and the golden glow shining from the windows.

Millie's words echo in my head. *Forget about the job stuff.*

Is that even possible? It's been a constant weight on my shoulders since my dreams of being an art teacher crumbled around me two weeks ago. I'd hoped that spending the holidays with Millie's family would be a breath of fresh air, a chance for something different.

Millie and her family have been the perfect distraction from all the negative thoughts in my head lately. At their house, everything is loud, joyous, and carefree.

Mine, on the other hand?

It's too quiet now that Millie and Pepper have moved out. Too calm and boring and void of friendship.

Maybe I should look into adopting a dog.

Don't get me wrong, I'm happy for Millie and Finn. I want to scream from the top of the Wilhelmina Natural Science Museum that I was an integral part of forcing those two clueless scientists together.

When Millie and Finn make eyes at each other across the room, and his lips kick up like he's completely smitten with her, it makes my heart warm and fuzzy. And when my other best friends, Micah and Emil, hold hands in the car while we drive to dinner, it makes me grin like a proud mom.

But my own loneliness still hangs like a collar around my neck, reminding me I don't have what my friends do.

I can be happy for them and sad for myself at the same time, I think. I've spent my whole life feeling that way.

My role is *best friend support system*. The one to help send that firmly worded text. The one who has their back against a bully. The one who pumps them up when they need a pep talk.

It's an honor to protect the people I care about.

But occasionally, I want my own person to help protect *me*.

I firmly believe I can make my way in the world without a partner, but that doesn't change the fact that sometimes I'm simply *lonely*.

Sometimes I wish I had someone to laugh at my ridiculous day and remind me to eat a real meal every once in a while. Someone to cuddle up to on the couch and have inside jokes with. Someone to lean on when I'm not feeling my strongest, and who can guide me in the right direction when I'm feeling lost.

And maybe some physical benefits too? Honestly, my lady bits might be amassing cobwebs at this point from the lack of contact with anything other than my vibrator.

Shivering at that possibility, I pull my rainbow beanie over my head. Then I slip on my sage-green gloves and stuff my arms into the sleeves of my puffy red jacket.

I take one more deep inhale for good measure before I get out of the car. Maybe the extra oxygen will relax all my tension-filled muscles.

My lashes are weighted with snowflakes when I finally make it to the front door, opting to leave the last-minute gifts I grabbed in the car so my five-year-old nephew, Jack, can't tear into them early.

When I push open the door, relief sweeps into my heart like a warm breeze.

I soak in all the little details. The garland twining around the banister, the phantom smell of sugar and vanilla, the faint Christmas music drifting to my ears.

Home.

I let my eyelids fall shut as I close the door behind me and drop my bags.

Despite the fact that I'd planned to stay away this year, I can't deny the comfort washing over me. I've missed it here.

"What the fuck, Lena?"

My eyes shoot open to land on my sister-in-law, Zara. A shocked smile brightens her blue eyes as she stands from the couch with her one-month-old son, Noah. "What are you doing here?"

"I heard it's Christmas." I shrug, grinning as we meet in the entryway.

"Did you have this planned all along?" Zara asks, tugging me into a quick, one-arm hug.

"No. Millie's family got sick, so I'm a surprise gift." My dark curls brush Noah's cheek as I lean toward him to leave a kiss on his forehead.

"Tia Lena," Jack screeches, his wild ringlets bouncing as he barrels toward me and collides with my legs.

Mama rushes in from the kitchen, hands waving excitedly. "Oi," she squeals. "You came! Merry Christmas, *amorzinho*."

Letting go of Jack, I pull Mama toward me, a wave of calm coursing through me as she squeezes me tight.

As Mama releases me, my grandmother, who we call Luci, rounds the corner. With tears glistening in her eyes, she frames my face between her palms. "*Menina*, you scared the shit out of me saying you wouldn't be here." She shakes her head. "Don't do it again." Her blunt words have me nodding in her grip. "I'll make you hot tea. It's freezing outside," she announces in the lingering Portuguese accent from her childhood in Brazil.

I huff a laugh. "It's okay. I'm really not that cold. I have a heater in my car."

She waves me off as she makes her way back to the kitchen.

Zara snickers, her blond hair swinging as she shakes her head. "She's a force to be reckoned with today."

"Where do you think I got it from?" I shoot her a sassy wink as I strip out of my cold-weather gear.

Zara nudges Noah toward me, and I settle him into my arms, a snuggly little bundle against my sweater.

"You're stuck with him now," she calls over her shoulder as she jogs up the stairs. "Auggie's at the store, and I need a shower more than you want to know."

Carefully carrying Noah into the living room, I navigate around Jack's doll collection in the middle of the floor.

"Where's your sister?" I ask him, lowering myself to the couch.

"With Daddy at the store," Jack says as he stuffs his doll's feet into a plastic shoe. "They had to get more bread for dinner."

I hum in understanding as I focus on the little guy in my arms.

New addition to my running list of jobs to look for: holding snuggly babies all day.

"We've only met once before," I whisper to Noah's sleeping face, soaking up every detail of his rosy round cheeks and long dark lashes. "But I'm sure you remember me. I'm the one who told you the secret about your dad actually being an alien."

He lets out a sigh that sounds an awful lot like a moody teenager.

"I know, but if you ignore the green antennae, he's a nice one, I promise."

Luci approaches with a mug nestled between her hands. "Raspberry. Our favorite."

"Thank you." I grab the tea, and she lets out a groan as she drops to the couch beside me.

"How's my Lena?" she wonders, patting my thigh.

I take a sip of my tart tea, trying to gain control of my emotions. "Good. Great." The words come out too loud, and the corners of my lips quiver.

I've felt so . . . adrift lately. Like I'm lost in a turbulent ocean without land in sight. And for some reason, the concern in her voice feels like she's thrown me a life preserver.

It makes me want to pour out all my thoughts and have her sort them out with me.

Her brow furrows, but before she can respond, the back door squeaks open and a commotion rises from behind us in the kitchen. My brother's voice booms through the house in greeting before my niece, Penelope, shouts, "Tia Lena!"

Craning my neck, I try to see her, but I don't want to wake

Noah, so I set the mug on the coffee table and wave her over. She bounds toward me and dives onto the couch beside me.

"There you are." I sigh, wrapping an arm around her shoulders. "I missed you, kid."

She grins up at me. "I missed you too. I'm glad you came."

"Me too." Pressing my nose to her chestnut waves, I breathe her in and grin. "Did you get the bread?"

"No, they didn't have the right kind for Gavin."

The last two syllables land like a bomb in my chest. I suck in a breath, but it does nothing to help me process the name she just said.

Gavin.

My stomach drops to the floor.

Anger and excitement swirl into a storm in my brain, mixing to the point that I can't distinguish them.

Pen's blue eyes blink up at me, and I must look as sick as I feel because she asks, "Are you okay?"

A tremor shakes my hands as I try to find the words to answer her.

It's not him. She must be mistaken.

But I can't confirm. I'm trapped on this couch, facing the wrong way, while unease churns in my gut.

In the mixture of voices behind me, one distinctive chuckle dances over my skin, raising every hair on my body. The deep, hearty laugh is a sound I've heard so many times, but not for the last three years.

They've been devoid of the man behind me.

Boots thud against the floors, ominously approaching. And suddenly, anger bursts out of my storm of emotions, and I know exactly where to direct it.

Chapter 2

Gavin

She's not supposed to be here.

That thought flashes through my mind like a bright sign on the Las Vegas strip.

It's the only reason I agreed to come back.

For a heartbeat, I consider sneaking out the door before she turns around and sees me. Everyone else would witness me running away, but at least *she* wouldn't.

But my legs don't move me toward an escape. Instead, it feels as though vines shoot up from the ground and wrap around my feet, holding me in place for whatever is about to happen.

Lena's chin tips up, and then she shakes her black curls before setting Noah in Luci's arms.

Anticipation burns in my chest as I wait for her to acknowledge me. Her reaction could be anything. She could turn around in a rage, or she could grant me the smile I've craved since the last time I saw her.

I'm desperate for anything at this point.

Slap me. Yell at me. Grin at me.

Anything, as long as I get to see her face while she does it.

With a deep breath, she stands, and even from the back, she's as beautiful as she was the last time I saw her.

Despite the couch between us, she feels so close, and my arms ache to hug her.

Can I hug her?

I follow the path of her long dark hair down her back. Those thick ebony curls have always fascinated me and had me wishing I could dig my fingers into them.

My gaze dips to the swell of her hips without permission. But thank god she turns around before it can drop any lower, because I don't know if I could have stopped myself from devouring every detail.

Unfortunately, I'm then forced to see the way her tight white sweater molds to her lush curves like a second skin.

Fuck my life.

I force my gaze up to meet her caramel eyes.

Something desperate and needy grips my throat. My lungs beg for oxygen.

All I can do is stare, mouth open and body tense.

I thought Lena was beautiful the first time I had the privilege of meeting her ten years ago.

But this version is *devastating*.

She crosses her arms and cocks her hip to the side, plump red lips pursed. "*What* are you doing here?" she grits out, her cheeks tinting pink.

There's no trace of that smile I missed. It has been replaced with a deep frown pressing down the corners of her mouth.

But for some reason, her sass feels like a win. Like she's looking at *me* and talking to *me*, and I should thank her for it.

I smother a smile and shrug. "It's Christmas."

The humor dies in my throat when her brows tighten and she growls, "This is *our* Christmas."

Her words sting like she sent a knife through my heart, and heat rushes up my neck.

"Lena Camilla dos Santos," Luci scolds, glaring up at her.

The color drains from Lena's cheeks as she blinks. Her lips fold between her teeth before she mumbles, "Sorry."

I open my mouth to reply, but Auggie bumps my shoulder on his way to hug his sister. He picks her up and twirls her in a circle as she gives him *that* smile.

The one I've ached to catch a glimpse of.

At least I got to see it before I leave, even if it was for someone else. I don't want to spend the next week around someone who's made it clear she doesn't want me here, but those vines are still holding me in place. I'm a deer in the headlights, watching Lena instead of moving to save my own life.

Auggie sets her down, and her head tilts as she asks, "Why didn't you tell me Gavin was coming?"

"Why didn't you tell me *you* were coming?" he throws back, playfully tugging on the end of her hair. "This guy"—he points a thumb in my direction—"got all mopey after a few drinks and admitted he was going to spend the week alone. So I told him he was coming back." Shame burns my cheeks as he continues. "He resisted until I told him you wouldn't be here and your room would be open."

Her gasp of betrayal echoes through the living room, and I bite back my grin at the sound of it. "He's in *my* room? Are you kidding me?" She shoves both hands into Auggie's chest, but he doesn't budge. Instead, he lets out a chuckle that only seems to make her nostrils flare.

In years past, when I was here for Christmas, I stayed in the guest room. But it has now been turned into Bea's quilting studio and Luci's knitting and crocheting headquarters. It's a tornado of creativity—stacks of fabric, spools of yarn, and half-finished projects everywhere.

If it wasn't so adorable that they share a mother-daughter creative space, I might've been devastated that they did away with my guest room.

But I left without a word. How were they supposed to know if I was coming back?

"I'll get my stuff and go," I concede, trying to dissolve the tension brewing in the room.

"You are *not* leaving," Beatriz, Lena and Auggie's mom, announces as she walks by and points at me. She nudges Auggie out of the way and wraps an arm around Lena's waist. *"Amorzinho, we thought you wouldn't be here. So when Auggie told me Gavin was coming, we let him have your room."*

"It's okay," I tell them, nodding toward one of the two couches in the living room. "I can move out here tonight, and then I'll leave tomorrow."

Bea scoffs and waves a hand in the air. "No you will not. Lena and her bad attitude can sleep on the couch."

Lena's hands prop on her hips, and she pins me with a glare. "Enjoy my bed," she offers with a condescending smile before she stomps to the bathroom.

My pulse skyrockets. "I don't mind sleeping down here—"

The bathroom door slams shut with a *bang*, cutting off the rest of my words.

The loud noise startles Noah, and he lets out a screeching cry from Luci's arms.

As Auggie picks him up to settle him, Bea wraps her arms around my waist and says, "I don't make it a habit of apologizing for my daughter's rude behavior, but this time it seems necessary. I'm sorry."

"Don't worry about it." I force a small smile, thankful that without Lena in the room, my ability to breathe is finally returning.

Following Bea into the kitchen, I fall into place at the counter, silently peeling and cutting potatoes for our dinner while trying my best not to think about *her*.

But, as usual when I try to avoid thinking about Lena, my mind brings her to the forefront instead.

My least favorite quality about myself is that I have lusted after my best friend's little sister for years.

Auggie and I met during our freshman year of college. We stayed friends after graduation but lived hours apart, so we didn't see each other much. A few years later, he was hired by the architecture firm I work for in Eugene, Oregon, and when he found out I was going to spend Christmas alone in my apartment, he invited me to Juniper.

That's when Lena entered my life, completely turning it upside down.

The first time I met her, she was sledding behind the house by herself. She rushed down the hill, a sprinkle of snow flying out behind her as she squealed with delight all the way.

Then she dragged her sled to where I was standing on the back porch, trying to get service to text my girlfriend at the time.

Even though I knew exactly who Lena was, I let myself admire her flushed cheeks and rosy lips as she walked toward me. I let myself have one blip of a moment to appreciate how goddamn beautiful she was before I shrank back into the reality of *who* she was.

My best friend's little sister. Nineteen years old. Ten years younger than us. And someone whose radiant eyes I shouldn't be staring at dreamily.

And since then, every time I've thought of her, guilt has seeped through my veins like a toxic chemical, killing me from the inside out.

I can hate my inability to make friends other than Auggie, I can despise my trauma-filled childhood, and I can loathe my incompetency when it comes to dating.

But the thing I hate the most? I want Lena's company more than anyone else's in the world, and it's quite possible I will die still wishing for it.

Even though I've kept myself away for the last few Christmases, my absence never stopped me from daydreaming about what they were doing here. I wondered what their tree looked like, if someone else made the cinnamon rolls, or if Lena still got her favorite lemon pie.

But at least I wasn't *here*. Watching her from across the room and wishing beyond all hope that she would look my way and gift me my favorite smile.

The one that lights up her eyes to a warm, soft caramel and pinkens her cheeks from the force of it. It forms adorable creases around her lips and somehow makes her entire body seem electric with happiness.

That smile is like a drug. Addicting, high-inducing, and deadly.

For me, at least.

Fuck. A sting burns through my finger as the knife slices into my skin. Blood gathers on the tip, proving to me once again how dangerous and distracting thoughts of Lena are.

Auggie saunters into the kitchen as I press a paper towel over my finger. He notices my hand and smirks. "Did Lena cut you?"

As I huff a laugh, she walks in behind Auggie and smacks the back of his head. "If I'd gotten to him, you'd be driving him to the hospital right now."

Auggie's eyes flare wide in a look that says *oh shit, man*.

Bea whips around from the stove and points her wooden spoon at Lena. A bit of creamy soup plops to the hardwood floors, but she ignores it. "Lena," she snaps, her brows stitched together. "He is family. We don't cut family."

I can't help the snort of laughter that escapes my throat.

Lena grabs a can of sparkling water out of the fridge. "You think I've never said something like that to Auggie?" She scoffs as she pops open the can and leans her hips on the counter beside her mother. "Pretty sure you were there when I told him I was going to cut his ears off if he didn't start using them."

Auggie's laughter gusts out of him as he snatches the sparkling water out of her hand and swallows a huge gulp of it.

She finally meets my stare from across the kitchen, and something warm and heady zaps between our gazes. I hold it as long as I can, my curious eyes pinned to her assessing ones, trying to stand up to the weight of whatever she's thinking, but I can't tell what's going on inside that brain of hers.

I used to be able to, but right now, it's a mystery.

And it's unsettling.

The cloth around my finger dampens as the blood soaks through, and I'm forced to drop my gaze, breaking the connection and leaving the kitchen in search of a bandage.

Chapter 3

Lena

"You either sleep in the studio or on the couch," Mama says, squinting as she studies the pot of what I'm guessing is potato soup, judging by the onion and garlic aroma filling the kitchen.

Groaning, I swallow a sip of my drink. "Your studio is a disaster. Do you and Luci just throw your supplies around the room when you're done?"

She waves this off with a frown. "I remember the desk in your classroom being a mess the last time I visited."

Guilt creeps up my throat at the reminder that she has no clue that I don't even have a desk or a classroom anymore.

"But if the mess bothers you, sleep on the couch." She heaves a deep sigh. "And be nice to Gavin."

Auggie swipes a kitchen towel over the soup Mama dripped on the floor, then loops his arm over my shoulders. "Yeah, sis, be nice to Gavin. Do you know how much convincing it took to get him here?"

"No, I guess I wouldn't since no one told me about it."

He grabs my drink out of my hand again and scoffs when he finds it empty. "Well, it took a lot. Weeks of it, in fact."

My brows lift. "It sounds like he showed up because he thought I wasn't."

"Maybe he's secretly scared of you." Narrowing his amber eyes, he tosses his shoulders up in a casual shrug before Zara calls his name from the living room. He ruffles the top of my head as he leaves the kitchen.

Mama sets the spoon down and pats my cheek. It's almost sweet until she pinches the skin between her fingers. "Please make my Gavin feel welcome," she orders before turning back to the soup.

Her Gavin. Geez. You'd think the sun shines out of his ass for how much she adores him.

But I can't argue with her. I won't.

Because of all the people in the world, I respect her the most. And if she wants me to be kind to Gavin, I will, at least when she's around.

She has been working to give Auggie and me the best possible lives she could since before we were born. After both of our fathers abandoned her in pregnancy, she spent our childhood working two jobs and getting a law degree. She commuted to Wilhelmina two days a week for school while Luci took care of us at home.

It may have taken her four times longer than normal, but she did it. And we were there, cheering for her as she walked across the stage at graduation.

She showed us how fierce her determination is and how much she could accomplish when she set her mind to something.

But that's why it's so hard to admit to her that I'm listless right now, with no clear path in front of me for what will make me happy. I don't even know what I want to work toward.

After living and breathing art for my entire life, becoming an art teacher was exactly what I thought I wanted my future to look like. I loved introducing children to their creative sides and watching them flourish.

But somewhere along the way, my own passion and creativity suffocated amid the school setting's bureaucracy and regulations.

So when they announced they were letting me go and downsizing their art programming, I felt . . . *nothing*.

I wasn't surprised or hurt or devastated.

Instead, I was just *empty*.

It feels as though I'm staring at a blank canvas, and I can't figure out what to put on it. There are too many options and not enough at the same time.

I haven't even picked up a paintbrush in weeks, so the thought of trying to paint out my whole future is overwhelming.

For the last two weeks, I've tried to come up with some new job ideas, but so far, the list of options is ludicrous at best.

1. *Target makeup consultant who helps match people with their most savage lip color.*
2. *Taylor Swift's bodyguard.*
3. *Taylor's fan-holder when she's getting overheated.*
4. *The woman who picks up Taylor's dirty clothes when she doesn't feel like putting them in the hamper.*
5. *Photographer who specializes in boudoir photos to send to an ex who jilted them.*

That one is extremely niche, and I'm still trying to figure out how the pictures can spontaneously delete within five seconds of the ex receiving them. Also, I don't know anything about photography, and that seems important.

Then the most recent addition is one of my personal favorites.

6. Holder of sleeping babies.

Obviously, the list needs some help, so I'm going to continue brainstorming.

The air shifts beside me as Gavin returns to the kitchen with a small Ninja Turtles bandage around his finger. Without looking my way, he grabs the knife he was using and brings it to the sink to wash it.

Leaning against the counter, I watch as he shoves up the sleeves of his black Henley, revealing forearms corded with muscles and covered in tattoos. He's always had them, but it looks like he's added a few more recently. I shamelessly stare at him, mesmerized by his movements, and if he can feel me watching him, he doesn't reveal it.

Our ten-year age difference is starting to show in the light dusting of gray hair around his ears, but he's aged like fine wine, and it only makes him more attractive to me.

His broad shoulders could hold a lucky woman slung over them, and his sharp jaw hosts a five o'clock shadow this evening. His dark-brown hair is artfully waved on top, and I'm mesmerized by those perfectly shaped lips that have no business being on a man.

When he turns back to chopping potatoes, I have a new view to be enamored with. His back and shoulder muscles shift under the shirt that seems to barely contain his strength.

Fuck. He's magnificent.

I want to climb onto his back and feel those solid muscles beneath my hands. Between my thighs.

A throat clears beside me, and I blink toward my mom. Heat blooms in my cheeks as I realize she caught me ogling Gavin. Thank *fuck* she can't read minds.

But when she looks at me over her wire-framed glasses and *tsks*, my whole body is engulfed in flames. My heartbeat jumps as I burst into movement, escaping the kitchen.

I flop onto the couch next to a sleeping Luci. Her quiet, rumbling snores echo beside me as I pull out my phone to text the group chat with my three best friends.

We Catan Beat Finn

> **Lena:** RED ALERT! Guess who showed up to Christmas!

Millie: The Easter Bunny.

Micah: Is it Emil? He hasn't come home from work yet.

Emil: Driving home, love. 😘

> **Lena:** 👀 GAVIN.

> **Lena:** Not to be dramatic, but did you see the name GAVIN??

Micah: We've never known you not to be dramatic.

> **Lena:** FOCUS! Gavin is here, and I don't know how to act around him.

Millie: Act like yourself.

Lena: That's not your best advice. I acted like myself and ended up being a bitch.

Millie: Well, then, transport back to three years ago before he left. How did you act around him then?

Lena: Like Auggie's annoying little sister. Probably flirtier than I should've been.

Millie: That seems like a good place to start.

Micah: That sure sounds like normal Lena.

Millie: What would you tell me in this situation?

Lena: That's tough. I would probably tell you to drag him into a closet and release some tension. 😉

Millie: Okay. Yeah. Go back to the "act like yourself" advice.

Lena: I don't even know what that means.

When no responses trickle in, I toss my phone aside on the couch, silently cursing my unhelpful friends.

How on earth am I going to make it through the next week in the same house as Gavin?

If I follow my friends' advice, I will *be myself*. Can I slip right back into the easy friendship we used to have? Years ago, my crush on him felt harmless. The teasing and flirting were fun, and I had a blast poking and prodding until I got under his skin.

But I'm not so sure it would feel the same now. Something about him seems strained and tense, and I don't know how to react to it.

My stomach sours as I remember how his face paled in the living room a moment ago.

I hate that I implied he wasn't a part of our family. I may have only seen him for one week out of fifty-two, eight years in a row, but he helped my mom cook our Christmas dinners, read Penelope countless books, and had snowball fights with us in the backyard.

He was absolutely a part of everything we did.

Until he left.

Mama's voice sings through the house, calling us to dinner, and my family's chatter fills the dining room. Drinks are made, bowls are set around the table, and seats are chosen.

But as I sit down, I notice Gavin standing awkwardly in the doorway, waiting for everyone to get settled. His focus bounces over the seats until it lands on the empty one beside me. He glances at me with a small shrug, like he's asking permission to sit there.

God, I wish literally anyone else had taken this seat.

The thought of his masculine scent filling my lungs sounds excruciating. But every other seat is taken now.

It will be my peace offering. Out of the kindness of my generous heart. I'm *being myself* now, at my friends' advice. I'm going back to three-years-ago Lena.

So I wave a hand in the direction of the empty chair to offer him the spot. With stiff shoulders, he walks over and drops into the seat. His spicy, woodsy scent invades my senses like I knew it would, and my brain scrambles like someone took a whisk to it.

Can I make it through this meal without breathing too much? Or I'll simply hover close to my bowl of soup the entire time and hope it'll mask the smell of him.

"Would you like some cheese?"

His deep voice startles me from my staring contest with my potato soup.

"Sure. Yes," I stammer.

He sets the dish above my bowl with a nod.

I'm going to have to force myself to be friendly to him. We have to spend a week in the same house. Surely, I can get over whatever had him disappearing three years ago, and we can fall back into the normal friendship we used to have.

Right? That has to be possible.

"Do you want some bread?" I offer, lifting the basket from beside my bowl. "Seems someone found the bread we were missing."

See, that's another peace offering. I'm the patron saint of peace and good relations.

And bread sharing.

He takes the basket and passes it to Auggie on his other side. "No, thank you. I was diagnosed with celiac disease last year. That's why we went to the store, but gluten-free bread does not exist in Juniper, apparently."

My skin prickles with this new information. Something *changed* while we were apart. And for some reason, I hate that I wasn't aware.

"Did you tell my mom? There could be traces of gluten in this."

One corner of his mouth lifts in an easy grin. "I told her. We went shopping for all the ingredients we needed."

An image flashes through my mind of Gavin and my mom at the grocery store together. He's more than a foot taller than her, and with his signature black ensemble, he would look like a looming shadow following my chattering mother down an aisle.

"Was she grumpy about changing her recipes?"

Gavin's warm gaze lands on my mom across the table. "No, actually. She's the one who dragged me to the store this morning. I told her I would just make my own food this week, but she refused." He looks back down at his bowl, a hint of pink on his cheeks. "She said I'm hired as her sous chef this week to make sure she gets it all right."

I can't stop my lips from twisting at the memory of my mom and Gavin in the kitchen every holiday. She's such a perfectionist about her food that she doesn't even let me do much.

But she lets Gavin help with anything. He was always there from start to finish, beside her at the stove or washing the dishes she used. They would laugh at their inside jokes while music drifted from the speaker in the corner.

"Well, don't forget to put the lid on the blender this time," I advise with a mock-stern look.

He laughs, deep and raspy, and my chest lurches. I've missed that sound so much. He rarely lets it out, but when he does, it's like a prize.

Those laughs are a secret weapon someone could use to make me submit to anything.

His eyes meet mine, the color of cool whiskey. "I've never made that mistake again."

"I'm pretty sure there's still a little peppermint milkshake on the ceiling all these years later."

Our gazes hold, my spoon halfway to my mouth and his twirling in his bowl. I take in the strong line of his jaw that I want to run my palm over. His perfect lips that look like they would feel silky soft if I touched them. Those shiny, thick strands of hair that I want to feel running through my fingers.

His throat works on a swallow, and for the life of me, I can't remember what we were talking about. It could've been elephants, for all I know at this point.

Because the only thing I can think about is how much I *missed* him. I didn't know how bad the pain of it had been until this moment.

"I need someone to drive to Fern River tomorrow." Mama's voice cuts through my thoughts like a blade, severing my connection with Gavin. "Our grocery store had everything we needed except for gluten-free bread."

"I can go," Gavin offers. "That way I can get a few more things I might need this week."

Mama stares at me across the table and lifts her brows in a way that says *you volunteer.* But I give her a subtle shake of my head, because like *hell* am I going to trap myself in a car with him for the hour-long drive to Fern River and then do it all over again on the way back.

"I can go with you," Auggie offers, his brunette curls waving as he nods to Gavin.

But to my horror, Mama says, "Lena will go." She points between Gavin and me. "You go to the store together and work out whatever is going on. Don't come back until you have."

Heavy silence settles over the table. Even the children, who have no clue what's going on, have paused to watch the scene.

I want to throw my napkin on the table and run away in a tantrum to rival one of Jack's. But Mama has already focused back on her food, having said what she wanted and knowing we will follow her instructions.

The heat radiating off Gavin warms my arm as the table returns to normal. But we both stay silent as we look over our bowls, and I pick at my food for the rest of the meal.

Chapter 4

Gavin

Let's go, sunshine," Lena grumbles as she stomps past me to the front door, her bright-red jacket and forest-green leggings accessorized by purple snow boots and a yellow knit hat.

I look down at my black boots, black jeans, black jacket, and, of course, black sweater.

Should be noted, my boxer briefs are also black.

She looks like she belongs at the North Pole, serving up decadent hot cocoa and at least five types of Christmas cookies. Probably doing some carol singing too.

Meanwhile, I look like the modern version of the Grinch as I trudge behind her.

In the driveway, she walks straight to her small SUV and opens the driver's door.

"How about we take my car?" I offer, surveying her nearly bald tires. I honestly can't believe she made it all the way here with the snowy road conditions last night.

She tilts her head and scowls at me, her fingers gripping the top of her door. "I'm not a passenger princess, Gav. I can drive."

My chest warms at the nickname, despite how cold it is outside. That's the first time I've heard it in years, and the sound of it in her sweet, raspy voice makes me want to get on my knees and beg her to say it again.

Stifling the urge, I shrug and tell her, "I was just offering to be nice."

Her lips curve up slowly. "Get in the damn car."

As I buckle my seat belt, I have the unsettling realization that I didn't think this arrangement through. When Bea ordered us to go to the store together, it seemed reasonable. Maybe we could clear the air between us and take one step back toward the playful friendship we used to have.

In the past, it was normal for us to drive to the store for the sixty-eighth forgotten ingredient for our holiday dinner. Lena would make fun of my strict sticking-to-the-list method of shopping, and I would tease her for her ability to turn our short list into a car full of groceries we didn't need.

I've never been able to tell her no, even if it meant we ended up with seven types of cheeses, ten cracker options, and more wine than our group could possibly drink.

But those car rides to the store never felt like *this*.

Like static tension covers my body, and the slightest touch to Lena or anything that belongs to her would shock me harder than a live wire.

Her tangy, citrusy scent drenches the car, and I'm surrounded by it, completely unable to escape.

An old to-go coffee cup with a red lipstick stain on the edge sits between us, and I'd be willing to bet my entire savings account that it was a peppermint mocha.

She swipes her sunglasses from the dash and slides them on, shaking her hair back. Tilting the rearview mirror down, she glides the pad of her finger over the corner of her mouth, perfecting her deep-red lipstick.

Admittedly, I know nothing about makeup, but from my minimal knowledge of it, I'm willing to bet she wears barely any.

Except that her lush lips are always coated in a tantalizing, bold color that draws my attention way more than it should.

That fucking lipstick has featured in way too many fantasies over the years.

As she pulls down the driveway, I study every detail of her. The smooth curve of her jaw as she checks the mirrors, the movement of the bones in her hands as she grips the steering wheel, the shift in her legs as she pushes the brake.

"You really don't have to watch me that closely," she says. "I promise I know how to drive."

I snap my attention forward, and my cheeks quirk in a grin. "Says the woman who ran into a stop sign with her own mother in the car."

She scoffs and sends a glare in my direction that I feel searing into my skin even through her sunglasses. "That was *one time*. And it was her fault for trying to convince me that Pierce Brosnan is the better James Bond. She *knew* I'd get worked up about that." She lets out a sharp breath like the memory is firing her up all over again. "Have you *seen* Daniel Craig? Hello, Daddy?"

A loud laugh barks out of me before I can stop it, and her returning smile is dazzling. Pink cheeks and tiny lines bracketing her mouth. Exactly the way I remembered.

It flashes me right back to my first Christmas morning in the Santoses' house, when that smile was just for me.

Five in the morning. I'm wide awake, like every day at this time, unable to sleep any later since my eighth year of life. That's when I had to train myself to wake up before the sun to complete the list of chores my foster family wanted me to finish before school.

Sliding out of the guest bed, I get up before everyone else and make a pot of coffee for the adults, since three-month-old Penelope will be waking them up earlier than they hope.

I sip my coffee and scroll through the news on my phone while powdery snowflakes fall outside the massive living room windows.

When soft footsteps pad down the stairs a few minutes later, I peek over my shoulder, and I'm met with the most adorable sight. Lena is dressed in a baggy flannel pajama set, her hair in complete disarray over her head as she rubs her eyes. She pulls her hands away and blinks a few times like she's trying to clear her vision.

And when she focuses on me, she gives me a radiant smile that lights up the whole room. Maybe the whole house.

That smile sends my heartrate galloping in my chest.

"Merry Christmas, Gav," she whispers, her voice hoarse from sleep.

I dip my chin with a small grin. "Merry Christmas, Lena. There's coffee in the kitchen."

Instead of making her way toward the caffeine, she plops on the couch beside me, dropping her head to the cushion behind her. "Too sleepy to make it right now," she says, her lashes fanning over her cheeks.

"I'll make it for you."

"My coffee requests are too complicated," she murmurs.

"I'm sure I can figure it out," I offer, not quite sure how to tell her that I already know how she fixes her coffee from seeing her do it for days. "Or you can go back to sleep. I'll make sure you don't miss the festivities."

She shakes her head and whispers, "I'm the one who gets up early on Christmas morning. I make the coffee and start the cinnamon rolls." She yawns, so big that she falls to the side until her head hits the pillow between us. "I have to check that all the

*stockings are done and the fire is going. Need to make sure every-
one has a perfect day."*

*Amid a few more murmurs about stockings, her breaths
deepen, and she drifts off to sleep.*

*I've spent the last few days witnessing her organizing family
games and keeping the festive music going, making sure everyone is laughing and having a great time. She's the bright light at
the center of this family—the one everyone looks at in complete
adoration.*

*But she's obviously exhausted, so I down the last sip of my
coffee and sneak into the kitchen. I don't know much about
stockings, but I pop open a can of cinnamon rolls and start a
fire before everyone wakes up.*

"I need some coffee. And food," Lena announces, shoving me
out of the memory. "I can feel the hangry coming on." She pushes
her sunglasses up into her hair as she slows down in front of Bear
Creek at the edge of Juniper.

A cozy coffee shop and bakery sits at the front of the property,
with lit garlands adorning the windows. Beside it rolls a field of
Christmas trees that's bordered by a row of rental cabins.

"That sounds great," I tell her, thankful for the break from the
tension in the car. It should be lethal in this dosage, and a small
breather before the rest of the drive to Fern River would be a
welcome relief.

Chapter 5

Lena

*H*e remembers my favorite drink without needing to be reminded, smoothly telling the barista, Rosie, exactly what I order every winter: a peppermint mocha.

I try not to let that affect me, but I can't ignore how my pulse sounds like a racehorse in my skull.

My heart could use a reality check, though. A reminder that I don't even know why he disappeared or where he's been.

I should be mad. I should be digging my claws in and cracking him open to find out what's going on.

But instead, I'm swooning over a coffee order.

For himself, he requests his usual boring black coffee. He's always been Mr. Plain Black Coffee, and I'm starting to wonder if that's why he's so moody sometimes.

Maybe he needs more sugar and whipped cream in his life.

While I wait for my drink, I drop into a cozy chair in the corner of the bakery and pull out my phone.

We Catan Beat Finn

> **Lena:** He remembered my coffee order.

Micah: Swoon.

Millie: Even the extra peppermint?

> **Lena:** Yep.

Millie: Swoon.

Emil: I remember all of your coffee orders.

Micah: And we all swoon over it.

> **Lena:** Am I in trouble?

Millie: What kind of trouble?

> **Lena:** Back to thinking about Gavin way more often than I should kind of trouble.

Millie: You might be.

"I'm not sure if there's any coffee in here or if it's straight sugar."

I look up to find a judgmental smirk on Gavin's lips as he offers me the drink, along with my bagel.

Shoving my phone into my jacket pocket, I stand and grab my coffee and breakfast. "You're just jealous." I peer at his cup like it's a virus I'm trying to stay away from. "If you keep drinking that, it's going to end up staining your soul the same color."

He huffs a laugh as he turns to walk toward the door. "Who says it hasn't already?"

As I step after him, I tuck my cup in my elbow to unwrap

my chocolate chip bagel with cream cheese. Inhaling the sweet scent, I open my mouth to take—

Oof.

Air rushes out of me as I slam into his back. My bagel smacks me right in the face, smearing the cream cheese all over my cheek, and a few drops of coffee splash out of the tiny hole in the lid and land on the arm of my jacket.

He goes rigid as I groan and step back, swiping the cream cheese from my face. "Fuck, Gav, why did you—"

"Hey, man," comes a drawled greeting from the other side of him.

"Brandon," Gavin says, his voice as dull as his coffee order.

Licking the cream cheese from my thumb, I scoot to the side to find my childhood friend standing in front of Gavin with a baby in his arms and a big, goofy smile on his face.

"Brandon," I squeal, giving him a one-arm hug and somehow managing not to hit the baby in the head. "What are you doing here?"

"We just moved back." He lifts the little girl, clad in a pink jacket and hat, adjusting her on his hip. "Jocelyn and I wanted to raise Evelyn where we grew up." He nods and looks between us. "Haven't seen you in forever," he says to Gavin, reaching out a hand.

Gav bites the inside of his cheek and looks at little Evelyn before returning Brandon's handshake. Neither of them says anything for a moment, and a tense silence hovers in the air, Brandon looking between us like he's trying to solve a puzzle.

"It's so good to see you," I tell him brightly, trying to alleviate some of the awkwardness that seems to have us in a chokehold. "I guess it's been since your wedding? You look great."

"You do too." Brandon gives me an appreciative grin.

Gavin runs a hand through his hair and lets out a loud breath that borders on a growl.

My moody architect must be antsy to leave.

I loop my free hand through his arm and grin up at him playfully. "I need to get this old man to the grocery store before his naptime." Gavin's face pinches before I look back to Brandon. "Will you be at the Christmas party?"

"Yep." He nods. "All three of us."

"Perfect. Can't wait to see Jocelyn," I say, leaving Gavin's arm to hug Brandon again before giving Evelyn an enthusiastic wave.

Once we're back on the highway, driving toward Fern River, I allow myself one glance over at Gavin. His dark brows are tense as he stares down the road in front of us, the paper crinkling around my bagel the only sound in the car.

Fiddling with the wrapper, I try to peel it away while keeping a hand on the wheel, but it almost fumbles to the ground. With a disgruntled sigh, Gavin grabs it from me. He unwraps my breakfast, offers me the bagel, and folds the paper into a neat square without ever saying a word.

I wish I could see inside his brain for a moment to know what he's thinking.

He's always kept most of his thoughts in a vault, hidden behind his serious expressions and quiet personality. Always a man of few words.

But we used to be good enough friends that sometimes I felt like I knew what was going on in his mind.

I guess I was wrong about that, though. Because I didn't know him well enough to predict he was going to disappear without telling me.

As I'm taking a big bite of bagel, Gavin's low voice rumbles through the car. "How long were you two together?"

Confusion knits my brows as I chew and swallow. "Who?"

"You and Brandon."

"Oh. We were never together."

I mean, we were technically "together" for one quick evening, but I definitely don't need to tell Gavin about *that*.

He rubs a palm across his freshly shaven jaw. "I, uh . . . I guess I thought you were."

A tense quiet blankets the car as I chew through another bite of bagel, then set the rest in my lap. "Nope. Just me, myself, and I for the last few years."

We reach for our cups in the console between us at the same moment, and when his fingers bump mine, he pulls back like I've burned him. The lid to my cup pops off when I try to grab it, and his hand stumbles to catch it before he presses it back on.

"Oops—"

"Sorry—"

"Oh—"

"Got it—"

Our words are all jumbled over each other, and I'm not even sure who says what.

Why is this so painfully awkward? It's like we don't even know each other. Like we're on some sort of blind date and have no clue how to act.

I don't know how to alleviate it other than shoving my way through it. Maybe if I pretend it isn't happening, we can get past it without dying of awkward tension.

Clearing my throat, I ask, "How about you? Any girlfriend updates while you've been gone?"

"No," he clips.

Nodding, I try to think through where to go next with that line of questioning. It's difficult to continue an interrogation with this tiny scrap of information. Finally, I let out a dramatic sigh and say, "Cool."

"Yeah."

I roll my eyes at his one-word answers. "What have you been up to since the last time I saw you?"

When you were angry at the Christmas Eve party and embar-rassed the hell out of me in front of everyone, then left without a word.

I don't say that, though, because bringing up *that* particular night seems the opposite of helpful, and we're already drowning in this tension.

He shifts in his seat. "Uh . . . Just work, mostly."

"How is work? Is architect life still nice and architecture-y?"

Let's be honest. I have no clue what he and my brother do all day at work. When Auggie talks about his job, I'm pretty sure my brain takes a timeout and fills with my favorite Lorelai-and-Rory banter from *Gilmore Girls* instead.

"It's okay. I don't quite have everything figured out yet, but I'm leaving the firm."

I blink and tilt my head. "You won't work with Auggie any-more?"

"He's, uh . . . leaving too," he says with a hint of evasiveness.

My mind whirs with these updates. I don't keep up with Auggie quite as much as I should. He lives five hours from me in Eugene, and when we talk on the phone, it's mostly to catch up about the kids. Combine that with the fact that all conversations adjacent to Gavin have been adamantly avoided.

That leaves me having no clue about Auggie's work updates, and I'm suddenly wishing I had been paying better attention.

"How is work going for you?" Gavin asks, and I'm so startled that he's trying to continue the conversation that it takes me a moment to respond.

My "fine" comes out several octaves too high, but I attempt to cover it with another lower one. "Fine."

Lying to him punctures my soul a little. It's not that I feel like I can't be honest with him. I'm just not prepared to talk about my plans yet.

So after a few deep breaths, I say something truthful to make up for my lie. "I just feel like something's missing in my life, and I want to find it. But I'm also not sure how."

Those words are more than I've admitted to anyone, and I bite the inside of my cheek as I wait for his response.

"I know that feeling well," he murmurs, nodding his head.

Surprise flickers through me. "Do you know what it is that you're missing?"

He rubs his fingertips over his lips, which is Gavin's telltale sign that he's thinking about something. I've seen him do it when he's trying to decide what he should add to a recipe and when he's contemplating his next move in a board game.

Since I'm driving, I can only give myself one second to watch, but he might as well have touched *my* lips for how intimate it feels for the briefest of moments.

Finally, he drops his hand and states simply, "I'm missing a home. A place that's finally mine."

Desperation colors his tone, and my throat tightens uncomfortably. I don't know all the details of Gavin's childhood in foster care, but I know he was in and out of homes regularly. And I've heard from Auggie that some of those homes didn't care for him as well as they should have.

My stomach churns with the memory of what I said when I

saw him last night, and suddenly the thought of taking another bite of my breakfast sounds nauseating.

How could I say that to him? How could I look him in the eye, after every moment he spent with us in the past, and make him feel like he wasn't important to us?

Forcing a deep breath through my lungs, I whisper, "I'm sorry about what I said yesterday. It was cruel, and I didn't mean it. Christmas wasn't the same without you."

He nods, fingers digging into his thighs. "Don't worry about it. Already forgotten."

Maybe for him.

But that pained, haunted expression on his face has been seared into my memory, and I don't know if I can ever forgive myself for being the one to put it there.

Chapter 6

Lena

*W*ho the fuck is *that*?

Stopping in my tracks at the edge of the bread aisle, I find Gavin crouched on the floor, a bag in each hand. But his eyes are on a woman in a tight royal-blue dress, jacket looped over her arm, and heels too high for a Washington winter.

How did she even get through the snowy parking lot wearing those?

Her burgundy-painted lips move as she points to the bread in his hands, but I'm too far away to hear her. He nods, and her cackling laughter drifts down the aisle to me.

I leave this man alone for five minutes in the Fern River grocery store, and he's already got a woman fluttering her eyelashes and probably asking to have his babies.

Digging my nails into my palms, I start toward them. On my way, I snatch a tin of cookie sticks off the shelf and toss them into the basket hooked over my arm, hoping they don't crumble to powder on the rough landing.

I paste on the brightest smile I can. Maybe my teeth will blind her momentarily, and we can make our escape.

When I reach Gavin, I set my basket beside his with a dramatic *thud* and shoot the woman a look that says *leave this man alone.* I'm not sure where the line is between that and *this is my man,* but I hope I'm getting it right.

It's not like I'm trying to claim him or anything. I'm simply trying to protect him from this—I scan down her body and back up—honestly very beautiful woman.

But frankly, I'm not in the mood for her.

"Did you find what you needed?" I ask Gavin, putting as much innocent sweetness into my tone as possible.

One side of her annoyingly perfect lips kicks up as she watches me. I try to keep my chin high, daring her to test me. I'm not sure what I'd do if she did, but I've been in a few fights in my life. I think I can handle her. As I learned in college, when an asshole was manhandling a girl at a bar, my curves are packing some scrappy muscle behind them, so I think I can take her.

Wait. Why the *fuck* am I even thinking about fighting this woman?

Gavin obstructs my view of her as he stands, turning to look at each of us. He gives me a knowing smirk with a stupid glint in his whiskey eyes.

I blink a few times, trying to clear away whatever he thinks he sees written on my face, because absolutely nothing about this situation should be smirked at.

"You done here?" I ask, lacing my words with a little more sass.

"Yeah," he chuckles, keeping his focus on me as he grabs the basket from the floor. "Let's go."

The urge to touch him as we pass Miss Blue Dress is so severe that I have to shove my hands into my jacket pockets to stop myself. She has a tight pucker on her lips as she glares at me, but it seems I've won this interaction.

I'll have to report this to my friends later. I've successfully protected Gavin from Christmas Barbie by perfectly executing my role as annoying little sister.

My heart twinges at the thought of being his little sister, but I brush it off, walking with my head held high toward the cashier.

As our checkout lady scans the food we've chosen, she offers each product to Gavin at the end of the station with a little *too* much attention.

Bag of gluten-free rolls. Her dark lashes flutter. My head tilts.

Box of butter. She bites into her bottom lip. My vision narrows.

Bottle of peppermint extract. She flashes him a wink. I see red.

Does she seriously not see me standing here?

To his credit, Gavin seems completely oblivious, his concentration narrowed on the groceries as he bags them.

But when she slides her fingers over his on *my* tin of cookie sticks, I lose it.

"We're in a hurry," I announce with a simpering smile in her direction.

She blinks as she focuses on me, like she didn't notice me this entire time.

The *audacity*.

I reach for the paper grocery bags, and they crinkle loudly as I heft them into my arms.

"So sorry that took a minute," she says, grinning at Gavin as her nails clack loudly on the register.

He bites back a smile, swiping his card through the machine before grabbing the remaining bags. "Don't worry about it. My friend here seems to be in a sudden rush for some reason."

And then he winks at her.

He. Winks. At. Her.

Like they have some sort of inside joke that I'm unaware of. Like they're best friends and I'm the third wheel.

My teeth grind against each other as I step outside and storm toward my car.

"What's the rush all of a sudden?" Gavin shouts from a few feet behind me.

"Trying to get away from the women around here who seem like they've never seen a handsome man before."

A deep laugh rumbles out of him, and I stop in my tracks to turn his way. His big, shit-eating grin makes his eyes sparkle and his cheeks pinken, and all of it together affects my ability to breathe.

"So glad I had you there to protect me," he teases, sauntering right past where I'm frozen.

"You should be," I scoff, pivoting to follow him. "Who knows what they would've done next." Stopping beside him at the back of the car, I pull out my keys and open the hatch, setting my bags inside. "Miss Blue Dress looked like she was about to strip you down right there next to the hot dog buns. Which is horribly un-sexy, if you ask me. And then Miss Blond Cashier looked like she wanted to check out way more than your groceries."

That infuriating smirk is still playing on his mouth as he sets his bags in the trunk. "And what would my big, bad Lena have done to protect me then?"

Chills race up my neck at the husky way he says my name, but I try to play it off by planting my hands on my hips. "Definitely would've defended your honor. Somehow." I shrug. "I could've at least shoved her out of the way."

"Mmm," he hums, nodding. "And then?"

I roll my eyes up to the cloudless sky. "I guess then I would take her by the—"

My words cut off when Gavin snatches the keys from my hand.

I lower my head in time to see him shove them into his pocket and declare, "I'm driving home."

"Like hell you are." I scowl up at him.

"You drove us here, I'll drive us home," he replies with his attempt at a convincing smile.

Unfortunately for me, all of his smiles are convincing, and my will to drive us home immediately frays around the edges.

"It's my car. I am not playing passenger princess."

His masculine scent surrounds me as he leans closer until he's only a few inches from me. "You're more like a passenger demon anyway."

My jaw drops open, and a silent battle rages between our gazes.

His seems to say, *come on, you know you want to give in.*

I really do.

That stupid fucking smirk is going to be the death of me.

Biting my bottom lip to smother a smile, I concede. "Fine. You can drive, but I get to be in charge of what we listen to."

His breath of sweet relief gusts against my cheek before he walks to the driver's-side door, completely unaware that he's about to regret making this arrangement.

Dropping into the passenger seat, I lift my chin and shimmy my shoulders with excitement. "My audiobook is right at the good part. The sexual tension is *just* about to snap."

When I throw a smug grin in his direction, his skin has paled to a snow white, and I add a new job idea to my mental list.

7. *Full-time role as the woman who makes Gavin lose his mind.*

Chapter 7

Gavin

*I*f you don't stop sassing me, I'm going to fuck that pretty mouth."

A bead of sweat rolls down my temple as I attempt to discreetly set my arm over my thigh to conceal how this audiobook has sent every ounce of blood straight to my dick. I can feel Lena's laser focus on me as she searches for any sign that she's successfully riling me up.

This is so wildly inappropriate to listen to together, but I'm determined not to give her the satisfaction of knowing she's winning this battle.

She's literally kicking her feet on the dash and squealing at whatever the fuck this book is. I can't even remember the main characters' names, but I can remember exactly how much squirming Lena and I have done over the course of this drive.

I swallow thickly and tug on the collar of my sweater as the female narrator's moans fill the car.

"You'd like that, wouldn't you?" a deep voice says. "I just can't decide if I want to fuck you like my princess or my dirty little slut."

My fingers slam over the volume knob right as the last word

comes out, ending in a dead silence ringing through the car. But after a beat, Lena's loud, cackling laughter erupts, echoing through the small space. I drop my arm back over my crotch right as she looks my way.

"It was just getting to the good part," she whines, fanning her flushed cheeks. "You didn't like it?"

My grip tightens around the steering wheel.

Of course I *liked* it.

Too much.

But I shouldn't be imagining the woman next to me while that scene plays out in my head. I shouldn't be picturing *her* on her knees, lips swollen and eyes pinned to mine while she takes me into her mouth.

Her vibrating groan as I hit the back of her throat.

Fuck, I have to stop thinking about it.

"I honestly didn't think you would last that long," she says with a sigh, pulling her feet from the dash and turning toward me.

Goddamn it. I wouldn't last that long.

I drag in a deep breath, trying to put all my concentration into making my blood flow back to all the appropriate places.

"Your cheeks are a little pink, Gav," Lena teases, leaning closer to inspect them.

As I slow to a stop at the first traffic light in Juniper, I shoot her a glare as severe as I can muster. "I'm never riding in your car again."

She barks out another laugh, throwing her head back.

Such a fucking menace.

The next stop light brings us in front of Bear Creek. Glancing out Lena's window, I spot the owners, Gary and Joe, shoveling the sidewalk up to the cabin they live in beside the bakery.

Lena rolls her window down, cool air breezing through the

car as she waves to them. "Hey, handsome men," she shouts, and their shovels pause as they turn with wide smiles.

"Lena! Happy holidays," Joe calls with a wave.

Gary bends down like he's trying to look farther into the car. "Is that Gavin?"

My gut rolls with guilt as I wave, hoping the conversation doesn't lead to them sharing all the details about my future before I can.

I'm not purposely keeping my and Auggie's plans to move here a secret from anyone, but I've promised him I wouldn't say anything until he does a big Christmas reveal for his mom and Luci.

But now Lena has been looped into that group of people who don't know about the plan, and I wish I could tell her about it.

The light turns green, saving me from having to weave my way through any awkwardness, and we shout a quick goodbye as I pull past their business.

Flicking my gaze to Lena, I find her concentration on her phone as she clicks to restart the audiobook. But fortunately, a call blares through the car speakers before that book can make my dick any harder than it already is.

With a swipe of her thumb, she answers her mother's call. "Hey. We're almost back to the house."

"Oh, good," Bea croons. "We're all ready to get the tree. Can you meet us at Bear Creek?"

Lena's brows crease as she turns to me and asks, "Did we get anything at the store that'll go bad while we pick out a tree?"

"No, we should be fine."

"Okay, we just passed it," she tells Bea. "We'll turn around and meet you there."

"Are you being nice to Gavin? If you were rude, he's not the one we're kicking out of the house." Bea's voice is stern, and it forces a chuckle out of me.

"I'm always nice," Lena says innocently, fluttering her lashes in my direction.

"That's a load of shit, Lena, and you know it," Bea says with a laugh before ending the call.

At the next road, I turn the car around to drive back to the tree farm. Lena doesn't restart the audiobook, pester me with more questions, or even look my way.

She just stares out the window, fingers drumming on her thigh.

Once I park beside the tree farm, I relax in my seat to wait for her family as uneasy silence cloaks the car.

The engine purrs lightly, and the heater hums from the dash, but we're both still and speechless.

And it's suffocating.

I don't know what happened in the last few minutes, but she seems completely closed off suddenly, like her mind is whirring with thoughts and I don't get to know them.

When I can't take it anymore, I ask, "Is everything okay?"

She shakes her head. "We're going to have to at least pretend to be friends again if there's any chance of my mom getting off my back," she blurts.

A breath of relief rushes out with a small laugh. "It has to be pretend?"

She tilts back to her headrest. "You tell me. It sure doesn't feel like we're friends right now."

My heart shrinks a little, and my laughter sobers. "Lena, I want to be your friend more than you know." I swallow tightly before admitting, "I missed you."

She turns to me with a heavy determination in the tense set of her brows. "I missed you too." Her shoulders lift in a quick shrug. "We used to be close, but now I know nothing about you. I don't know why you left, why you're back, what's been going on since. And I feel like there's a dark shadow over our friendship from all these things left unsaid."

As my chest constricts, I spot Auggie pulling up to park beside us. He smiles and waves through his window, oblivious to what's happening inside the car.

I only have a moment to wrap this conversation up, even though I need days.

"I wish I could explain everything. It would make this so much easier." Emotion catches in my throat. "Just know that I really want to be friends with you again." My lips tug up in a grin. "Pretend it's my Christmas wish."

A soft "okay" whispers from her lips. Then she clears her throat, and her voice sounds steadier when she adds, "Friends, then?"

She reaches out her hand for me to shake, and I slide mine around her soft skin without hesitation. She meets my stare, a small grin tweaking the corner of her lips. And with one jerky lift, our agreement is settled, and she releases my hand to pull on her gloves.

"I'll be right there. I need to answer a few emails," I tell her, picking up my phone from the console.

But instead, after she gets out of the car, I stare blankly at the screen.

I just agreed to be friends with Lena, when only moments ago, I had a goddamn hard-on while imagining my best friend's sister with my dick in her mouth.

Smearing that lipstick. Gripping her hair tight. Groaning her name.

Fuck. How do I look Auggie in the eye five minutes after that?

I've worked with him every day for years, and I see Zara and the kids at least once a week in Eugene. But even they don't know where I've been the last two Christmases.

They don't know I desperately wished I was with them while also hating myself for it at the same time.

I spent my entire childhood bouncing between foster homes, always a little too *something* to be loved. Too old, too big, too boy, too hard to care for at every turn.

I've never felt important. Or good enough. Or worth the effort it takes to love me.

After getting to know Auggie in college, he encouraged me to go to therapy. I put it off for years, always giving some excuse as to why that wasn't the right time.

But when I graduated, I finally called someone. Auggie drove me to my first appointment, waited for me, and then took me out for a beer after.

He's taken care of me since the day we met, and I owe him everything.

He and his family are the only true home I've ever known.

Yet here I am, spoiling it with my feelings for Lena.

She's always been a shameless flirt. I've witnessed her act the same way with other people, so it's not like I think it's something special for me.

But my heart and dick don't seem to be getting that message. They're enjoying her attention way more than they're supposed to.

I should probably avoid being alone with her. We can be friends who keep a buffer around us at all times. That's normal, right?

Through the windshield, I watch as she pulls her hat over her ears and swoops an arm over Luci's petite shoulders, a field full of trees rolling down the hill behind her. Pen and Jack have pulled their dad and Bea off in one direction, and Zara holds Noah beside Lena.

This is fine. We have buffers. I can handle this.

Snapping open the car door, I join the group just as Lena steers them toward the foggy windows of the bakery.

"I need a peppermint mocha first," she announces.

"It's only been three hours since you had one," I grumble, shaking my head as I follow after her.

"And my blood sugar is feeling a little peaky," she snarks, batting her lashes at me over her shoulder.

My lips twitch without my permission.

And when I watch her raven curls bounce as she skips up the bakery steps, the smile only grows.

Taking Luci's hand, I guide her inside, and we wait by the door while Lena and Zara place their orders.

As usual, my attention stays on Lena. While she pulls her gloves off with her teeth, while she flashes her sunny smile at the barista, while she runs a hand over Noah's head.

It's somehow utterly mesmerizing to watch her do mundane things.

"Beautiful, isn't she?" Luci's voice startles me.

I blink a few times, grinning down at her curly gray hair. "What was that?"

She gives me a knowing grin, her eyes crinkling in the corners. That look says *I know more than you think I do*, and it shoots an icy chill down my spine.

"Just commenting on the view," she says as her attention flicks to Lena.

The view.

The view is only the most gorgeous woman in the goddamn world.

Lena's head is thrown back, her raspy, uninhibited laughter echoing off the wood walls of the bakery. I want to wrap my arms around her and breathe that laughter right into my lungs and live off it.

Once the barista hands her a drink, Lena saunters toward us and out the bakery door. Zara's right behind her as Lena sings "Jingle Bells" loud enough to turn a few heads.

I'm dazedly watching them stroll away when I remember Luci by my side.

"We should probably get on our way, don't you think, young man?" She raises an eyebrow. "We don't want to miss the main event."

I huff a laugh, pulling her hand to my forearm and guiding her down the steps. "I'm not as young as you think I am."

"Oh, age is all relative." She lets out a small grunt on the last step. "Did you know my Davis was sixteen years older than me?"

Surprise flickers through me. "I did not."

Her thin finger pokes into my chest. "He may have been sixteen years older, but he was always energetic in the bedroom, where it counts."

Laughter tumbles out of me, loud and gravelly.

Inky curls whip in my direction a few yards down the path as Lena hears it, and her sparkling gaze meets mine. A brilliant smile takes over her whole face, lifting her cheeks and making her skin glow with joy.

The sight of her zings right through my body like I've been shocked by an electric jolt.

Do I get that smile just for laughing?

Fuck, I should laugh more often.

"For consenting adults, age isn't important, dear," Luci whispers as we continue toward everyone gathered at the front of the tree field.

"Who's picking the tree this year?" Lena squeals.

"Is it my turn?" Jack bounces on his toes so high that he has to spin his arms to stay upright.

"Think you can handle this very serious tradition?" Lena grins down at him while Zara zips up his thick coat.

"Yes, yes," he squeaks, grinning proudly.

Lena pulls a small scarf out of her jacket and whips it through the air beside Jack. Then she turns around and hands me her peppermint mocha with a wink.

While she's tying the scarf over Jack's eyes, I peer down at the drink in my hand. The little red cup has lit Christmas trees decorating the sides, and the smell wafting from the opening is honestly . . . intriguing.

The imprint of her red lipstick on the edge holds my attention for way longer than it should.

A surge of curiosity builds in my chest, and I lift the cup to sneak a tiny sip. As soon as the sweet peppermint flavor hits my tongue, I recoil, scowling down at the opening.

What the fuck? It's way too sweet.

But I let the chocolate and peppermint melt on my tongue a little, and then, checking to make sure Lena's still not looking, I steal one more sip, just to try again.

Bleh. Still too much going on.

"Okay. What's your favorite number?" she asks Jack.

"Thirty-seven." He beams.

"I didn't know that," Auggie says as we all laugh. "Are you sure? Because that's going to make this process a little—"

Lena cuts him off with a sharp look. "You cannot interfere with fate, Auggie. If he wants thirty-seven, that's our number."

Auggie puts both his hands in the air, conceding, as Jack's little legs twitch with excitement.

When Lena still hasn't looked my way, I steal another sip of the coffee in my hands and minimally enjoy it that time. It really does taste like someone liquefied the entire holiday season and poured it into this cup.

As I lower it from my mouth, Zara's gaze snaps in my direction, and her lips curve up knowingly.

"How many times should we spin him?" Lena asks Pen.

"Five hundred forty-three times," she answers with a mischievous grin.

"How about five?" Zara offers, and Pen rolls her eyes.

"Okay, everyone knows the drill, right?" Lena says, the ringleader directing her troops. She turns around as I'm pulling her cup away from my mouth for the fourth time. Her adorable nose scrunches as she sends a mock glare in my direction.

Then she spins Jack five times before steadying his shoulders. "Thirty-seventh tree you hit is the one. Ready? Go!"

She releases him, and he wobbles on his feet for a moment before reaching his hands out and stumbling like Frankenstein toward the tree lot. Laughter ensues from the rest of the family as he crashes into his first tree, the pine needles prickling his cheeks.

"One," everyone cheers, and Lena holds a finger in the air.

They've been doing this tradition since I met them. Apparently, Lena wanted to choose the tree this way when she was six years old, and they've kept it alive since then. One year, the Juniper Gazette followed a sixteen-year-old Lena around the tree farm, snapping pictures and cataloging the whole process until she hit her thirteenth tree.

Jack's thirty-seven is definitely the biggest number I've been a part of.

My first holiday with the Santos family, Lena tried to convince me to do it. She thought her dancing lashes and hands clasped under her chin would convince me, but it didn't. The next year, she tried threatening to never speak to me again, and that one was a little harder to refuse, but I managed it. Then the final time, she offered to make my favorite cookies if I did it.

"Please? I'll make you those crinkle cookies you like."

"I can make those for myself," I argue, patting the top of her head.

She growls and crosses her arms. "But everyone in the family does it."

Exactly. That's not me.

As Jack bumps into his seventh tree and falls over, Lena reaches for her cup. "Totally forgot about this," she says, pulling it from my hand. Then her gaze jumps to mine. "Gavin. Mr. Plain Black Coffee. Did you drink half of my peppermint mocha?"

She grins broadly, and warmth pools in my cheeks.

"You did," she squeaks, pointing a finger at me. "You left me two sips!"

"I think it was Luci." I shrug, and Luci's hand smacks my stomach as she passes us to follow Jack to the next tree.

Lena's teeth dig into her perfect bottom lip. "You liked it, didn't you? Admit it."

"It's atrocious." *It's not.*

"It's delicious."

Maybe. It's decent.

She lifts the cup and plants her mouth right where mine was, watching me as she takes a sip. "It's growing on you. Pretty soon you'll be begging for it."

My knees falter as a sudden rush of heat spreads through my veins.

You'll be begging for it.

It feels like I already am.

Chapter 8

Lena

*T*wisting into a new position on the couch, I squeeze my thighs together, attempting to snuff out the throbbing ache between them. My body has been on pins and needles since the audiobook this morning, and as the clock on the mantel ticks toward midnight, the arousal refuses to dissipate.

I'm *almost* ashamed of how much I loved watching Gavin fidget in his seat, but there was something satisfying about being the one to make him squirm.

Flipping onto my side with a dramatic huff, I scan our perfectly imperfect Christmas tree. The thirty-seventh tree Jack ran into is lopsided and missing quite a few branches from one angle, but I love it.

The flawed trees are my favorites. You can tell they've been through some shit, but they're still trying and growing and putting themselves out there, just begging someone to love them.

And isn't that a little like all of us?

We brought it home, filled the house with Christmas music and laughter, and passed ornaments around as we decorated.

Gavin spent most of the time in the corner of the couch, watching everyone move around the living room. But when it was time to put the star on top, Mama pulled him up and forced him to do it.

His cheeks had turned scarlet, but he stood, set his whiskey down, and lifted onto his tiptoes to reach the top of the tree. As he positioned the star, the entire house erupted in cheers and a huge smile broke out over his face.

Remembering that smile makes me restless again.

I kick the covers off in frustration and tiptoe to my luggage in the guest bathroom. My strappy maroon swimsuit sits at the top, and I slip it on before grabbing a towel and sneaking out the back door.

The cold air burns my skin as the steam escaping the hot tub lures me closer. I fold over the cover and slide it to the side, leaving only half of it open.

My muscles immediately relax as I lower into the water, like I'm releasing all the pent-up tension from today into the bubbles. I tuck my fingers under my thighs, lean my head back, and squeeze my eyes shut, forcing deep breaths through my lungs.

Today has been mentally exhausting. If someone could see my brain's search history, they'd be confused by what they found. It would be a blend of *how to stifle a crush on the man I shouldn't be thinking about* and *how to make him look at me like I want him to* with a sprinkle of *how to convince him to tell me why he left*.

For the record, all of those searches turned up no results. I still don't have the answers.

A soft *snick* from the door has my eyelids popping open, and Gavin's wide gaze lands on me.

I can't deny the tiny thrill that shoots up my spine at the sight of him, his sturdy shoulders cloaked in shadows and the dim light from the kitchen illuminating the sharp lines of his face.

"Sorry. I didn't know . . . I'll go back upstairs," he mumbles as he ducks back toward the door.

If I were a responsible person—a good sister and *friend*—I would let him leave.

But instead, I say, "No," probably too brightly. "You don't have to go."

He shifts uncomfortably, tilting his head back to focus intently on the beams overhead. "It's probably best if I do."

My heart rate beats quicker in my ears. "I really don't mind."

His conflicted thoughts play out over his face. He looks at the hot tub, the patio, back to the beams, down at the towel in his hand. Everywhere but at me.

"I don't bite." I laugh, trying to break the tension as he rubs a hand over his neck.

Goose bumps prickle over my skin when he takes a tentative step in my direction and asks, "Are you sure?"

My snort of laughter echoes through the quiet night. "I mean, I'd bite someone if they asked me to."

He shakes his head as he continues to avoid my gaze, so I drop the flirting and put him out of his misery. My throat feels like sandpaper as I sober and tell him, "Join me. It's not a big deal."

But as he grips his shirt to pull it off, my stomach flips with the realization that I was wrong. It is, in fact, a very big deal.

As he reveals every rippling inch of his abdomen, chest, and shoulders, I can practically *feel* the glittering delight in my eyes. His muscles flex and roll as he lifts his shirt over his head, the dark lines of his intricate tattoos visible but unrecognizable with such little light.

And *god*, I wish I could see them. Trace them. Lick them.

This hot tub has only been here since last year, so this is the first time I've been around Gavin like this. I've never had the thrill of seeing any of the tattoos on his chest or back. The details of the snake on his forearm are vividly etched in my mind, and I could draw the vines around his wrist from memory.

But I want that kind of familiarity with the tattoos over the rest of his body too.

It's probably for the best that I can't see those, though. Even being this close to a shirtless Gavin is pooling heat between my thighs, the throbbing arousal from earlier skyrocketing right back up in his presence.

I force myself to shut my eyes while he gets into the hot tub. He sits beside me, the water rising enough that I tuck my legs under me to lift myself up.

He lets out a low groan that makes my heart stutter, but then he goes silent, sitting perfectly still. The only movement in the water is from the jets around us.

After a moment of tense silence, I peep through one slitted eyelid. Mostly because I can't help it.

He's making this hot tub feel claustrophobic, his shoulders spanning more than twice as much of the side as mine. With his head tilted back, lips parted, and lashes fanned over his cheeks, he appears utterly relaxed.

Meanwhile, I'm the exact opposite.

Gavin Moore is sitting beside me in nothing but swim shorts, and my entire body is *buzzing*.

If I scoot a little closer . . . *no*, I can't think about that.

When I turn my head to get a better view of his face in the moonlight, all the oxygen rushes from my lungs.

Dark tendrils of hair brush his forehead. Droplets of water

stream down the planes of his neck. A five o'clock shadow dusts his jaw.

My thighs clench at the thought of that stubble scraping between them.

That would never happen. But I'm not above admitting that I've fantasized about it a few times.

More than a few times.

It's fine, right? It's totally normal to have a ten-year crush on a man you can't have. This happens to people all the time.

As he swallows, I'm fascinated by the way his Adam's apple rolls in the long, thick column of his throat.

Fuck. All he's doing is breathing and swallowing, and I can't look away from him.

"I can feel you staring," he murmurs, peeking in my direction.

I choke on a breath as I turn to face forward again. "It's because you're too goddamn big. You barely fit in here," I lie, scooting an inch farther from him to reinforce the fake point.

He lifts his head and stretches his legs out to the bench across from us. "I'm the perfect size, actually."

Our conversation lands in my brain, and my cheeks catch on fire. I know we're talking about this hot tub, but my mind pretends for a moment that we're talking about something entirely different.

Water laps at my neck as I squirm from the pressure building in my core at the thought of Gavin's *size*.

In my fidgeting, my knee accidentally bumps against his thigh, but I don't move it. I let it rest there, testing myself in a way that might kill me later.

Why am I putting myself through a *test*? I don't even like tests. I don't agree with them being an appropriate way to assess knowledge. So why am I doing it to myself?

Is it:

A. Because I like how it feels to touch him?

B. Because I enjoy torturing myself by pretending this is normal?

C. Because I like pushing him, teasing him, flirting with him?

D. All of the above.

The answer is obviously D, and I have no idea if that means I pass or fail this test.

A trickle of sweat rolls down the back of my neck as the bunched fabric of his shorts rubs against my bare knee. I didn't know knees had so many nerve endings, but right now it feels like all my focus is on that tiny bit of skin.

He seems unbothered, with his relaxed face and steady breaths puffing from his lips.

Not flustered and jumping out of his skin like I am.

This entire damn hot tub is boiling.

The urge to say *fuck the rules* and crawl into his lap is pounding in my chest.

I need a distraction.

This knee-based sexual tension is about to make me combust. I don't know if that's ever happened before, but I refuse to be the first.

Distraction. Distraction.

"Did I tell you Millie moved out?" I ask loudly, cursing the rapid heartbeat in my ears that's keeping me from speaking at a normal decibel.

A muscle ripples in his jaw. "No. Are you okay?" he asks, his gentle voice sliding over me like silk.

"Oh, it's not like a friendship breakup or anything. She just moved in with her boyfriend. And I'm okay. I think?" As I'm attempting to sound sure and steady, his brows press together like he doesn't believe me. "Well, that's a lie. I miss her more than I thought I would. But I'm happy for her at the same time," I admit.

"I'm sorry." His big hand wraps around my knee under the water, and a flush of adrenaline coils through my body.

The drastic shift in hormones pulls more words from my lips. "Her boyfriend, Finn, has custody of his nieces. So they have their own little family now. I'm at their house a lot, and I adore all of them. But when I'm at home, everything feels lonely." I lift a shoulder in a shrug. "And maybe it's a little bit of jealousy . . . I don't know. Seeing them happy is amazing, but I know I'm not the kind of person who gets a romance like that. I'm doomed to be the side character to my friends' love stories forever, and that's fine. At least I get to see them happy."

I suck in a deep breath after that string of rapid sentences, embarrassed that I sound as flustered as I feel on the inside.

His thumb rubs the line where my calf meets my thigh, and I don't know if he realizes he's doing it, but it makes my pulse pound in my throat and my knee feel like it's on fire.

"You'll get your own love story one day," he whispers, like it's a fact. Like he knows for sure that it will happen. And I can hardly focus on his words when his finger makes another slide over my knee. "You're a lot of things, Lena Santos, but a side character is not one of them."

Chapter 9

Gavin

I had two rules for myself before I got in the water.

1. *Do not look below her face.*
2. *Do not touch her. At all.*

But fuck if I didn't break both within minutes.

The no-looking-below-her-face rule was shattered when I let my eyes trail over the flimsy straps on her shoulders, the little dips above her collarbones, the elegant neck that I'm buzzing to kiss.

Then I touched the bare skin of her leg like an absolute fucking idiot.

I must have a death wish.

It takes a concerted effort, but I manage to pull my hand away from her knee and slide my arm behind her on the side of the hot tub.

Spinning toward me, Lena tucks her knees up to her chest. Her voice drips with bleak uncertainty as she says, "I don't know if I'll get a love story. Lately it feels like I might be defective. Aside from my core group of family and friends, everyone else leaves. Like I don't matter that much to them."

Two fists squeeze around my heart.

I know how that feels.

She scoffs before continuing. "Starting with my sperm donor of a father, then every person I've tried to build a relationship with. And I know Millie didn't *leave* me, but when I'm sitting in my empty house, it still feels a little bit like I got left behind. Everybody always leaves."

Even you left.

The words are unsaid, but they loom over me.

My throat tightens, and I try to swallow the pressure as images from many years ago flash through my mind.

My own people leaving me.

Lena's hand slaps over her mouth. "Fuck. I'm sorry." Her legs drop as she sits up straighter. "Oh god, that was so insensitive. I don't know everything about your story, but my mopey one has to be nothing compared to yours. I'm so sorry."

I shake my head. "It's all right. I know you didn't mean it that way." My voice sounds unsteady in my ears, even though it's the truth.

"I still shouldn't have said it." Her lips press into a flat line.

A thread pulls tight in my chest, tugging me toward her.

It seems to say, *closer. Tell her. Trust her.*

With a slow inhale, I follow my instincts to open up my heart a little. "Our dads had similar roles in our lives, and I never met mine either." Lena's brows crease as she nods. "And my last memory of my mother is the view of her taillights after she left me on my grandmother's front porch."

A strangled gasp rips from Lena's throat, and my arms ache to hold her. Hug her. Comfort her, even though I'm the one sharing painful memories.

"What happened to your grandmother?" she whispers gently.

"She left me with a social worker a few months later." With a sympathetic whimper, she reaches across me and somehow finds my free hand under the water, pulling it to the bench between us. Encasing my hand in hers, she holds it tenderly while she waits for me to continue. "She said I was too much to handle, and they couldn't find my mother anywhere, so I went into foster care."

Her thumb glides over my knuckles. "I'm so sorry, Gav. I didn't mean to sound so callous about having a shitty parent when you had it so much worse."

Turning toward her, I slide my hand from the edge of the hot tub to tuck a stray curl behind her ear. "Your trauma isn't invalid because you think mine is bigger. Your hurt matters too. And you're allowed to talk about it, even with me."

Her lips part as silence blankets the space between us.

My whole life has been a lesson in how unworthy I am of love. There has never been anyone who chose me wholeheartedly or put me first, and I have a feeling it's never going to be in the cards for me.

I'm never going to find someone who embraces me exactly the way I am.

But it *destroys* me that Lena has similar thoughts about herself. I may be unlovable, but she's not.

Loving her has never been the problem. In fact, it's the easiest thing I've ever done.

Clearing my throat, I allow myself one more moment of her touch before I pull my hands back and rub my tense shoulder instead.

"Can I ask you a question?" she murmurs, setting her chin on her knees.

"Always."

"Is this why you left us?" she wonders, tilting her head to the side. "Because of something to do with your parents?"

A shaky breath leaves my lungs as I meet her concerned gaze.

My throat aches to tell her. To let all the words blaze the space between us like wildfire, cleansing everything and leaving room for new growth.

But I can't.

"No, it's not. I wish I could tell you."

She groans, rolling her eyes. "I think I deserve *something*, Gav. You abandoned us at that party. You were my designated driver, and you didn't even care if I was safe." Her voice cracks on the last few words.

The atmosphere shifts as this new version of that night slams into my mind.

"I told Auggie I was leaving. He was in charge of getting you home." A sharp pain burns in my chest. "I found him before I left, and he said he was fine to drive."

She shakes her head. "He wasn't."

I clench my hands into fists as my voice cracks like a whip through the air. "What?"

"It's not his fault." She lifts one shoulder half-heartedly. "I encouraged him to have another drink with me because I thought you were still there somewhere."

My teeth grind together. "How did you get home?"

"I called Mama to come back and get us."

Guilt sours my stomach. Everyone was asleep when I rushed back to the cabin that night to shove my things in a bag and leave. That means Lena had to wake her up.

"So please," she begs, "tell me the truth. I don't want to be mad at you right now. Not after you told me about your past and promised we're friends. But it feels like there's a missing piece, and I want the truth. I don't want this big secret looming over us anymore."

Dark images from that night blaze through my mind like a torture device that my brain cycles through on my worst days.

Greedy hands on her thighs, inching up her dress. Hips pressing into hers, grinding her against the wall. Soft moans echoing through the hallway. Her back arching as the straps of her dress slip down her shoulders.

I let out a deep, heavy breath, trying to force the memories away.

This entire setting is intoxicating me. The quiet night and the warm water and the dim lights through the window from our crooked tree and the way Lena's hair is curling around her temples from the humidity. All of it melds together and puts me under some sort of spell that I can't fight against.

"You think knowing why I left will fix it?" I ask, and she nods in confirmation.

Maybe I'm tired of keeping everything bottled up inside me. Maybe I'm dying to get out of my own thoughts.

So the words seep out of me.

"I saw you." I clear my throat. "I saw you with Brandon in that hallway."

The color drains from her face, but I keep going.

"His hands up your skirt and his face in your neck." Shame burns on my cheeks, even though I've only given away a tiny bit of information.

Not enough to reveal my jealousy and damn me.

"I didn't know you saw that." She bites her bottom lip and puckers her brow with confusion. "I know you're like . . . my big brother, but even *he* isn't that angry when he's seen me kissing someone. And he definitely isn't mad enough to skip Christmas for years."

I know you're like my big brother.

Fuck. I hate every word of that sentence.

I want to burn them, tell her I'm not like her big brother at all. I'm the opposite.

I think about you constantly. When I'm in a work meeting with your brother. When I'm at the gym, trying to drown out the sound of your voice in my ears. When I'm eating dinner and wishing you were across from me. When my dick is in my hand and I'm dreaming that it's you wrapped around it. When something funny happens, I want to tell you about it.

It never. Fucking. Ends.

I'm walking an ultrathin tightrope right now. On one side, I could fall back into safe territory. *Big brother* territory.

On the other side, I could tip toward something else. I could finally tell her what my mind does when she's around and how miserable it was to watch her writhe against a wall and moan someone else's name.

But it's safer to stay on the tightrope than fall to the wrong side.

Saying those words would change everything. It would threaten the only family I've ever truly loved. It would put the life I'm trying to build in jeopardy and risk my only friendship.

The truth endangers *everything*.

So instead, I whisper, "Do you really see me as your brother?" A stabbing ache builds in my chest in anticipation of the answer.

I don't quite know what response I'm hoping for. I want her to see me as part of this family, to say I belong here, because I've never belonged anywhere in my life.

But secretly, way down in the hidden parts of my heart, I want to be nowhere *near* her brother.

She hesitates for a moment, her shoulders lifting with short breaths. Then she slowly nods and says, "Yeah. You're a part of our family." Her lashes flutter a few times before she finally looks at me. Her eyes are clear, like she's putting all her energy into making me believe her words. "You'll always be my brother, Gav."

A crack splits right through my soul, causing me to lose my balance on the tightrope and topple off.

I'm careening, tumbling, falling into eternal brotherhood, and she has no idea.

Her lips twist into an uneasy grin. "I'm getting tired. I'm going to attempt to get some sleep."

I nod and try to school my features. "You should go upstairs and take the bed," I offer, because it's not like I'm getting much sleep in there anyway.

She hums in acknowledgment, scooting through the water past my legs.

As she lifts herself out of the hot tub, I let myself have one heartbeat to watch her body. I give myself that one second to memorize every curve of her ass and strong thighs. Her toned calves and all the way down to her delicate ankles.

Just one flash of an image that I can keep forever.

That's all I get.

Chapter 10

Lena

Shhh. You're okay, buddy."

A gentle voice floats through my dreams, and I blink myself awake. The sun barely illuminates the windows as the sound of running water makes its way from the kitchen, followed by a soft shushing and the distinct *click* of the coffee pot settling back into the machine.

A smile touches my lips. I know without looking that it's Gavin, that comforting medley a familiar soundtrack to our Christmas mornings together.

Last night after leaving the hot tub, I slipped my pajamas back on and ignored his offer for me to take the bedroom. Instead, I tucked myself under my blanket on the couch, trying as hard as I could to block out the intoxicating memory of Gavin's body and voice and presence.

When he came inside a little while later, he stepped up to the back of the couch and whispered, "Lena. Go take the bed. I'll sleep down here."

Of course, I was still awake, failing at not thinking about him, but I refused to acknowledge his words. Because there's no way in hell I was going to be able to lie in a bed that's probably drenched in his scent.

Sleep would've been the furthest thing from my mind as the temptation to sink my fingers between my thighs wreaked havoc on my body.

With a frustrated groan, I throw off my blanket and tiptoe into the downstairs bathroom to take a shower. As I lather shampoo into my hair, the conversation from last night bursts back into my mind, and my hands pause.

Gavin saw me with Brandon.

I imagine him scowling down that dark hallway, and my skin flushes hot. But it has nothing to do with his brotherly concern about what's happening.

No, my pulse is spiking for a different reason.

Fantasies fill my head with what could've happened instead.

Gavin storming toward us, ripping Brandon away, and pinning me against the wall. Growling into my neck. Crashing his lips to mine. Burying his fingers in my hair.

I shove my face into the water, trying to shatter the delusion.

Just last night, I told him he was like a brother to me.

It might've been the biggest lie I've ever told.

The reality is, I've seen him as a friend, a crush, a companion.

But I've *never* seen him as a brother.

When I emerge from the bathroom a little while later, dressed in leggings and my favorite cookie-themed holiday sweater that says *Let's Get Baked*, I'm not prepared for what I see through the doorway into the kitchen.

My stomach flips at the sight of Gavin in black pajama pants, muscles bulging out of his black long-sleeve shirt, with Noah cradled in his arms. He's pouring some half-and-half into a coffee mug while doing that bouncy dance people tend to do with a baby in their arms.

Noah makes a cooing sound, and Gavin murmurs, "Is that right?"

He turns in my direction and pads toward me, his dark-brown hair sticking up on one side in the most adorable way. A lazy grin plays on his lips, and it turns my insides to mush.

"Here you are," he says, handing me the mug. "Noah made this for you."

I drop onto the couch sideways and carefully pull my legs under me so I don't spill the contents of the mug. The scent from the coffee hits me immediately, and my brows draw together. "I didn't know he knew how to make peppermint mochas."

One shoulder kicks up in a shrug as he sits beside me. "Apparently, he knows how to Google things already. Kids these days." He pulls a pillow behind himself and leans back, letting Noah lie against his chest, a big hand wrapped around his back to hold him in place.

Suddenly, a new job idea flickers in my mind.

8. *Woman who watches Gavin hold babies.*

My ovaries are aching at the sight.

"Did anyone check your references before they gave you this babysitting gig?"

His face pinches as he scowls at me. "I'll have you know, I come with great references. I watch this guy all the time. We're good buds, aren't we?" He looks down at Noah's face as he adds, "Zara came downstairs half-asleep. So I told her I would hang out with him while she went back to bed."

I have to dig my nails into the couch cushion to keep from melting into a puddle on the floor. "You really babysit?"

My breath stalls in anticipation of his response. I'm pretty sure his answer is about to get me pregnant.

"I like kids." He shrugs. "I watch them sometimes while Auggie and Zara go out to dinner." Warm pressure gathers in my chest as he kisses the top of Noah's head. "Noah and I have an arrangement. He stays happy as long as I hold him, so I keep him in my arms the entire time."

"Do you want kids one day?" The words startle me, even though they came from my throat. I pinch my lips together, trying to keep more inner thoughts from popping out.

"Yeah." His lashes lift as he meets my gaze. "I'd love to be a dad."

My mind betrays me. It makes a mockery of my sanity by producing images I didn't know could exist.

Gavin touching my swollen belly. His strong hands assembling a crib. His whispered voice soothing *our* newborn. His broad shoulders with a baby carrier strapped to them.

And for some reason, that vision *aches* as it burrows its way into my heart.

"Do you?" His voice cuts through the daydream, and I immediately want it back.

I feel like I'm already mourning the loss of something that never existed.

My answer clogs in my throat, making my "Yes" sound like a squawk.

But he must understand me because he nods before motioning to the mug in my hands. "You gonna try that?"

I blink down at it, thankful for the subject change. "How many sips did you steal?" I tease, lifting an eyebrow.

"Zero." A muscle in his jaw ticks as he tries to control a grin.

Shaking my head, I bring the mug to my lips. "Mm-hmm. Sure."

His dark stare watches me closely as the chocolaty peppermint flavor washes over my tongue and down my throat. Just that little bit of liquid sends warmth throughout my entire body, and a hum of pleasure rumbles from my chest.

I don't know what kind of sorcery he has put into this, but it's even better than the one at Bear Creek Bakery.

Gavin clears his throat, dropping his attention back down to Noah. "How is it?"

"Perfect." I swallow another sip as I pull my legs up to hug my knees.

Leaning his head back, he turns to me, his dark, thoughtful gaze sliding lazily over my face. His eyes have always had this foxlike intensity to them.

That focused attention is almost predatory, like he's studying me intently, tracking every detail, and it sets my entire body buzzing and my pulse pounding in my neck.

Grinning over my mug, I wonder, "Do you remember that Christmas I made everyone drawings of the animals they remind me of?"

He nods. "Of course."

"And I made you a fox?"

One corner of his lips quirks up. "I believe your words were 'intelligent and cunning.'"

I snort a laugh. "Among other words, yes. Adaptable, independent, observant."

He swallows as a blush coats his cheeks. "I remember." His whiskey eyes drop to watch me take another sip of coffee. "And you chose a tiger for yourself."

He remembers.

Surprise flutters through me. "Yeah. Strong-willed and intuitive."

"Unpredictable," he adds with a smirk.

"But you"—I poke him in the shoulder playfully—"told me I was more of a tiger *cub*."

"I stand by that," he says firmly. "Fierce and ferocious on the outside, soft and cuddly on the inside."

His dark gaze pins me in place like he has seen straight into my soul.

My lungs constrict, cutting off my airflow.

He couldn't be more right. I am a fierce protector of the people I love, ferocious when I need to be. Unpredictable most of the time, even to myself.

But when the rest of the world isn't watching, I soften. I relax. And insecurity and vulnerability creep into places I didn't know they could.

Can I find a job I love?

Will I be adrift like this forever, searching for my passion?

Am I unlovable? Destined to be alone for the rest of my life?

Swallowing those thoughts, I try to push them away. I can't wallow in them, or I might never pull myself out.

So I summon a bit of confidence into my features and take another sip from my mug. "This might be the best peppermint mocha of my life. Try it." I hold the mug in his direction. "You know you want to."

He lifts a hand from Noah's back. I try to ignore the zap of electricity that shoots up my arm when our fingers brush. But it's impossible as the jolt travels all the way to my heart.

I can't drag my attention away as he brings the cup to his

mouth. My gaze wanders over his smooth lips, sharp jaw, and strong hands.

A low groan rumbles through him, and I want to drown in it. I want to hear nothing but his laugh and *that* groan for the rest of my life.

Chapter 11

Gavin

Lena grabs the mug from my hand and pulls it to her mouth. Pride bubbles in my chest as I watch her lashes drift closed in pleasure.

It took some time to make the homemade chocolate and peppermint syrups this morning, but I know it was worth it as she lowers the cup and a peaceful smile lifts her lips.

Those perfect, plump lips. They're bare right now, no red lipstick darkening them, but I find them even more tempting. That lush coral pink makes me want to find out if they taste like peppermint right now. And I'm dying to know what they would look like puffy from kissing.

Last night in bed, I tried so hard not to think about those flimsy straps around her collarbone and how easily I could've slipped them off. I tried not to imagine what it would feel like to slide my hand further up her thigh. And most of all, I tried not to fantasize about tugging her into my lap to see how perfectly we fit together.

But I failed at every *fucking* bit of it.

"Gavin?" With my attention on her lips, I get to see the way they move when she whispers my name. The way the tip of her tongue is visible when she says the syllables.

My throat is dry when I sigh, "Lena."

Her raven curls shine in the sunrise through the window as she tilts her head to take another sip. "I missed this. Drinking coffee with you early in the morning when the house is quiet."

"I missed it too. Last Christmas, no one berated me about how soon the cinnamon rolls would be ready." I try to hide my small grin, but it sneaks out around the words.

Her gaze flicks up, and she groans. "They just make the house smell *so good*. It's hard to wait for them. We had to go back to canned cinnamon rolls without our Gavin here to make them."

Guilt lands like a lead weight in my stomach. My cinnamon rolls are also Penelope's favorite, and I hate that I wasn't here to make them.

Noah stirs on my chest, his arm flying out before he settles again. As I run a hand over his back, I scan the line of stockings on the mantel.

Mine is at the very end, Rudolph's red nose protruding from it. Bea got me that stocking with my name embroidered across the top on my second holiday here. At thirty years old, it was the first time I ever had one with my name on it.

That night, I cried into my pillow as silently as I possibly could.

I had made it through twenty-nine Christmases without the kind of memories and family I saw in holiday movies. Twenty-nine years of wishing I could have what Ralphie from *A Christmas Story* had. Or, hell, I'd be content with two parents fighting for my attention like Charlie from *The Santa Clause*.

Instead, I had two biological parents who wanted nothing to do with me and foster parents who couldn't care less.

"We hung yours up even though you weren't here," Lena whispers, like she can sense where my thoughts are.

Pressure builds behind my eyes and burns down into my throat as that information lodges in my heart.

They included me even when I couldn't show up. Even when I didn't deserve it.

"Did you know that's my first stocking?" I can't pull my gaze away from the white stitching of my name across the top.

"Really? Your first one ever?"

"Yeah. Every Christmas was lonely except for one until I came here." I swallow thickly and kiss the top of Noah's head for something to do. "The year I was ten, I had just been placed with the Lornells a few weeks before. There were three other foster children in that home who already knew each other. They had their own friendship going on, and I had spent most of my time reading in my bed when I wasn't at school."

When I pause, Lena wordlessly offers me her cup. Without thinking, I take a sip and hand it back to her. "But that Christmas evening, my foster sister pulled me out of bed. She convinced me to come to her room, where she was going to read a book to the rest of us. Who knows what the hell the Lornells were doing, but this sixteen-year-old read every page of a gilded copy of *Christmas Stories for Children* that she had gotten from the library." I let out a small laugh that cracks on the edges. "That was my favorite Christmas until I came here."

Lena sets the mug on the coffee table, and the cushion dips as she scoots next to me. Her head lands on my shoulder, and she nestles her hand into mine on the couch, twining our fingers together in a perfect fit.

My breath gusts out of me as her touch brings a rush of relaxation to every muscle in my body. Relief washes over me like a warm breeze, and my fingers clench around hers, holding tight like she might keep me safe with her small grip.

"We want you here for all your Christmases from now on," she says, sighing as she cuddles closer to my shoulder.

My eyelids drift shut slowly. "I want that too."

Chapter 12

Lena

The hair stands up on the back of my neck as I stare at the image Zara AirDropped to my phone.

Gavin's head is tipped back, lips parted in sleep, with Noah on his chest. Gav has one big hand around Noah's back and the other on the cushion between our thighs. My sleeping face is pressed against his bicep, which ended up making the perfect pillow while we were curled up together.

The picture doesn't have a clear view of my hand, but it's still wrapped inside Gavin's, exactly the way it remained until Noah woke up a while later with hungry whimpers.

We look way too comfortable. Like a tiny family.

Damn it. I'm in so much trouble.

I click the little arrow at the bottom of the screen and send it to my friends.

We Catan Beat Finn

> **Lena:** Zara took this picture earlier.

> **Lena:** Houston, we have a problem.

Lena: I don't think I'll ever recover from this.

Emil: Oh shit. This is the cutest thing I've ever seen.

Lena: I know.

Micah: Those forearms, though.

Lena: I know.

Millie: That looks so cozy!

Lena: I know.

Lena: You are all saying the good things, and I need you to say bad things.

Millie: Okay.

Millie: I just hate how peaceful you look.

Micah: Are you two holding hands? Ew.

Emil: Hot guys cuddling babies. Gross.

Lena: I need new best friends.

"How many pounds of butter are we going to need?" Zara's muffled voice breaks through my concentration, and I turn to find her entire upper body inside the refrigerator, hunting for ingredients.

Mama, Zara, Luci, Pen, and I are teaming up to bake enough cookies to feed an army before the Bear Creek Christmas festival this afternoon.

I shove my phone away from the baking headquarters and scan the stained and tattered pages in Mama's homemade cookbook. These cookie recipes are her prized possessions. It's quite possible she loves them more than me and Auggie.

"At least three?" I call to Zara, flipping between recipes.

Zara drops three boxes of butter on the counter and mumbles, "This seems excessive," as I move to the sink to wash my hands.

Through the window, I catch a glimpse of Gavin and Auggie in the large empty lot next door. They pace back and forth through the snow as I lather my hands.

"What are they up to?" Mama wonders, putting a hand on my lower back.

Suspicion crawls up my spine as we watch them turn in a circle.

"Boring stuff, probably," Penelope says, wedging between us to look out the window.

Gavin's expression is serious as he stands and nods. He doesn't have a hat on, so his dark hair is being blown about by the winter wind, and even from here, I can see his nose and cheeks are rosy from the chill.

Auggie, on the other hand, is like a puppy in the snow, bouncing around and pointing in every direction with a huge smile.

"Zara." I turn to find her unwrapping a stick of butter. "Do you know what—"

"Wanna help me?" she interrupts with a too-bright smile, holding one in my direction.

I squint at her before looking back over my shoulder to find the guys trudging back to the house. I'm definitely missing some information here, but Christmas isn't the time to go poking around. It's probably some sort of surprise for the kids, so I'll pester Zara about it later.

As I'm pulling the measuring spoons from a drawer, Gavin and Auggie walk in the back door, filling the kitchen with their deep voices.

Mama leans in front of me and snaps her recipe book shut. Then she walks to the corner of the kitchen where clutter tends to accumulate and sets her notebook down. She picks up a flawless, hardback book and sets that in front of me.

Gluten-Free Baking for the Holidays.

My brows jump to my hairline as I blink between the book and my mother's retreating form. I'm a gaping fish in the middle of the kitchen, utterly in shock that she's not using *her* book.

I'm pretty sure she wants to be buried with those recipes. She won't even let me make copies of them to share with Millie.

And yet she's tossed them aside to make something Gavin can enjoy.

I spin to find her helping Penelope crack eggs into a bowl, with Gavin beside her, slinging a red apron over his neck.

"The book is next to Lena," Mama says, patting his arm.

Gavin douses me in his masculine pine scent as he steps up to the counter and flips through the book. I'm mesmerized as the pads of his fingers glide over his lips while he scans a cookie recipe. Then, with a nod, he sets down the book and shoves the sleeves of his black sweater up his arms.

My vision tracks in slow motion as the fabric moves to reveal his thick forearms, covered in lines of tattoos. The snake on his skin coils around his muscles, and I wish my hands could do the same.

"Spritz or crinkle first?" He flashes me a brilliant smile that tilts my stomach on its axis.

"Yeah. Yes," I stammer.

His lips curve in a confused grin. "Okay. Both, then."

* * *

"WE'RE GOING TO need one person at the cookie decorating station, someone helping Rosie make drinks, and then we should probably get one of you over here at the coloring area." Joe points around the bakery, directing Gavin, Auggie, and me to different spots in the room. "The kids will be here in about"—he flips his wrist to check his watch—"twenty minutes."

"I'm taking cookies," Auggie calls, making a run for the table covered in icing and sprinkle containers.

As Joe gets called away by a disgruntled volunteer, Gavin shrugs to me, hands shoved into his dark jeans. "I guess the choice is obvious here. You take the coloring, and I'll take the drinks?"

"Are you implying I can't handle the drinks?" I cross my arms over my chest and lance him with a glare.

He tilts his head. "I definitely think I could handle being Rosie's assistant, and you'd be better at the coloring station. No doubt in my mind."

"Just for that." I poke him in the chest, and his gaze lowers to where my red-tipped nail presses into his black sweater. "You're on coloring duty. Isn't that all you do for a living, anyway?"

A ghost of a smile flickers over his lips. "Yeah, I make all my plans and blueprints with crayons, actually." He leans down, bringing our faces to the same level. "Have fun with that drink station, Lena."

His voice sounds like a dare, and it only makes me more adamant to prove I can succeed.

But an hour later, I officially decide there should never be any food service or coffee-making jobs on my list. There's a quarter-size burn on my palm from a mishap with the espresso machine, the rug behind the counter almost sent me careening into the trash can a few minutes ago, and a sweet little boy is now covered in chocolate milk because I didn't get the lid secure before I handed it to him.

The *only* benefit to this particular task is the scenery. From the espresso machine, I have the perfect view of Gavin as he sits surrounded by children, his big, hulking frame towering over them like a bodyguard. They laugh and snag crayons out of the box in the middle while Gavin colors his own picture, the crayons dwarfed by his broad hand.

I've seen him with a kid on his lap, helping a crying child find the color they were looking for, letting a little girl draw on his picture, and using a piece of tape to hang a coloring page on the wall.

Why is all of that so goddamn *hot*?

"Lena, do you have that double shot?" Rosie calls over her shoulder with a warm smile.

Honestly, this woman is a saint. How has she not kicked me out of here yet?

"Yes, yes, I'm on my way." I shuffle up beside her and set the warm cup next to the register.

As I'm struggling to dump the espresso grinds and start again, Gary rushes into the bakery, bringing a blast of cold air with him. He frantically searches the room until his gaze lands on Gavin, and his snow boots beat on the hardwood floors as he trudges toward him. When he reaches the coloring station, Gary motions toward the back hallway with a nod. Gavin whispers to the boy beside him, ruffles his hair, and then follows Gary into the back of the bakery.

Being the unapologetic snoop that I am, I lean over the counter to see what's going on, but they're out of my view.

A moment later, Gary appears again, his gray hair mussed like he's been running his fingers through it. "Rosie. Can you come back here for a moment?"

She gives me an unsure shrug and follows Gary down the hall.

What the hell is so serious that they need to have this secret meeting?

By the time I've warmed up a blueberry muffin and made a hot chocolate for a customer, Gary is rushing back out the front door.

"Lena," Rosie hisses from the corner of the kitchen. "I need you."

My curiosity peaks as I turn and follow her long blond hair down the hall.

But Gavin is nowhere to be seen. The space is empty, with only a back door and a supply closet to the left.

"Listen," Rosie says, grabbing my shoulders. "I need a Mrs. Claus. Can you do it?"

Confusion prickles in my mind. "Me?" I look down at my black leggings and green sweater dress that look nothing like Mrs. Claus. "Right this second?"

"Yes and yes." She picks up a zippered canvas bag from the floor and shoves it toward me. "Just put this on."

I nod, but my brows tighten as I try to sort out the puzzle pieces of this situation. She nudges the bag into me, pushing me toward the storage closet. "Once you're dressed, go out the back door," she says, pointing over her shoulder. I think she tries to reassure me with a smile, but her wide eyes look rather manic.

She reaches around my hip and turns the handle, and before I can ask another question, she shoves me blindly through it. As I stumble back, two big hands grab my arms, and a masculine pine scent hits my lungs.

"You have five minutes," Rosie whispers before she slams the door shut.

Chapter 13

Lena

*W*hat the fuck is happening?" I whip around, my fingers still clutching the bag.

Gavin reaches behind me to flick on the light, bathing us in its dim glow. He has a knowing glint in his eye like he finds this whole situation hilarious, and it's disorienting.

"We're playing dress-up." He shrugs like that statement is a completely normal thing to say.

I feel like an error code is whirling in front of my face while I try to understand. Which is exceptionally frustrating because I like to think I have a firm grip on reality most of the time.

But instead, I'm stuck in a poorly lit closet with a man who makes the space feel like a tiny suitcase, and I'm supposed to be playing *dress-up*?

He bends to lift a bag from the ground. "I'm Santa, and I'm pretty sure you are signed on as my Mrs. Claus."

The words *my Mrs. Claus* burrow under my skin. The idea of Mrs. Claus is not inherently sexy. Hell, neither is Santa, but something about being called *his* warms my cheeks.

"What happened to the original Santa and Mrs. Claus?"

"Stomach flu," Gavin says with a wince, kicking off his shoes.

"Oh shit."

"Literally," he deadpans, and a giggle bursts out of me.

Gavin's sock-covered toes draw my attention, only a few inches from my purple boots. "Probably have about four minutes left at this point." The zipper buzzes on his bag as he opens it and rifles through its contents. "I'll turn around," he says as he faces away from me.

My brain feels like it's crawling through sludge, but it's finally making sense of things.

Closet. Dress-up. Gavin.

I'm going to change in this closet with Gavin.

My pulse beats like a drum in my skull, and I can't decide if it's from excitement or nerves.

He stands there a moment, perfectly still, before his hands move to the bottom of his sweater. With a deep breath, he pulls the fabric up his body, over his shoulders, and off his head in one quick swoop.

The room immediately transforms into a sauna, the air so thick with heat that I almost can't breathe. Maybe we should've turned off the lights for this, because with his back and shoulders on display, every muscle showcased a foot away from me, I can't think clearly anymore.

Dark lines of ink cover his back, and I let myself take in as much of the details as possible. I swallow hard as I track the raven covering one shoulder blade, wishing I could feel the feathers beneath my fingers.

But then a clink of metal ricochets through the tiny room as he flicks open his belt. I'm frozen in place as the soft sounds of his hands against the leather send a flush of arousal through my body.

A quiet gasp leaves my lips, and I force myself to whip around and face the door. Leather rasps through belt loops, and I squeeze my eyes shut as hot, heady, forbidden images flash through my mind.

When I hear the zipper, my heart stops. The metallic buzz echoes through the room, and my core aches with need.

Fuck. This is Gavin.

I'm not supposed to be thinking about him like this. There are children outside, waiting to meet Santa and Mrs. Claus. I shouldn't be in here listening to every goddamn detail of his undressing like he's putting on a show for me.

The thought hits me like a snowball to the face.

Is he doing this on purpose? Is he trying to make me lose my mind with the sensual sounds of stripping out of his clothes?

Maybe it's payback for that audiobook.

I press my lips together to stop the mischievous laugh that wants to sneak out.

Oh, Gavin, two can play at this game.

If he wants my cheeks flaming and my pulse beating in my ears, he's already won.

But I'm betting I can make the same thing happen to him. I want to see what it takes for him to give up that cool composure he keeps in place. It's a game I've played half-heartedly since I met him, but I'm dying to see what happens when I give it my full effort.

I'll dig my nails in and crack him open until he admits I've won.

This game is called: *How far can I push Gavin before he snaps?*

His pants hit the floor with a rustle of fabric. A hint of copper brushes my tongue as I bite my cheek to stop myself from peeking over my shoulder. I'll just imagine what he looks like standing there with nothing but his briefs over his amazing ass.

Focus, Lena.

My breathing picks up as I pull off my shoes and tug down my leggings. Then I grab the bright-red fuzzy-lined tights from the bag and pull them on. Luckily, they're stretchy enough to fit as I hop a few times to get them all the way up.

When I pause, I realize Gavin isn't making noise anymore. I cast a glance over my shoulder and find him still facing the other direction in his Santa suit, his shoulders lifting with quick breaths.

Good. Maybe this is affecting him too.

A smug grin blooms on my lips as I pull my sweater dress over my head and fling it backward. I'm not quite sure where it lands, but Gavin's choking cough makes me think my aim was perfect.

"Sorry," I breathe, trying to sound as innocent as possible.

"No problem," he mutters, his deep, gravelly timbre sending flames licking over my bare skin.

I pull on the red dress with white faux-fur trim. The fabric is a little tight around the waist and chest and hits about mid thigh.

Geez, how tiny is the usual Mrs. Claus? This would fit Luci way better than it does my curves.

I peek over my shoulder again, and, of course, he still has his back to me because he's a complete gentleman. He appears calm, other than the staccato beats of his breath.

Biting into my bottom lip, I brace myself for the next step. Then I turn and whisper, "Gav?" His shoulders freeze at the sound of my voice. "I need your help."

"What kind of help?" His voice cracks in the middle of the question.

"With the zipper." My breathy words aren't even for show at this point. I may be trying to make him lose his mind, but I'm not immune.

He rakes a hand through his hair, tugging at the roots. Then he tilts his face up to the ceiling, letting out a deep sigh.

Fuck yes. This is working.

When he turns, my gaze lands on his dark, fathomless eyes. They're like a trap, luring me closer until I'm lost in their depths forever.

His gaze stays pinned right to mine, not dropping to see the way my breasts are spilling out of the gaping neckline of this dress.

But I want his eyes to drop. I want him to see. I want his composure to *snap*.

So I flash him a flirty grin. "Do you approve of your Mrs. Claus?" I ask, pulling the bottom of the skirt out and fanning the ends to capture his attention.

He finally gives in, his whiskey eyes dipping down my body in a slow path, practically burning right through the fabric. I watch every twitch of his jaw until he reaches my socked feet and drags his gaze back up.

His eyes are almost black, his jaw tight, but to my disappointment, he ignores my question. "Turn around," he orders, his voice low and smooth.

My body obeys without a second thought, baring my back to him. A gasp leaves my throat as the tips of his fingers brush over me when he grabs the zipper. With his other hand gripping the bottom of the fabric, he glides it up, reaching a little resistance at the tightness around my chest.

Just before the top, he pauses. With utter gentleness, his fingers sweep under my hair and move it over my left shoulder, leaving a trail of goose bumps where his skin touches mine.

His warm breath fans against the back of my neck as he brings the zipper up the last bit, but his fingers stay exactly where they are. Neither of us moves while my blood turns to lava in my veins.

Somewhere in the last few moments, I forgot that I was trying to tease him. I may have been attempting to push him over the edge, but I threw myself right over with him.

I would give *anything* to see his face right now.

With a stuttered exhale, he takes a step back.

Chest rattling, I suck in a breath and then a few more, trying to stabilize everything in my body.

I turn to face him, whispering, "Thank—"

But my words die on my lips at the *tortured* expression on his face. His dark eyes are wide, his cheeks flaming the same color as his outfit.

Oh, I've won. I've fucking won this game.

His composure has slipped enough that I can see the *need* burning through his body.

He licks his lips, his attention dropping to my mouth for a beat.

Swallowing my nerves, I take one step toward him, my toes bumping his. His whiskey gaze darkens on my lips like he can't look away from them.

Fuck it, we're already over the cliff together. We might as well crash at the bottom in each other's arms.

I lift my chin, putting as much determination into my expression as I can.

If I could beg for one thing right now, it would be for Gavin to dip his head and bring his mouth to mine.

Just a taste.

His wide hands land on my waist, and every bit of focus in my brain is taken away from helping me breathe, and it's all rerouted to the spots where we connect.

We're pulling toward each other like there's a force dragging us closer. Only a few inches separate us, and our collision feels unavoidable.

His grip tightens, and his eyelids flutter shut. "You're a menace," he breathes, but nothing about it seems like an insult. Instead, it sounds like the sweetest compliment.

My heart races as I grip the front of his suit and—

Tap, tap, tap.

Three hard knocks rattle the door behind me, and we jump away from each other, breathing heavily.

"You two ready?" comes Rosie's sweet voice from the other side.

Chapter 14

Gavin

*M*y mom doesn't want me to have a BB gun, but can you get me one?"

This kid on my lap—maybe his name is Felix, I can't remember—blinks up at me, flapping his lashes like he thinks that might convince Santa.

Running a hand over my fake white beard, I deepen my voice to ask, "How old are you . . ." *Is it Felix? Shit. I have no clue.*

He flicks his fingers up one at a time until all five are out. Then he holds them in my face with a proud smile between his round cheeks. "Five. But my birthday is coming."

I shoot a questioning look at Mrs. Claus, who's standing next to the giant sleigh I'm sitting on. Elevated a few feet above her, I have to make a concerted effort not to look down the front of her dress. There's only about an inch of her cleavage showing, but it's enough to draw my attention every time I look her way.

Lena winces and gives a subtle shake of her head.

"Well, sometimes even Santa has to give Mom and Dad the final say. So hopefully next year we can try again for that BB gun," I tell maybe-Felix. I brace myself for a fit, maybe even a few tears, but he nods and climbs out of my lap. Lena helps him down the sleigh steps, then lifts a little girl up to the same spot.

"Santa, this is Julia." A secret grin tugs at Lena's lips.

Julia's long blond hair shields her face as she makes her way slowly up the steps.

"Hi, Julia." I lean down until I'm low enough to draw her gaze to mine. Reaching out a black-gloved hand, I introduce myself. "I'm Santa. How are you?"

Her orange-mittened hand lands in mine tentatively as she shakes her head. "You're not the real Santa."

The abrupt delivery has me fumbling for a moment, trying to gauge what my response is supposed to be.

Her assertive gaze studies me like I'm simply another adult trying to lie to her face. She looks like she's as sharp as a tack. Like she can see right through this fake beard and wiry white hair around my face.

She reminds me of myself as a kid.

Scanning out over the field around us, my eyes land on the only other adult left besides Lena. Shannon's at the front of the sleigh, offering me a small, happy wave.

Gary and Joe introduced us a few years ago, and we've kept in close contact since. I haven't seen her in a few months, but the way her focus is pinned on Julia tells me two things.

One, Julia is under Shannon's care and in the foster system.

Two, Julia *is* like me. A little lost, a little too grown-up for her age, and a little skeptical of adults.

She slips her hand from mine, then sticks them in the pockets of her coat.

"Did the beard give me away?" I whisper, adjusting it on my chin.

She tilts her head, assessing me. "Yeah, it looks like a goat's beard."

I lean toward her and whisper behind my hand. "It smells like one too."

Her cheeks lift in a grin before she turns, looking in every direction until she spots a group of kids running between the trees on the edge of the clearing. "You can't take it off yet, or those kids will see." She climbs onto the sleigh's bench beside me.

Out of the corner of my eye, I spot Lena walking toward Shannon, maybe to give us some privacy.

"How old are you?" I ask, watching the way Julia's hands twist together in her lap.

"Six. How old are you?"

"Thirty-nine."

Her brows shoot up. "That's old."

"Yeah. Any minute, this white beard is going to be real."

Her small laugh sends a wave of comfort through my chest.

"Is there anything you want for Christmas?" I ask.

She shrugs. "I wanted to see my mom, but Shannon said I might not get to. But she said we could have pizza for lunch on Christmas Day like I used to do with Mommy."

My throat tightens as a wave of protectiveness bleeds through me. I know that ache she's feeling in her heart because I've been dealing with it for my whole life. I wish I could soak all her pain into myself to save her from a lifetime of it.

"That sounds like a perfect lunch. Do you have a plan for breakfast? Because I make some really awesome cinnamon rolls."

Her blue eyes brighten. "I like cinnamon rolls."

"Then I'll make you some and bring them to Shannon on Christmas Eve."

She nods and kicks her feet a couple times. "I guess if you talk to the real Santa, you could tell him I want art supplies."

"Absolutely. I'll let him know."

Slowly, she untangles her hands and sets one in mine. She seems to steel her spine, but her cheeks wobble as she says, "And if he can talk to my mom, can you tell her to get better soon so I can see her?"

My chest caves in, all the air rushing out at once, but before I can respond, she hops off the sleigh and goes to stand by Shannon's side, staring at the ground beneath her little feet.

* * *

THIS SUIT IS suffocating me. I can't wait to get out of it. For every step I take toward the bakery, I say a silent prayer that nothing else is required of me once we get inside.

I managed to have a conversation with Shannon after my chat with Julia. Even though I was dressed as Santa, it gave me a chance to talk to her about how things were going at home and if she needed anything now that I was back in town.

In addition to a new job with Auggie, helping Shannon is a big incentive for me to move to Juniper. She doesn't know about it yet, but I'm excited to be around to help her more. Since her husband died, things have been difficult, and I know my financial help isn't making up for her loss, but at least I feel like I'm relieving some of the burden.

As my boots hit the steps of the bakery, my hopes of getting out of this suit are immediately destroyed as Joe waves me over. The deck is crowded with people as he beckons me to where a porch swing sits on the edge with a cameraman positioned in front of it.

I stifle a groan. I've let at least forty kids sit on my lap today, and while most of them were wonderful, if I have to spend one more minute in this suit, I might be stripping out of it right here in front of everyone.

But kids are lining the porch, so I put on my best Santa-like smile and wave to them as I walk by.

Joe puts a hand on my arm and leans into my ear when I reach him. "I can tell you're over this," he says for only me to hear. "But I need a picture of you and Mrs. Claus for the newspaper." He winces a smile. "Please? I'll make that gluten-free chess pie you liked last year?"

Fuck, that pie was good. I tilt my head like I'm thinking it over, but Joe sees right through my bullshit as usual and shoves me toward the bench with a laugh.

As I settle into my assigned spot in front of the camera, Lena snags my gaze. Her broad smile lifts the apples of her cheeks as she walks through the crowd toward me, patting children's heads along the way.

They all preen under her attention.

She has this magnetic ability to bring everyone into her orbit, and sometimes I want to succumb to it. I want to stop fighting and let her drag me in.

She almost had me in that closet a few hours ago. I was drowning in the tension and *so close* to giving in to it.

"Can you sit down with your husband?" Joe wiggles his brows at Lena, and her cheeks pinken, the blush flooding down her neck.

My skin tightens as I pat the spot beside me. "Here you are, my wife."

Her teeth dig into her cherry-red bottom lip as she sits beside me and sets a hand on my thigh. "My husband."

It takes every ounce of self-preservation I have left to not think about that hand being inches away from my cock. We are *literally* in front of a camera and a bunch of witnesses, but the pressure growing in these stupid red pants doesn't seem to give a single fuck.

Lena turns her head, blinking innocently as her fingers clench on my thigh.

My stomach bottoms out when I register her expression.

She's doing this on purpose. The little menace is fucking with me.

I hold her gaze as we both paste on a smile, and I hope mine borders on the side of sinister. A warning to stop testing me in front of these people.

But her smile only grows bigger. More devious.

"If you could both look this way," the cameraman calls, drawing our attention.

As I grin and he clicks his camera, I repeat a mantra in my mind.

Ignore her hand. Do not get hard.

The cameraman peeks from behind the lens. "Santa, can you put your arm around Mrs. Claus?"

With a stiff nod, I move my arm up and around her shoulders, and she scoots closer under the protection of it. But, fuck my life, that readjusts her a bit closer to—

Ignore her hand. Do not get hard.

Ignore her hand.

It's not working. Goddamn, it's not working.

My heartbeat thunders in my ears as she smirks up at me, that inch of smooth cleavage snagging my attention again. I want to dip a finger into it. I want to slide my tongue—

"You okay, Santa?" she murmurs, her low, raspy tone making me anything *but* okay.

Cameraman forgotten, I visually trace the outline of her sensual lips. Her tongue slides over them, and I have to stifle a groan.

She's trying to kill me. That's what this is. She's trying to drown me in her caramel eyes in front of all these people, and I'm helplessly falling into them.

"You're a little menace," I whisper, shaking my head.

"That's perfect," calls the cameraman. "Now both of you look this way."

Reluctantly dragging my eyes away from hers, I focus on the lens, giving the best smile I can muster while wanting none of these people to look at me. I want my focus to be on how perfectly Lena fits under my arm like a missing puzzle piece slid into place.

"How about a kiss for Santa?"

When I flick my eyes to Joe at the sound of his voice, his hands are clasped under a radiant smile.

I shoot him a death glare, but Lena doesn't hesitate. She leans toward me, and her sweet, citrusy scent floods my senses. I stay perfectly still as her lush lips land high on my cheekbone, above the fake beard lining my jaw.

I wish I could see her. I wish I could have an out-of-body experience right now to watch us together. Does she have her eyes closed? Does she look annoyed to be doing this?

But I can't see her, and in my search for something to focus on to keep myself from floating away, my eyes land on Bea and Luci. They're standing at the back of the group watching us, and they're both . . . *smiling*.

Not running to stop Lena from pressing her lips to me. Not shaking their heads in dismay. No, they're full-on smiling like this is the most adorable thing they've ever seen.

Lena stays glued to my cheek for a few moments, long enough to let the cameraman snap a few photos before she pulls away, sauntering toward her mom.

Joe snaps a picture on his phone, then he steps closer, breaking my view of Lena's swaying hips as she walks away. With a knowing grin, he holds his phone up for me to see the screen.

There I am, filling the frame with a dazed expression, a scraggly white beard, and a perfect imprint of Lena's red lips on my cheekbone.

Chapter 15

Gavin

*M*y rolling suitcase catches on the railing with a *thud* that echoes through the silent house, drawing Lena's attention away from the couch she's preparing for the night. She crosses her arms and cocks her hip, sass pouring from her in waves as she watches me descend the stairs. Her sleep shorts are so small that they're almost invisible beneath her baggy long-sleeve shirt, and I'm so busy devouring the sight of her bare legs in the lamplight that I almost trip down the last step.

"Running away again?" She tilts her head, sending her messy bun flopping to the side.

"Sleeping on this other couch tonight." I shoot her a grin as I drop my bags and sit down on the middle cushion.

As I was heading upstairs a few minutes ago, listening to her set up her couch for the night, I knew I couldn't do it anymore.

I had to give up that room, even if Bea scolds me about it tomorrow.

"No you're not." Lena bends to spread her blanket out, and my gaze drags over her thighs again like it can't stay away.

I have to force myself to stare at a candle on the coffee table instead. "Yes, I am. That bed was doing something weird to my back," I lie.

"That's the most comfortable bed I've ever slept in."

"You need to sleep in better beds, then."

I swallow hard when I hear my own words. *Goddamn it.*

"Are you offering up yours?" she snaps, turning to me with a slow, sexy grin, and fuck. She's not wearing a bra.

Her nipples are peaked against the front of her shirt, and I don't think I'll survive this.

Tiny shorts. Long legs. No bra.

I might be dying.

My control has been slipping rapidly the last few days. Every promise I've made and every rule I've laid out for myself have been bent and broken until I don't recognize them anymore.

I can't play along in this game she's tempting me with. No matter how badly I want to flirt back with her. I have to hang on to these final shreds of my control, even if it kills me.

"No," I croak, then clear my throat. "No. I'm not," I repeat firmly, just in case anyone is still awake and can hear this conversation.

With a barely concealed smirk, she asks, "Did I fluster you?"

My teeth grind together so hard that I might crack a tooth.

"It's okay, Gav. I already know the answer." She throws her shoulders up in a casual shrug. "But I'm not going upstairs." With a wink, she spins back to arrange her blanket.

She bends over the couch again, her shorts lifting enough to reveal the bottom curve of her perfect ass below those goddamn shorts.

For fuck's sake.

My hands ache to grip her curves, tug her toward my already-hard cock, and see how quickly I can replace all her sass with needy whimpers.

I want to show her how goddamn flustered I can make *her*.

A man can only take so much before he snaps, and my composure feels paper-thin tonight.

As I fit my own couch with a sheet, I studiously avoid looking at Lena, and I ignore her sigh of relief as she settles under her blanket. When I lay down, I block out the sound of her soft huffs as she repositions.

To distract myself, I plan the house I want to build one day.

Cabin surrounded by trees. Huge back porch. Hot tub. High ceilings and tall windows.

"Stop breathing so loud," Lena hisses across the moonlit living room.

"I'm breathing like a normal human trying to get to sleep," I whisper-yell back. "Maybe it's all your wiggling and squirming over there."

Honestly, it's me too. My whole body is restless and hot. I'm burning up, palms clammy and cheeks warm, because I'm across from Lena in those flimsy shorts.

The ones that could so easily be pulled aside for me to press my fingers into her—

Fuck.

There's no way I am getting any sleep tonight.

"You're letting a perfectly good bed go to waste," she grumbles, throwing her blanket off. She walks across the room and leans behind the tree to turn the Christmas lights back on.

I stare up at the ceiling while I try to think of anything other than those fucking shorts riding up again.

Blueprints. Sustainability. Floor plans. Spatiality. Clean lines.

The clean lines of Lena's bikini top over her collarbone last night. The simple knot behind her head that would've been effortless to undo and drag down her golden skin.

I throw a hand over my face.

This isn't working.

Chapter 16

Lena

*A*fter plugging in our lopsided tree's multicolored lights, I turn around to find Gavin covering his face. I let out a snort of laughter. "That's a little dramatic. It's not that bright."

With a sigh, he sits up and plants his feet on the ground like he's giving up all pretense of trying to sleep.

"I can't sleep," I admit, walking to his couch and sitting cross-legged beside him.

Having trouble sleeping has been routine for the last few weeks. My brain has been full of so many restless thoughts about life and work and my future that I haven't been able to let it go at night.

But that's not the problem this evening.

It's the man beside me.

The man who I have teased and flirted with endlessly today. But in the process of attempting to torture him, I've also been torturing myself.

He drags a hand through his hair. "I'm pretty sure I mentioned there's a queen-size bed upstairs. You could try that."

"I don't want to risk the mysterious back problems." I quirk a disbelieving brow in his direction. "Besides, I feel . . . jittery. Wide awake, for some reason."

"Maybe you shouldn't have had that late-afternoon peppermint mocha."

Well, he might have a point there. I turn ninety degrees to face him and smile sweetly. "But I had this really nice guy who was willing to make me one."

His lips twitch. "A nice guy who is now regretting his choices."

My vision narrows. "I feel like Santa probably makes excellent peppermint mochas for Mrs. Claus. He's got to be smitten enough that he does anything she asks." My brows dance as he shakes his head at me. "So you were really just continuing to nail your role as Santa."

He snorts a laugh. "I wasn't doing a great job of that when I almost dropped Brandon's kid."

"She was squirming out of your arms." I shrug. "Santa can't be blamed for that."

"Yeah. The whole force-a-kid-to-sit-on-a-stranger's-lap thing is ridiculous to me. She just wanted her mama. That's why I had to give her back to . . ." Wincing, he looks to me for her name.

"Josie." I cast him an unimpressed glare.

His chin dips in a nod. "Right. Josie. She seemed nice."

"She is. I guess they got together really soon after the Christmas party hallway moment." A bitter laugh bursts out of me. "Which is honestly about how my dating life goes." I lift my hand to pretend I'm waving at an imaginary person. "Hi, I'm Lena. The woman you meet on the way to the person you're looking for."

Gavin's brows crinkle. "That's not true."

"It is. Remember Rachel? My girlfriend I brought to Christmas a few years ago?" A muscle in his jaw shifts as I continue. "She got married *six months* later." Tugging the elastic out of my hair, I shake out my curls, letting them fall around my shoulders. "It's fine. I've gotten used to the idea. I try to think of it like I'm helping them learn what they don't want on the way to what they do."

Thoughts flicker behind Gavin's eyes as his face sags with a frown. "They just weren't the person for you."

He states it so matter-of-factly, like he just *knows* without a doubt.

I wish I could scoot closer and have him whisper those words right against my ear. Maybe that would put them in my permanent memory bank to reassure myself when I'm feeling like the only lonely person in the world.

My heart rattles against my chest as a question bubbles to my lips. "How do I know who the right person is?"

Chills race up my neck as I watch him slide his fingers over his lips.

Finally, after what feels like an eternity of waiting for his response, he drags his gaze to mine, and my stomach bottoms out at his expression. Determination paints his tense jaw and furrowed brow, and certainty seeps through his whiskey eyes.

"The right person would be steady and dependable. A partner who sees you just the way you are and loves every tiny piece. They would need to be a lighthouse for you to come back to after you've braved the seas." His voice slips over me like the softest velvet caressing my skin. "And they would need to be protective of you. Because you spend so much time protecting everyone around you that you need someone watching *your* back."

A raw ache grips my throat as his words bleed with the truth of exactly how I feel.

I've been adrift for months. Cast out to sea, hopelessly floating and searching for land.

For a lighthouse to guide me home.

"They should know that you like to push people's buttons sometimes," he continues with a small smile. "But it's easier to just roll with it." A breathy laugh trembles through me, and his molten eyes dip to my mouth for a beat. "Also, they should love your tigerlike stubbornness and unpredictability," he teases with a wry grin.

"Tame the tiger," I add.

His expression sobers. "No, Lena. You don't need to be tamed." My heart leaps in my throat as his fingers graze my ear to tuck a loose strand of hair behind it. "You're perfect just the way you are. Wild, free, passionate, warm."

Each word lands in my chest like a promise.

Like they're a vow he's swearing his life on.

You're perfect just the way you are.

Tears push at the edges of my eyes, and I try to blink them away. But one makes it past my lashes and tumbles down my cheek.

He has cut straight to the core of who I am and what I need, and it seemed effortless for him.

Like he has sliced right through the seventy-five layers of cellophane protecting my heart.

He's just revealed who I am underneath all of it, and I'm breaking through. I'm gasping for breath.

I'm seeing things clearly for the first time.

I don't want to be alone. I don't want to be adrift.

I want to land in the arms of the person who sees me exactly as I am.

Gavin.

A shiver racks my shoulders before I ask, "Do you know why I took Brandon down that hallway three years ago?"

Breaking his gaze from mine, he pulls his hand away to slide it down his thigh. "No. Why?"

My throat feels coated in sand, but I force my answer out. "Because 'Have Yourself a Merry Little Christmas' came on."

Recognition flickers over his face as he turns to me.

"And I asked you to dance, but you said no." A scorching fire sears through my chest at the memory of that heartache. "Well, you *rudely* said no."

The sound of his gruff words echoes in my ears like it was just a moment ago.

With a pained expression, he'd shouted over Frank Sinatra's voice, *"That's an awful idea, Lena. No."*

He shakes his head and lets out a deep breath, a grumble mingling with the air.

"It broke my heart," I tell him. "It kinda broke *me*, I guess, and I wanted to get back at you. Or forget about you. I'm not sure which one. So I kissed Brandon."

The couch dips as he turns his body my way, leaning a shoulder into the backrest. "Do you know why I said no, though?"

Trying to keep him from seeing my pain, I stare at the stockings on the mantel, eyeing his next to Penelope's where she demanded it hang.

"It was just a dance. I wasn't asking you to . . ." I drift off, letting the unclear end of that sentence hang between us before I add, "I danced with a lot of people that night, made a lot of good memories. But nothing stands out as sharply as your refusal."

Dragging in a deep breath, he sits forward, setting his elbows on his knees. He pulls both hands through his hair, looking down at the rug. The sprinkle of gray strands around his ears almost glows in the lights from the tree, and I wish I could run my fingers through them. Touch the evidence of the years that have passed since I saw him. Those years I wasted searching for someone who could replace Gavin's spot in my heart.

Nerves skitter through me as he stands and lifts his phone from the coffee table. He swipes through it as he approaches the mantel, and when the first few notes of "Have Yourself a Merry Little Christmas" drift from the speaker, he sets it next to the nutcracker above his stocking.

Then he holds out a hand to me, palm up in offering. "Let's fix that memory." He quirks a grin. "Will you dance with me?"

My heart bursts with a *yes*, craving any opportunity to be near him. But my brain keeps my limbs pinned to the couch.

I watch him skeptically as he holds his steady hand out for me. Unwavering. Sure.

"Please," he whispers.

That simple word snaps all the threads holding me in place, and it feels like I float toward him.

Like he's my lighthouse, guiding me in.

When my palm settles against his, heat winds its way up my arm and into my chest. He lifts our joined hands and wraps his other one around my waist, leaving a little space between our bodies.

As Frank Sinatra's voice croons from the phone, Gavin sways us to the slow beat. I try to remind myself to breathe, but the stars dancing in my vision make me think it's not working.

His warm exhalations fan my cheek as I skim my hand up to his broad shoulder. Tilting my head back, I take in the sight of his eyes sparkling with the reflection of the tree lights.

"You're good at this." My words end on a sigh when his thumb makes a smooth glide over my ribs.

"Yeah. My dance card stays pretty full," he deadpans, pulling me toward him until his hand splays over my lower back and my hips bump his.

"I've never seen you dance with anyone else."

He swallows, and I watch in fascination as his Adam's apple rolls in his throat. "I don't normally."

"So I'm the exception to the rule?" I whisper, sliding my fingers to sit beside his neck.

His palm trails up the center of my back, pulling me closer until my chest presses into his, that masculine pine scent invading my lungs.

"I wish you were," he sighs, lowering his cheek to the top of my head. "I really wish you were."

My breath hitches, but neither of us says another word as we sway to the beat for the rest of the song. His fingers never stop gliding over my back like a comforting caress.

Vivid images flash through my mind as I imagine what it would be like if I *was* the exception to the rule. If I got to see his dark gaze as he moved toward my lips. If his tongue was sliding against mine. If his hands were under my shirt, molding to the shape of my breast.

Frank's voice fades out, and the music ends. But before we can stop moving, Gavin's voice fills the silence, humming the same song, deep and gravelly in my ear.

My skin buzzes with pleasure as he moves us in a slow circle. I release our joined hands to wrap my arms around his shoulders, and I breathe him in like an addict.

Hell, maybe I *am* an addict, because from this moment on, I don't know how I'll survive without touching Gavin like this. I'll be desperate for it.

"Lena," he sighs, dragging out the last syllable until it sounds like a moan.

"Gavin," I whisper back, coasting the word across his neck.

His hand knits into my curls, and when his fingers touch my scalp, a small whimper leaves my throat, my head falling back into the pressure.

He stares at me with an intensity I've never experienced before, like nothing else exists in the entire world.

Our synchronized slow, steady exhales are the only sound between us as his gaze falls to my mouth.

My lips tingle with anticipation.

Fuck the rules.

Damn them to hell.

I want him.

Chapter 17

Gavin

*G*avin," she breathes, and my cock twitches at the sound of her low, needy voice. "Please kiss me."

My feet stop. My breath leaves my lungs.

I shake my head, even though my gaze lingers on her wet lips. No tormenting red lipstick tonight. Just that perfect pink mouth I've been dreaming of tasting for ten years.

But I can't.

I can't.

"Why?" Her nails graze over the base of my neck, and I hold in a groan.

It's all fucking agony. Her shorts, her smooth back, her lush tits pressed against me, her begging mouth.

I don't know what I've done so wrong in my life to deserve this torture, but I want to drop to my knees and beg for forgiveness.

"You know why I can't kiss you." I lower my forehead to hers and breathe her in. Sweet citrus and temptation and broken rules.

"You're too scared to play with tigers?" she taunts.

"No, little menace," I groan, my fingers gliding against her scalp.

She tilts her head, drawing my attention to her neck, and the long, smooth offering is irresistible. I groan as I drop my nose to the silky skin of her throat, my eyes drifting shut as I glide my lips over her pulse. Lust surges violently through my veins when her soft moans land in my ear.

I've dreamed of what her moans would sound like in that sweet, raspy voice, but it's so much better in real life.

Her panting breaths are hot against my neck as she melts in my arms. "Gav, please."

The need burning in her voice is about to ignite a fire. It feels like at any moment, we could burst into flames from the unstoppable tension pulling us together.

And I can't even prevent it. It's inevitable.

She's in my arms, and she's begging me.

This strong, fierce woman is begging *me*.

And all I can think is *finally*.

"Fuck it," I growl, lifting my head to bring our mouths together in a gentle kiss.

The startling relief weakens my knees. Her lips are soft, supple, intoxicating. I glide mine back and forth over hers, savoring the little puff of air that escapes through them.

Reluctantly, I pull back to make sure she's okay. Though this is Lena. If she wasn't okay, I'd be on the floor with my balls kicked up to my throat. But I still have to check.

"More," she grits out, tugging me back greedily.

A breath of laughter leaves my lungs as we kiss again, and the moment is so tender and gentle that it's impossible for it to feel illicit.

This feels like the most *right* thing I've ever done.

Like after years of searching, after a lifetime of wondering where I belong, here it is.

Her lips feel like *home*.

She parts them, granting me access, and as our tongues brush, I moan into her mouth, pouring years' worth of pent-up frustration into the sound. Her arms wind tighter around my neck as I tangle my fingers into her hair like she might leave at any moment.

She tastes like peppermint and something so inherently *Lena* that I shudder with pleasure.

"Fuck," I whisper against her lips. "You taste so good. You *feel* so good."

Her nails scrape against my scalp, dragging a hiss from my mouth, but the prickle of pain only strengthens the storm raging through me.

I grip her hair and pull her head back to the angle I want her. Where I can devour her best.

This kiss is pure need and desperation, and I'm drunk off it.

Nothing else in the world matters other than Lena and her whimpers and the need to capture all of them.

Grabbing the sides of my face, she pulls our mouths apart. Our panting breaths punctuate the silence as I drink her in.

Dark, heavy-lidded gaze. Wet, swollen lips. Wild, mussed curls.

I did that to her, and the primal need to do it again sears through my veins.

My heart pounds against my ribs as I slide my hands along her waist and down to grab her warm, smooth thighs. I dig my fingers in and lift until her legs wrap around my waist.

"Hold on tight," I command. With one arm banded across her lower back, I glide my fingers down her neck in a featherlight touch. "You're so fucking beautiful like this, Lena."

She whimpers, tilting her head to offer me the silky column of her throat. I dive forward, licking and kissing the sweet flesh, pulling it between my teeth and sucking on her pulse.

Her nails dig into my shoulders, and she uses her grip as leverage to writhe into my stomach with an adorable grunt. Desperately, I turn and press her back into the sliver of open wall between the fireplace and the Christmas tree. A little bell jingles from an ornament, but I quickly forget about it when Lena pushes her hot core against my stomach again.

"Gav, I need more," she urges, tugging me toward her mouth.

"I know. Me too." Pinning her against the wall with my hips, I pull back enough to watch my hands glide up the outsides of her smooth thighs. "These fucking shorts," I groan, teasing the hem. "Were you torturing me with these on purpose?"

"Yes," she sighs, tightening around my waist.

When I slide my fingers under the fabric to grab two handfuls of her curves, I groan at what I find. "For fuck's sake. Nothing under them, either?"

Her whimpered "mm-mm" makes me want to smack her ass red for all the agony she's made me endure. All the burning need every time I'm in her presence.

I lift a hand to slide my fingers over her neck as she whispers, "Please. Gavin." I relish the way her throat shifts as she begs for me. The way her caramel eyes shine with need.

Fuck. I'm so gone for her. I could wreck every bit of the future I have planned to get lost with her forever.

My body and soul *ache* to make her mine. Claim her. Love her. Worship her. Tell her every day how perfect she is.

"You're awfully sweet when you want something, little menace," I whisper, sliding my thumb over her pulse.

She drags her teeth over her bottom lip. "You're awfully bossy when *you* want something."

My smile is wicked as I lean closer. "That's fucking right, baby."

With a desperate whimper, she lunges, crashing her mouth to mine. Her foot bumps the Christmas tree with the movement, and needles rustle behind me.

"Careful," I purr.

"Okay." Her hands tangle in my hair as my tongue dives into her mouth, tasting as much of her as I can.

My control is rapidly dissolving, but I have no desire to hold on to it. This is everything I've ever dreamed of, jammed into one perfect moment that I never want to end.

The rug is soft beneath my feet as I dig my heels in to push harder into her. The pressure hits perfectly, and our moans filter through our kisses.

I could just pull these flimsy shorts aside and sink into her. Feel her come around my fingers or my tongue or my cock. I'm desperate for any of it.

"You have to be quiet," I whisper against her lips. "I wanna make you feel good, but I'm going to have to cover your mouth if you're too loud. You don't want to wake anyone up." I press into her again, and her head falls back to hit the wall with a *thud*.

We both freeze at the sound, holding our breaths for a moment to see if it woke anyone.

When the house remains silent, we both snicker, fighting to contain our laughter.

"I said to be quiet," I remind her, squeezing her hips and pulling her tightly against me.

"I will. I promise," she says. "Just touch me. Please . . ." Her voice fades out as I suck at her neck and tug, brushing my fingers along the hem of her shorts to the warmth of her inner thigh.

"Yes," she moans, kicking out her leg and—

A rustle sounds behind me, and a snap from the outlet cloaks the room in darkness. We both go perfectly still at the *whoosh* of a ten-foot Christmas tree, ornaments, and lights crashing to the ground behind me.

Neither of us breathes, shock and fear engulfing my body.

A snicker snorts out of Lena, but ice crawls through my veins, clearing away the lust-filled fog.

"Goddamn it," I hiss, pulling back and setting her safely on her feet.

I immediately dive for the tree. Guilt infuses my spine as I listen as hard as I can for anyone moving in the house.

Lena crouches beside me, brushing my arm with hers.

She can't be down here. If someone comes out, she needs to be as far away as possible.

On a different continent would be preferable.

"Go upstairs," I blurt. "I'll take care of this."

"I can help." She scoffs, reaching for the broken pieces of an ornament by the coffee table.

"Get. Upstairs." The bite in my voice burns as it leaves my throat, but I can't find it in myself to care right now. Someone could've caught us moments ago, making out like desperate teenagers who don't have a fully developed prefrontal cortex.

In the darkness, Lena stills beside me. "I don't mind—"

"No. Stop being stubborn and listen."

She stands and casts me a long look before turning and jogging up the stairs.

And it's a good thing she did, because a moment later, Bea's voice carries around the corner. "What's going on?"

"It's okay." My voice shakes, but I try to calm it. "I was unplugging the lights and lost my balance." Shame sours my stomach.

"I'll help you clean it up," she mumbles, walking toward the utility room.

As I lift the tree back into place, trying to steady the already-wonky structure, I briefly consider if I should leave again.

Because what just happened between Lena and me has the potential to destroy the only place I've ever felt truly welcome.

Chapter 18

Lena

"Do you mind if we run a quick errand?" Gavin asks, tension radiating from him in the back seat as we approach Bear Creek for the Christmas Eve Eve party.

My brows pucker as I glance at him in the rearview mirror. "Where do you need to go?"

His broad frame fills the entire reflection, and he has to be uncomfortable squeezed back there, but Luci claims her age earns her front-seat privileges.

After last night, he has avoided me all day. Other than a trip into town with Auggie, he's been in the same house as me, pretending I don't exist.

But the biggest sign something is bothering him is the fact that he didn't even argue when I told him I'd be driving us to the party in my car.

"Just downtown." He points for me to turn right. "I don't think they'll be open tomorrow."

Luci taps a finger to the clock on the dashboard. "They're serving dinner in thirty minutes," she says sternly. "I tend to pinch people when I'm hangry."

He snorts a laugh, lifting a brow in the reflection. "Must be hereditary."

Snowflakes land softly on the windshield as I pull into a parallel parking spot—masterfully, I must add—on the side of Juniper's rundown historic Main Street. A few businesses still occupy spaces on the main drag, but there are many more empty ones than there used to be. With collapsing awnings and bricks in a pile from the corner building, this area of town has seen better days.

"I'll stay in the car," Luci says, leaning back on the headrest. "Just enough time for a nap."

"Me too," I announce, even though he didn't invite me.

"I'll hurry. No pinching." His door snaps shut, and I watch him jog across the street to Peter's Pizza.

Pizza? That's the emergency errand that couldn't wait?

Un-fucking-believable.

I pull out my phone and swipe open my messages, typing furiously.

We Catan Beat Finn

> **Lena:** I kissed Gavin.

> **Lena:** He kissed me back.

> **Lena:** I accidentally kicked the Christmas tree and knocked it over.

> **Emil:** 🌮

> **Micah:** 😧

Millie: OMG no you didn't.

Lena: I did. Broke four ornaments.

Emil: How are you feeling about the kiss?

Lena: On one hand, it was the hottest kiss in the history of time, and I would do it again in a heartbeat.

Lena: On the other hand, he's barely spoken to me since.

Micah: You think he regrets it?

Lena: I have no clue.

Lena: But probably.

Lena: I'm just tired of pretending.

As the sound of Luci's deep, sleepy breaths fills the car, I set my phone on the console and lean my head back, squeezing my eyes shut tight.

But just like when I tried to fall asleep last night, all I can hear, see, feel, and smell is *Gavin*.

His moans against my mouth, his mocha hair gripped between my fingers, his lips dragging over my neck, his masculine scent everywhere around me.

All the lines are blurred. Lines I've been hoping to blur for years.

But now I'm on one side of that line I can't distinguish, and I'm terrified he's still on the other.

He's on the side of *no*, and now I'm fully on the side of *yes*.

Last night, I heard the need in his voice and saw the longing in his eyes and felt the desperation in his grip. But in the time it took for that tree to hit the ground, he had rebuilt an impenetrable wall around himself.

Tap. Tap. Tap.

My eyes open to find Gavin with a knuckle on my window, motioning for me to open it. As I hold the button down to lower the glass, he leans closer.

"Want to come into the last place with me?" he asks, tiny snowflakes landing and melting against his cheeks. "You'll like this one."

"You came back with no pizza, and now you have *another* store to go into?" Crossing my arms over my stomach, I glare up at him.

A burst of pleasure zips through my veins when his eyes dip to the vee of my emerald-green dress before he snaps them back up quickly.

Oh, Gavin, you may not like that you want me, but you want me.

Clearing his throat, he straightens and mumbles, "I'll be right back."

Anticipation flutters behind my rib cage as he jogs across the street. Maybe the lines are blurring in his mind too.

He passes a small market and stops in front of the art gallery, then casts a glance in my direction before opening the door and disappearing inside.

Damn it. Of all the places he could go, he enters the *one* that intrigues me.

Ugh! I throw open the door, grab my jacket, and walk toward the gallery, careful not to let my heels slip on the pavement.

The familiar scent of paints and clean canvases welcomes me as I step into the shop. I haven't been here in years, but upon a quick scan, it seems the new owners have kept the setup about the same. Art supply store in the front and gallery in the back.

"She just said art supplies, so I'm not sure." Gavin's voice drifts to me as I make my way deeper into the shop, trying to keep my heels as quiet as possible on the hardwood floors.

"Well, over here," comes an older woman's voice. "These paints are all washable, so that might be best for a child."

I bypass their discussion, drawn to the welcoming coziness of the small gallery in the back. Canvases and a few sculptures line the walls, with instrumental holiday music echoing softly through the room.

As I wander down one side of the gallery, I stare at each piece for a long moment, trying to absorb the feelings they elicit and hear what the artist is conveying. There are detailed landscapes, a beautiful portrait of a father holding a baby, and an abstract piece full of bright colors.

When I reach the last painting on the wall, my breath pours from my chest.

A beautiful older woman is depicted before me, her dark skin glowing against the dim background. Her gray hair is braided over her shoulder, and her eyes are closed with a peaceful smile covering her lips.

But from the center of her chest radiates a medley of colors. Swirls and spirals and hearts and flowers, like they're erupting out of her chest.

Creativity, inspiration, excitement.

I instantly envy her.

My hand settles over my own heart, aching for what the woman in this painting is feeling.

I wish I could touch it—feel the texture of the paint beneath my fingers and absorb some of the passion through my skin.

This. This is what I'm missing right now.

A dark, toxic cloud has been looming around my head, and I haven't been able to clear it. But looking at this painting, I *yearn* to. I want to shine a light so bright that it obliterates the darkness entirely.

New job idea:

9.   *Find whatever it is that makes me feel this inspired.*

Leaning closer, I read the small card beside the painting.
Self-portrait
Victoria Adams
"What do you think?"

I turn my head at the kind voice and find a carbon copy of the woman in the painting. But in person, her sparkly brown eyes are open, watching her reflection in the artwork.

"I love it," I whisper, glancing over her shoulder for Gavin, but the space is empty.

"He went to the car," she says with a grin. "That's a wonderful man you have there."

The urge to correct her never arises, so I smile back before turning to face the painting again. "It feels . . ." I tilt my head. "It feels like it's speaking right to my soul."

"Are you an artist?"

"I used to think I was." I sigh, shoving my hands in the pockets of my coat. "But lately, I don't know."

Her palm lands softly between my shoulder blades, and the comfort of it has my chin quivering. "You're always an artist, even if you haven't done it in a while. I like to think everyone has an artist in them. You and I have simply explored it enough to let our passion flourish."

I press my lips together to hide their shaking as I nod toward her self-portrait. "I think I'm missing that passion right now."

She slides her hand in a circle on my back. "Well, I had misplaced mine when I started that piece, honey. Sometimes you have to force yourself to start, and the inspiration comes later."

My face scrunches in a wince. "I haven't picked up a pencil or a paintbrush for myself in months," I admit.

The weight of those words lifts from my chest as I let them out. They land heavily in the air before me, but the relief of saying them out loud loosens my shoulders.

"Can I show you something?" she asks gently.

I nod, and she guides me through a door at the end of the gallery and into a work studio. The back wall of windows overlooks a line of snowy trees, and the room is filled with easels, paints, stools, and canvases.

Following behind Victoria, I'm careful not to brush against anything in my dress and coat as she leads me to the back. Dim snow-reflected light shines through the windows, showcasing a landscape in progress on an easel.

"You're welcome here anytime you want," she offers, dumping a jar of paint water into the nearby sink. "It's usually just me here, but on Thursdays, a few other artists join me in the evening for a little get-together." She fills the jar with clean water and sets it beside the canvas. "Sometimes everyone works, sometimes we all chat, and sometimes we sit in silence. But it helps us refill our store of creativity." Her arm brushes mine as she joins me by the window.

"I would love that," I tell her, the possibility already cultivating in my head.

Could I drive two hours here once a week to join them? It sounds just wild enough to be a great idea.

She laughs warmly. "I'll see you Thursday, then, honey."

Chapter 19

Lena

"Have you seen your newspaper photo?" Zara asks, raising a brow in my direction.

"No," I reply, watching Pen's dark curls trailing around her as she spins on the dance floor in the center of Bear Creek Bakery.

The tables have been cleared away, and the counter is filled with Christmas desserts. Gary, Joe, and Rosie have covered the ceiling in hanging snowflakes and white strands of lights, making the space feel like a wintry wonderland.

Zara sets her phone in my hand. "You should see it."

The headline reads "Mr. and Mrs. Claus Visit Bear Creek Tree Farm," and when I scroll down and see the photo, my lungs constrict.

They didn't use the smiling one. They didn't even use the cheek-kissing one.

No, in this photo, Gavin and I are looking at each other, his arm around my shoulders and me leaning toward him like I'm a flower growing toward sunlight. My hand is settled on his thigh a little too intimately, but it's the expression on our faces that twists my stomach into knots.

My cheeks are pink as I smirk up at him playfully, and his returning grin is like a secret only I can hear. His eyes are focused on me like I'm the only person in the world, with that little swoop of his mocha waves over his forehead that I got to run my fingers through last night.

I lift my attention from the phone, searching the room, and when I spot him, my knees wobble. Even with his shoulders hunched while he talks to my mom, he's taller than everyone else here.

I let my gaze rake over him shamelessly. His black sweater sits over his burgundy-and-green plaid dress shirt, just the pop of color on his collar making his eyes glow brighter. Fitted dark jeans mold perfectly over muscular thighs, ending at his ankles to meet his Chelsea boots.

His mouth is moving in conversation, but he's unabashedly watching me. It's like a tether is strung across the busy room, linking us together, and all I can see are those sparkly whiskey eyes tugging me in.

Blindly handing Zara her phone, I keep my focus on him as I cross the room. The small crowd seems to part for me, clearing a path to the man I want, and Gavin's smile widens in slow motion as I approach.

Swallowing my nerves, I stop a few feet away from him, my mom's voice pausing mid-sentence. But I don't have the capacity to apologize for interrupting or worry about how she might see what's happening between us, because right now, there's only one thing on my mind.

Gavin.

"Will you dance with me?" My voice is unwavering as I repeat what I asked him three years ago at this party.

A split second passes before Gavin clears his throat. "Of course." He nods to Mama. "Excuse me."

I distantly hear her say, "Go right ahead," but I can't concentrate on it as Gavin's palm lands on my back, guiding me to the middle of the dance floor.

When we stop, he pulls me toward him and slides his other hand in mine. Silence lodges between us as we move to the slow beat of the music, so much more stiff and robotic than our dance by the Christmas tree.

He keeps his gaze over my head, his lips tight. Nothing like how he looked last night.

But I want *that* Gavin back. I want undone, passionate, greedy Gavin, whose eyes were molten for me.

"What are we doing?" I breathe out as quietly as I can.

"Dancing. People move their feet to the music," he mutters.

"No. I mean what are we doing after last night? You've barely spoken to me."

"I spoke to you at breakfast."

Frustration steels my spine. "To ask if I wanted orange juice," I grit through my teeth, hiding the anger in my words behind a strained smile.

"And you said 'no thank you.' It was a perfectly reasonable conversation," he says, biting back a grin.

The sudden urge to knee him in the balls bleeds through me, and I plant my feet. "Nevermind. I don't want to dance with you." I try to drag my hand away, but he holds it tight.

"Sorry. Fuck. I'm sorry." He pulls me to move again, and my feet shuffle involuntarily. "I just have no idea what to say about last night."

Flicking my gaze to the hollow of his throat, I ask, "Why did you shut down so quickly?"

His exasperated sigh sends a gust of breath by my ear. "Because it was a reminder of all the reasons we shouldn't have been doing that. It was a shock to my system that brought me back to reality."

"Reality," I repeat with a bitter laugh. "That kiss seemed pretty real to me."

I watch the column of his throat as he swallows. "Yeah, it was *too* real," he says, voice full of gravel.

"But I'm just supposed to forget it? Move on and pretend it never happened?"

The song filters out, and a new one starts, a similar slow tempo that we keep moving through. "Yes. We both forget it," he agrees with a definitive nod.

"Why?"

He tips his head toward me as he sighs. "Because you're going back to your life in Wilhelmina. And one day you'll meet someone closer to your age." His fingers tighten around mine. "Someone who isn't tangled up with your family the way I am. Someone who knows how to love you the way you deserve."

"But I'm not expecting forever. Remember? I'm the one people meet on the way to their forever person." My hollow laughter echoes between us. "Who knows, maybe if we got together, you'd find your future wife the next day."

"I won't," he announces firmly. "But you deserve the kind of love your friends have. You deserve better than me, Lena."

I swallow the raw sting in my throat. "You'll be able to forget last night like it never happened?"

His smooth jaw works like he's grinding his teeth together. "No. I will never forget a single *fucking* second of last night." Agony bleeds through his words as he says, "I've been trying to push you out of my mind for years, and it has never worked."

He drops my hand, and my stomach caves in from the force of his statement.

"I'm sorry," he mutters before turning to leave me on the dance floor.

* * *

"WE'RE GOING TO head home. Everybody's tired," Auggie says, lifting Jack's sleeping body from my lap.

Behind him, Pen and Gavin are spinning on the dance floor, her feet atop his and her twirly dress fanning out behind her. Zara taps Pen's shoulder and motions that it's time to go, and my niece wraps her arms around Gavin's waist.

With a sleeping Noah in her arms, Zara gives me a side hug goodbye. "I think Luci's riding home with your mom, and we're going to take our crew."

I nod, looking around the room. "I think I might stay for another hour or so. I promised Gary and Joe a dance, and"—I hold up my empty cup—"I've only had one glass of Rosie's famous eggnog."

"I'll stay with her." Gavin's deep voice startles me enough that I blink a few times as he approaches.

"I don't need a chaperone," I counter, not looking his way. "I'm sure you can ride home with Mama and Luci." I run a hand over my silk dress to have something to do.

"Then pretend I'm your designated driver. You can have as many eggnogs as your heart desires."

Zara's gaze bounces between us as Auggie claps Gavin on the shoulder and thanks him for staying with me.

I meet Gavin's stare and give him a sinister smile. "Fine. But I get to pick what we listen to on the way home."

* * *

GARY PULLS ME into a fancy spin, and my dress swirls around my ankles.

"What are you all doing tomorrow for Christmas Eve?" I ask when I'm back in his arms.

I'm happy to report that the second cup of eggnog did wonders for my mood. I've forced Rosie to stop working long enough to dance with me, eaten way too many Christmas cookies, and organized a round of the macarena.

I feel so much better than an hour ago.

It must be the sugar.

"We have a Christmas Eve tradition in our house," Gary says as he turns us in a circle. "We have a holiday movie marathon, cover the coffee table with snacks and hot cocoa, wear Christmas pajamas, and spend the whole day lounging." His wrinkles stand out with the force of his smile. "My favorite day of the year."

"How have I never been invited to this?" I shove playfully at his chest. "What do you watch?"

"Last year, it was *The Holiday*, *Home Alone*"—he twirls me again—"and *Miracle on 34th Street*."

"Oh, I love that movie."

"Me too." He pulls me close, and we sway for a few beats before he lowers his voice to ask, "How's Gavin doing this year?"

My gaze immediately snags on the man in question at the edge of the room, where he's talking to Shannon. There's possibly something wrong with my brain because it feels like some sort of radar has been installed that makes me constantly aware of his location. Even without conscious thought, I can turn my head and find him. When he's in a group of people or snagging a cookie or dancing with Julia. My eyes land right on him like my mind knew where he was all along.

"He seems okay," I say, pulling my attention back to Gary. "We're glad he's back."

"That's good to hear. He's had a rough life, and I'm happy he's found some people to spend the holidays with."

The song's melody fades away, and Gary pulls my hand into the crook of his arm, guiding me toward Gavin. He has his phone to his ear, a tense expression across his handsome face.

"Yeah, her tires are in bad shape," he says into the phone, and worry prickles at the back of my mind. "Thanks for letting us know. I'm sure we can find somewhere in town."

Gary's head tilts as Gavin hangs up and slides the phone into his pocket.

"That was Auggie. He said even though the roads were getting icy on their way home, the bridge was still passable. But your mom just heard from the neighbors that they couldn't cross it. And with your tires . . . I really don't want to risk it." He shrugs, worry creasing his brows. "I think we're stuck in town for the night."

Gary perks up. "We have your . . . er, one cabin left open if you want it."

A tense, silent conversation flickers between Gary and Gavin, and the hair stands up on the back of my neck.

Gavin's fingers slide over his lips in that tantalizing way I love. "Okay. Do you mind if I sleep on your couch, though? Lena can have the cabin."

Gary winces, turning toward Joe as he approaches. "Gavin was just asking if he could sleep on our couch tonight, but isn't your cousin staying with us?" His nose wrinkles and Joe's brows jump to his hairline.

"Oh yeah," Joe sighs. "Eesh. Yeah. The couch is booked."

Adrenaline pumps through my veins, vibrating my whole body with excitement.

But Gavin frowns as he looks between the men. "What cousin?"

Joe waves a hand over his shoulder. "Patrick. I don't think you know him."

"Yeah, it's Patrick," Gary adds, nodding quickly. "But there should be plenty of room at the cabin. It's a big bed."

With his hands on his hips, Gavin glares up at the ceiling, an aggravated groan rattling from his lungs. "Fucking hell."

I can't deny the breathless feeling in my chest at the thought of staying the night in the same bed as Gavin.

But for his sake, I try to stifle the giddy smile on my face. "I'm going to take a trip to the ladies' room," I tell them, pointing toward the hallway that leads to the bathrooms. "I'll let you all figure this out."

On my way, I pass the exact spot where I kissed Brandon three years ago. I slide my fingers over the wall where I moaned his name but imagined the man I've been dreaming about for ten years.

Ten years.

That seems like enough time to get over someone if it was going to happen.

Ten years of hoping the ache to be with him would dull over time. Ten years of wishing I could taste his lips. Ten years of thinking about him in ways I shouldn't.

Scanning myself in the bathroom mirror, I press my fingers into my red lips and remember the feeling of his soft mouth against them last night.

With only two glasses of eggnog in my system, I feel perfectly sober.

Perfectly clear to make the decision rippling through my head.

I've been trying to push you out of my mind for years, and it has never worked.

Same here, Gavin.

Chapter 20

Gavin

As we make our way up the steps to cabin four, the familiar front deck and lights around the railing feel like a welcome home sign.

The buttons are icy under my fingers as I punch in the code, but when I open the door, the warmth inside greets me like an old friend.

The cozy cabin has a plush king bed and two armchairs by the large windows overlooking the forest in the back. The fireplace is already crackling with heat; Gary or Joe must've come over to warm it up for us. In the small kitchen, they've placed a T-shirt and a pair of sweatpants on the counter.

Lena kicks off her heels at the end of the bed and makes her way to the back windows. She presses her fingers to the glass and squeals, "There's a hot tub."

My gaze slips down her frame. I've spent the entire evening trying not to devour the sight of her in that silky dress. It hugs every fucking curve of her body in ways I wish I could.

She spins toward me, raven curls swinging out around her. In the fire's glow and the dim lamplight beside the bed, I let myself stare at her. Really take her in.

And the sight of her wrenches all the oxygen from my lungs.

I feel like I'm drowning. No air left in my body because my lungs are filled with Lena instead.

She's all sass and softness. Forbidden and perfect.

The pads of my fingers itch to feel that smooth skin under mine as I touch her slowly. Desperately. Possessively.

"Want to relax in the hot tub for a bit?" Her small smirk makes my stomach clench.

"Lena," I practically growl. "I don't have a swimsuit, and I'm pretty sure you don't either."

She lifts a shoulder carelessly. "We could just not look at each other."

A laugh tumbles out of me. "I'm *always* looking at you." At my words, her cheeks flush pink, and I follow the color as it cascades down her throat. "Even when I tell myself not to, I can't help it. So getting in that hot tub wouldn't be relaxing at all."

Her chin dips in a nod as she takes a step toward me. "I have an idea," she offers. "Can we pretend for this one night that we can be together?" She lifts her head, drawing another step closer. "We pretend my family doesn't matter. We don't worry about where we live. We don't think about any of the shit standing in our way. We simply give in for one night."

I go still. My pulse hums in my ears.

The words hang in the air. They strangle me when I try to take a breath.

"It doesn't have to mean anything tomorrow." She scoffs a hollow laugh. "Hell, remember, you might meet your soulmate tomorrow. But tonight, we could just be . . . us. Together."

My stomach tilts like I've dropped into the steep descent on a roller coaster. I'm tumbling down like it's completely inevitable, and I can't *fucking* stop it.

My gaze jumps between her dark caramel eyes, then down to her tempting lips. God, she probably tastes like sugar cookies and eggnog right now, and my mouth waters to find out.

The tension churns like a winter storm, clouding my judgment and obscuring the lines.

I hear myself say, "I don't know," like I'm in a trance. Like her goddamn curves have drugged me without even touching them.

She nods and whispers, "Okay. I'm going to wait in the hot tub, and you can either join me or . . ." Her words flicker out as she shrugs. Then she turns around and looks coyly over her shoulder at me. "Can you unzip me, please?"

My jaw clenches, but I move closer anyway.

The buzz of the zipper fills my ears as I lower it slowly. It's excruciating to watch every centimeter it moves down, but I'm careful not to let my fingers touch her body.

This is a reversal of our movements yesterday. Instead of zipping her dress up, covering her body, I'm revealing it, and that absurdity almost makes me laugh. How did I get here?

The zipper travels past the strap of her bra, down the silky skin of her back, and then reaches the top curve of her ass.

My mouth dries out as I reveal the tiny strap of her black thong. "Lena." The word scrapes out of my throat, raw and jagged.

Without thinking, I press the knuckle of my index finger into the warm flesh right above her thong. I drag it up in a slow line, relishing the goose bumps that peak under my touch. Her skin glows in the firelight, smooth and creamy, and I desperately wish I was doing this with my lips.

When I reach her hair, I tuck my hand underneath and let my palm settle against her neck. My fingertips graze her pulse, and it flutters rapidly beneath my touch. Her breath hitches as she tilts her head, her wild curls gliding to the side to give me better access.

Just this point of contact is so perfect that I want to crumble. I want to take all the bricks around my heart and hand her each one as an offering.

"Go get in the hot tub." My voice is unrecognizable as I pull my hand away. It's all I can think to say when my brain power is flowing south with all the blood in my body.

My heart stops beating as Lena slips the dress off her body, and it pools on the floor. The tiny black strip of her thong disappears between the round globes of her ass, and the dim light casts shadows in all the places I want to sink into.

She works her shoulders playfully like she knows exactly what she's doing to me. The little menace.

Tossing a smirk in my direction, she steps out of her dress and opens the back door, parading her perfect body through it.

After it clicks shut, a gust of air rips from my lungs.

I want to collapse to the bed. The physical, mental, and emotional strength it takes to stay away from her is almost more than I can bear.

I've spent years with a near-constant ache to touch her. To watch her unravel for me.

Fuck. I want to take what she's offering.

Just give in for one night.

I don't know if I can handle it, though. I'd be a greedy asshole when it comes to her. If I had one whole night with the woman I've been in love with for years, I don't know that I could let her go.

Could I live through the agony of it ending? Could I drag myself away from her and pretend it never happened?

But if this is it, if this is truly my one shot with her, do I really throw it away?

Goddamn it.

I kick off my shoes and shrug out of my jacket. Then my

sweater, shirt, belt, pants, and socks, until I'm standing in the middle of the cabin in black briefs, my hard cock begging me to step outside.

For a moment, I almost put it all back on. I almost reach for my pants again.

But then my gaze catches on Lena through the hazy window, and my heart leaps in my throat. Her silhouette is illuminated by moonlight as she pulls her hair into a knot behind her head. I visually trace the long column of her neck and the slope of her shoulders, and before I can think better of it, I'm drifting closer to the back door.

I'm walking toward the woman who will be my doom or my salvation.

The turn of a knob, the blast of chilly air, the click of the shutting door. I'm in a daze for all of it, until I reach the dark hot tub, and I focus intently on Lena. Her head is tilted back and her eyes are shut as I slip into the warm water and sit on the opposite side.

An electric current zaps through the water between us, flooding my body with nervous energy.

"You joined me," she states softly, a knowing grin painted on her lips.

I swallow the bubbling apprehension in my throat. "I did."

She sits up and crosses her legs under her, lifting enough for me to see the wet swell of her tits. "What does that mean?" she asks, small wisps of hair around her face curling tighter in the humidity.

"I have to make something clear first." I track a bead of water as it runs down her collarbone and straight into her vee of cleavage. "You are not the person people find on their way to meet someone else. You are the whole damn package, Lena, and anyone would be lucky to love you and take care of you."

"But not you?"

The water laps around my shoulders as she rises and stands between my feet. She tilts her head, and it takes a concerted effort to keep my eyes pinned to hers instead of letting them dip down to see everything she's revealed above the water.

"Not me." A sharp ache pierces my heart as I say the words. "But not because I don't *want* to be that person." I finally allow myself the pleasure of looking down, taking in every curve above her waist and trying to download every detail into my mind as quickly as possible. When I drag my gaze back up to hers, there's a deep crease between her brows. "I can't, Lena. As much as I want to, I can't ruin the only family I've ever had." I blink up at her and shake my head. "You're so young, so full of life, and I'm just a moody asshole whose whole world is a mess."

It feels like clawing my way through a list of reasons that I'm going to ignore for one night. But I have to say them out loud anyway so I don't forget them.

She leans forward to grab my hands under the water and plants them on her hips. Her smooth curves are warm in my grip as I dig my fingers in a tiny bit.

Tilting her head, she bites back the smirk playing over her mouth. "You said nothing has ever worked to get me out of your mind." She takes a small step forward, her thighs bumping my knees. "Maybe we need this one night to get it off our minds. Then we'll move on tomorrow."

Her tongue darts out to lick her lips, leaving a perfect bit of wetness there that I want to taste. I squeeze her hips under the water, memorizing how they feel in my hands.

I'm smart enough to know this plan won't work. It's absurd to think I could stop wanting her the way I do. It's laced so tightly into who I am that it's just become a part of me.

Gavin. Architect. Foster child. Introvert. In love with Lena. Adamant she deserves better.

They're facts. They're inescapable.

She's burrowed so far into my heart and soul that there's no moving on. Ever.

But at least if she gets it out of *her* system, it'll be easier for me to stay away. Maybe without her teasing and flirting, there won't be this magnetic pull dragging me closer.

Then she can go back to Wilhelmina. Back to her friends and her job and her vibrant life there.

And I can stay here, drowning in the agony of having her for one night, only to lose her.

Chapter 21

Lena

*G*avin looks like he's starving and I've just put a buffet of his favorite foods in front of him. And he's *so* tempted. So close to taking a bite.

But all those thoughts of *shouldn't* are still playing in his mind, and I need to silence them.

Because I want this one night with him. I want to mindlessly fall and let him catch me.

Deep down, I know I won't recover from this night. There's no getting him out of my head, but it would be ecstasy to surrender.

So I give him the nudge we both need.

His gaze sparks like fireworks as I lower myself onto his lap, straddling his thighs. I keep my hips lifted, but I know there's only a thin layer of my thong and his briefs separating us, and it makes my pulse pound in my core.

I'm craving that pressure of grinding myself against him, but he looks like he needs small steps.

"Lena," he breathes like a prayer, focus glued to the bit of skin swelling out of the top of my bra.

Sliding my nails through the hair behind his ears, I tilt his head back until he meets my gaze. "Can we make each other feel good tonight?"

His fingers tighten on my hips. "Fuck," he mutters, dropping his head to my shoulder, hot breath puffing over my collarbone.

I let out a whimpering laugh. "Yeah, that's what I'm asking for."

He tugs me an inch closer, and his lips skate over my neck. "Okay," he sighs, and my heartbeat hums in my ears. "Don't worry. I'll take care of you."

Logically, I know he means that he's going to make me feel good, but my heart bypasses that information and charges straight into *forever* territory.

He's going to take care of me. Always.

My body tingles with anticipation as he slides his hands up to my ribs, stroking over them with the pads of his fingers. He lifts his head, pressing gentle kisses to the corners of my mouth, his lips like velvet as he glides them over mine leisurely.

"Just tonight," he whispers against my mouth. He pulls my bottom lip between his teeth gently before releasing it. "One night with *my Lena*."

He growls the last two words, and pleasure buzzes over my skin.

I'm trying so hard to be patient, letting him set the languid pace between us, but then his tongue slides over the seam of my lips.

And languid is the last thing I want. I'm craving *wildfire*.

My mouth drops open on a greedy gasp. As my tongue slides against his, I moan at the taste of those chocolate crinkle cookies I saw him sneak at the party. My hips pop forward, seeking any pressure I can find, and his groan rumbles through me when I hit his hard length.

Yes, that's exactly what I need.

Grinning against him, I do it again, and his fingers tighten on my upper thighs, his grip vibrating with tension.

"Little menace," he breathes, and it's like a reward.

My lashes flutter shut as he kisses me, and I dig my nails into his shoulders like I'm clinging to him for dear life. This kiss is bruising and desperate, and when I press my hips closer again, he moans and nudges me back.

"Lena, baby." He drops his forehead to mine, panting sharp breaths over my lips. "We have to slow down. I want to take my time with you."

He lifts his head, and I finally get to see Gavin on the edge of control, losing his mind.

Puffy lips, heavy-lidded eyes, sharp jaw, flushed cheeks.

It's my favorite version of him yet.

"Slow down. Okay," I sigh, pushing away from him. When I reach the opposite bench, I fan my lashes with the most innocent smile I can muster. "What should we do, then? The ABC game? Practice our knock-knock jokes?"

He bursts out a laugh, deep and devious, and it brings me so much unbridled joy that I add another job to my list.

10.   *Follow Gavin around and find new ways to make him laugh.*

"No, none of that." His chuckle falls into an arrogant smirk as his eyes flicker over my face, down to my shoulders. "Sit on the edge of the hot tub for me. Let me look at you."

Goose bumps race over my arms at his deep, commanding tone.

My body obeys immediately.

When I lift myself out of the water, there's a firm wood surface below me, from where the hot tub is built into the deck. The cold slats bite into my bare flesh, but it's easy to ignore with the heat radiating from everywhere else in my body.

And Gavin's dark gaze is as hot as any fire.

"That's perfect, baby," he says, devouring every inch of skin. The weight of his desire leaves a blazing path as it trails over my collarbone and down my stomach.

When he reaches my hip, his forehead crinkles. A prickling sensation shoots up my spine as he steps toward me with rapt focus.

A gentle hand wraps around my hip. "What is this?"

My heart pounds in my ears as I lean back on my hands, and he swipes a thumb over the tattoo on my hip bone.

"A tiger," I whisper, watching his lips part as he sucks in a breath.

"A tiger *cub*," he corrects, brushing his fingertips over it like he's petting the fur.

I nod as the memory of sitting in the tattoo parlor floods my mind. Millie holding my hand and trying to keep me laughing through the pain.

Gavin leans toward me, palms on the boards beside my thighs. My breath stutters in my chest as he presses a soft, reverent kiss to the tiny tiger. "Fierce." He leaves another kiss a little lower. "And soft."

In that moment, that tiny flash of a minute, my unsettling reality becomes clear: no one will ever compare to Gavin.

No matter how many years I spend searching, every new person I meet will be analyzed against him in my mind, and I already know none of them will hold a candle to him.

Stepping back, he turns to the side, showcasing his masterpiece of tattoos. Flowers, vines, feathers, a moon and stars. Then he lifts his arm, and sitting right on his rib cage is a—

The world around me tilts as recognition flares in my mind.

I *know* that drawing.

A regal fox stares back at me, with its observant, intelligent eyes that took forever to get perfect. I spent hours detailing every single hair on its body, and it's reflected here with precision.

The back of my eyes sting as I lean forward and trace my fingers over the fox on his rib cage. "You liked my art that much?" I settle a palm over it, my hand not even covering the entire thing.

When my gaze lifts, it collides with Gavin's. "I *love* your art."

My heart *sings* at his words.

He continues, unaware of the chorus in my chest. "Everything you've ever made is perfection. But I got this because you made it for *me*. You could've drawn me a spider, and I would've wanted it inked on my body forever, because it was for me."

Pride unfurls in my chest, like petals blossoming in the light.

He lowers himself back to the bench across from me, his dark gaze roaming over my body as he spreads his arms along the edge of the hot tub. The tattoos over his thick shoulders and arms shift with the movement, and droplets of water run down his throat and chest.

"Spread your legs, Lena." He stares at my knees with an intensity that sends heat surging in my core.

Playfully biting my bottom lip, I part my knees an inch just to toy with him.

As I expected, he glares up at me, his thinning restraint rippling across the hot tub. "Wider," he grits out.

I grant him a few more inches, revealing a tiny glimpse of the black lace between my thighs.

A low groan escapes his control. "All the way open for me. I'm not going to ask again."

Watching every flicker of his jaw, I widen my legs until my knees bump the edge of the hot tub.

"That's my girl." He hums with satisfaction as his attention settles on the apex of my thighs.

That's my girl.

My heart turns to liquid at his claim.

Looking down, I try to imagine what I look like for him, leaning back on my hands, legs spread wide, thong disappearing under me, hard nipples pushing against my black lace bra.

Ragged breaths puff from his parted lips, his arms spanning the side of the hot tub like a king as he watches me with feral delight. All he has to do is look at me like that and I'm throbbing with anticipation.

New job idea:

11.   *This. Just this.*

"Have you been aching for me? Needing me between those pretty thighs?" he asks, and all I can do is nod. "I've been aching to be there too. Now take off your bra."

"Bossy," I murmur, reaching behind me to flick open the clasp. The straps slip from my shoulders, and I cover myself with one arm while I drop the fabric behind me.

He lets out a dark chuckle. "I think you like bossy." When I bite back a grin, it's all the answer he needs. "Move your arm, Lena. I want to see what I've been missing."

As I uncover myself, his shoulders move with unsteady breaths. The cold air hits my peaked nipples, and my breasts grow unbearably heavier as his hungry gaze roams over them.

"You're fucking gorgeous, baby. More perfect than I imagined." He leans forward on the bench eagerly.

I can't help but preen under his compliment. I've wished for his undivided attention like this for years, and to finally have it is making every nerve in my body buzz with pleasure.

"You imagined this?" I tease, lifting my fingers to rub soft circles over my cold, tight nipples.

He chokes on a breath. "Fuck yeah, I have." A breathy sigh sneaks past my lips, and his control dissolves further. "Pull your thong to the side, Lena."

Swallowing my nerves, I slide a hand down my stomach until it touches fabric. I can't resist letting my fingers circle my clit once through the lace, and a low moan rattles from my chest.

His eyes flare, and a wicked smile coats his lips. "No touching yet, my little menace."

My whimper sounds like a whine as I follow his orders and drag my thong to the side, baring myself fully for him.

That earns me a reward when he goes eerily still, his greedy gaze devouring the sight of me. He moves to his knees in the middle of the hot tub like he's desperate for a closer look, and my legs drift even wider like my body instinctively wants him to see *everything*.

His tongue flicks over his lips as he stares between my thighs. "One finger in. Tell me how wet you are."

I huff a laugh. "I don't need to touch myself to know I'm soaked."

His teeth dig into his bottom lip as his gaze lifts to mine. "Do it anyway. I want to watch your finger disappear inside that pretty pussy and come back out dripping."

My heart hammers against my ribs as I obey, slipping a finger inside. My arousal coats it instantly as I push in as far as I can, watching his steady gaze consume the movement.

"That's not enough for you, is it?" he asks with a smirk. "My girl needs more. Add another finger."

This time I watch myself as two fingers disappear inside my core, the pressure better but still not what I crave. I groan as I pull them out and bring them up to circle my clit.

But Gavin snaps a hand out. His strong grip wraps around my wrist, and he brings my fingers to his lips, pulling me forward to accommodate the movement.

With his eyes anchored to mine, he pulls them into his mouth, his tongue laving across my flesh. He groans, his lashes falling to his cheeks as he sucks hard. A deep ache sweeps through my muscles as his hot tongue glides between my fingers, licking them clean. Then he drags them from his mouth with a *pop*.

"You taste like heaven. I knew you would."

A thin puff of air seeps from my parted lips, and when I try to inhale, there isn't any oxygen left in this entire state.

He sets my hand gently on the deck and inches closer, his palms spreading my legs open even wider for him. His focus flits up to me before he presses a kiss to my inner thigh, near my knee. It's not a particularly pleasurable spot, but as I learned that first night in the hot tub, any part of my body can be sensitive when it's *him* doing the touching.

When Gavin's lips press there again, his lust-filled eyes linked to mine, I consider if anyone has ever orgasmed from knee kissing. It really might be possible.

His tongue flicks out, and he runs it a few inches up my thigh before he sucks. He pulls my skin between his lips, and I whimper, wanting to let my head fall back but also trying with all my effort to keep watching him. The tugging pressure feels like it's pulling right on my clit, sending pleasure zinging through my whole body.

My nails dig into the wood planks as he sucks harder, his tongue moving against the tender skin and making my thighs ache to close. But he must hear my thoughts because he pushes a firm hand against my other leg as a low moan grinds out of his throat.

"Oh my god." I pant the words desperately.

He releases my thigh and surveys the tender spot, gently sliding his thumb over it. Then he leaves a soft kiss, and I melt into a fucking puddle.

Here lies Lena Santos, liquefied from leg kissing.

From between my thighs, he flicks his lashes up to me, and his expression sobers. "I need to know if you want to keep going. But you can change your mind at any time."

"Yeah . . . yes. Please keep going."

A ghost of a smirk lifts his lips. "You're sure?"

"Positive."

He stands and pulls back, keeping a palm on each of my knees as he looks at me. "I don't even know where to start, then."

"Anywhere," I whine, wiggling my hips. "I just need something. Soon."

He cocks his head with a rakish grin. "You mean to tell me, after days of torturing me—after *years* of flirting with me and antagonizing me—you want me to *hurry*?" A devious laugh bubbles from his throat. "Hell no. I'm taking my *fucking* time with you. If I only get this one night, I'm savoring every second."

"It was torture for me too." I straighten my shoulders, and he tracks the way my breasts shift. "I'm losing my mind. I haven't been able to touch myself for days because the thought of imagining you while we're in the same house is humiliating."

His grip flinches on my knees, and he leans forward with predatory intensity. "Show me."

"Show you what?"

"Show me what you do when you think about me." His gaze drags down my body as he bites his bottom lip. "I want you to whisper my name like a secret. Like I've whispered yours for days in a house full of people so no one knows what I do to you in my mind." He shakes his head as fire blazes through my blood. "Then I want you to moan my name like I do yours every time I stroke my cock, even though I hate myself for it."

My breath hitches.

"And then I want you to scream my name because I *finally* get to scream yours."

A helpless moan escapes my throat as his intense stare tempts me to picture what he's painting for me.

My imagination runs wild.

Soft grunts slipping from his lips, one palm on the shower wall, his stomach clenched tight, muscles rolling in his arms as he pumps himself hard and whispers my name. Like a secret.

"Let's see it, little menace."

My limbs are heavy as I bring my hands to my breasts, pinching my nipples and sending a flush of warmth to my core. His gaze stays glued to my movements as I mold my breasts to my grip.

Then he watches closely as I slide them down to my wet heat. My skin is slick with my arousal as I tease myself with light movements.

I don't actually want to get myself off. I want to convince *him* to do it. I want to see him snap, make him shred all that restraint and touch me.

I dip a finger inside as slowly as I can and roll my hips against it. "Gavin." The soft moan drags a whimper from his throat, his bottom lip gripped between his teeth.

Adding another finger, I call out his name a little louder as my eyelids fall closed. His hands slide up my thighs to hold them open.

"Eyes on me, baby. I want to see 'em when you come apart for me." I force them open, and he rewards me by pressing another kiss to the inside of my knee. "That's my girl. Now touch your clit," he orders, and I follow his directions. Pleasure spirals through my stomach, hot and heavy. "You're doing perfect."

I'm already trembling, and yet his control is still in place. When I apply more pressure, my swirling movements drag me closer to oblivion.

My nerves sizzle as he runs his fingers over my nipple, just like he does on his lips when he's thinking. I circle my bundle of nerves again and grind against my hand.

"Do you know how much I've thought about you like this?"

"No," I whimper, heat spreading to my limbs at the deep timbre of his voice.

"All the *fucking* time." He tracks my fingers as they slide over my clit. "But none of the fantasies lived up to this, Lena."

Pleasure shoots up my spine and washes down to my toes. The thought flickers through me that I should slow down or lighten my touch if I want this to last longer, but my fingers aren't listening.

I need more. More pressure, more hands, more lips. More Gavin.

He pinches my tight nipple between his fingers, and I moan his name into the night. The cold weather means nothing as flames lick every bit of my skin while I crest higher and higher toward the peak.

"Harder, baby. Show me how bad you want me."

My fingers move against my clit and into my pussy with precision. With the skilled movements of someone who has done it hundreds of times to the thought of Gavin's voice in her ear.

"You're perfect, Lena," he rasps. "Fuck your fingers and call out my name."

My breaths heave faster and faster as swirling pressure builds up my spine and out to my extremities.

As I scream his name, Gavin grabs the front of my throat possessively, using just enough pressure to get my attention as he pulls me toward him. With a growl, he crashes his lips into mine, his tongue diving between them as white-hot pleasure ricochets to every bone in my body.

He devours my mouth like he needs me to survive. Mewling whimpers leave my throat as I ride my fingers, my walls fluttering around them. His grip on my throat loosens, but he keeps a hold on me, stopping me from falling into the water when my muscles go slack.

As the final spasms clench in my core, he releases my lips and brings his forehead to mine. Warm breath exhales over my lips. "Lena, baby. You're beautiful, you know that?"

Clasping my cheeks, he kisses me through my breathy laugh, and I soften in his embrace. I'm as limp as a ragdoll when he lifts me and wraps my legs around his waist, my head buried in his neck. His strong arms support me as he stands in the middle of the hot tub, holding me and breathing me in like I'm precious to him.

Like he's never letting me go.

Even if it's only for tonight.

Chapter 22

Lena

"Don't turn around," Gavin grumbles as I slide my thong down to my feet and step out of it.

"Why?" Squinting over my shoulder, I try to catch another glimpse of his hard length straining against the front of his briefs.

"Because if you keep looking at me like that"—he settles his hand on top of my head to turn me toward the running water—"I'm going to fuck you in this shower before I've gotten a chance to take it slow."

Warm water cascades down my body as I step far enough under the stream to wet my hair. "I see absolutely no problem with that plan," I tell him.

The curtain scrapes against the rod as Gavin steps in behind me. His hands land on my arms, his hard cock bumping into my ass as he presses a soft kiss to the back of my neck. "The things I want to do with you are endless, and I've been thinking about this for so long. Don't rush me."

My back arches at the thought, arousal burning through my veins again despite what happened in the hot tub only moments ago.

"Yes, sir," I snark, and he smacks a playful tap to my ass.

"That's right, little menace." He holds the shampoo bottle up in front of me, letting it slowly fill his hand. "How much do I need?"

I let a little more land in his palm before I murmur, "That's good."

The lid clicks as he snaps it shut and sets it down. Then he brings his hands to my hair. He lathers my curls, fingers sliding over my scalp and sending a tingling sensation down my spine. His movements make my eyelids drop shut, and a soft groan threads from my lips as he washes my hair better than any stylist on the planet.

Then he leans into my ear and whispers, "Turn around with your eyes closed."

Once I spin, he uses his grip on my hair to pull my head back slightly to rinse it.

"You're good at this," I whisper. "Are there a lot of women on your roster whose hair you wash?"

"Same number as there are on my dance card," he murmurs, sliding his fingers through my curls.

"So it's only me, then?"

He's silent for a long time, hands rinsing my hair carefully. And I almost open my eyes to check on him, but then his voice rumbles over my skin. "It's only you, Lena."

A rush of possessiveness bleeds through my heart.

This is mine. Hair washing is mine. He's mine.

But I bite back those words, instead saying, "Well, you're pretty good at it. For an old man." I beam at him even though I can't see his reaction.

"Old man, huh?" His grip tightens in my hair, and he kisses my cheek.

"Practically a dinosaur." Peeking one eye open, I find his lips curving in a devastating grin as he looks down at my body.

"Oh, little menace," he growls, tugging my head back by my wet strands. His lips land on the shell of my ear as he says, "I may be ten years older, but I can still make you come so hard you forget your own name. So you might not want to test me."

A flurry of butterflies gathers in my stomach. "But I love testing you." I blindly press a finger into his abs. "Pushing your buttons to see what happens. It's my favorite game."

He huffs a laugh, his warm breath fanning over my face. "Oh, I know. And I can't wait to ruin you tonight as your punishment."

As he conditions my hair, my mind whirs with the heady possibilities of what that would feel like. What it would mean to be ruined by him. And every time his skin grazes mine, my blood surges faster in my veins in anticipation.

After he rinses my hair once more, he whispers, "Open your eyes. Let me see them."

When I meet his dark whiskey gaze, it's focused on me like I'm the only thing that matters. Like he would burn down the world for me if I asked him to.

His lips are silky smooth as he kisses each of my damp cheeks. "They're my favorite color."

A disbelieving laugh pulls from my chest. "Your favorite color is black."

He stares right at me, like he's looking deep inside my soul as he murmurs, "My favorite color is the warm caramel of your eyes." His thumbs glide over my cheekbones as emotion clogs my throat. "I'm going to get out. You stay as long as you want."

As he leaves the shower, my heart pounds against my chest like it wants to escape my ribs and follow after him.

How is it possible that he can balance being so hot and so soft in the span of a few minutes? He's rocked me to my core, and as the water rains down over my naked body, I wonder if I'll ever be the same after one night with him.

Or if he really *is* going to ruin me.

When I step out of the bathroom a few minutes later, with my towel wrapped around me, I find Gavin at the edge of the bed, elbows on his knees and face in his hands. A fire crackles through the room as I take him in, hunched forward like the weight of the world rests on his shoulders.

I'm not sure what's changed in the last few minutes, but he suddenly looks like he's rethinking everything.

Stepping in front of him, I run a hand through his thick hair. "What's going on?"

Frown lines mar his handsome face as he stares up at me. "Are we making a mistake?"

I grab his chin firmly so I have his attention. "This is not something to feel bad about. We're two adults making a consensual decision." Saying the words out loud makes them ring even more true in my ears. "I don't think this is a mistake at all, and I'm never wrong." I shimmy my shoulders, trying to lighten the mood.

Gavin grabs my hips and pulls me between his thighs, pressing his forehead to my towel-covered stomach. A potent mixture of desire and nervousness trickles through my bloodstream as I stroke my hands through his damp hair.

God, what if he changes his mind? What if he's about to pull away after we only got a tiny taste of each other?

"You were wrong that time I asked for a flathead screwdriver and you brought me a wrench," he murmurs against my stomach.

"That was one time."

"You were also wrong about the rules to Catan when you

taught me how to play." He lifts his head, a grin shining up at me. That light in his eyes is back, and relief rolls through my chest.

I shove his shoulders lightly, but he exaggerates it and falls back to the bed. The sight of him sprawled out, mine for the taking, is too tempting to pass up. "I was wrong two times, then. That's still a pretty solid record." I climb over him, straddling his thighs, and this view is even better. Hovering over him like this and feeling the breadth of his body between my legs is making my core pulse with need.

He covers his face with his hands and groans, "Auggie's my best friend. How can I face him after I've slept with his sister?"

Pulling his hands away, I place them on my thighs. "Oh, so we're going to sleep together?" My brows dance, and he gifts me his sexiest deadpan stare. "It's one night, Gav. One night to get it out of our systems." I untuck the corner of the towel by my shoulder and let it fall open. "One night to spend together however we want without worrying about anyone else. This is just for me"—I toss the towel to the floor—"and you."

His chest heaves as he sucks in a breath, grip tightening on my legs. I watch his gaze slip down my shoulders, breasts, and stomach until it lands on the small tiger cub curled up on my hip. Warmth blooms from his touch as he brushes his fingers over it reverently.

"I can't believe we both did this," he whispers.

Pressing my hand against his fox, I feel his heart thumping under my palm. "Me either."

The weight of it is more significant than I can fully process, but it somehow feels like fate played a part.

His throat shifts as he swallows, staring back at me intently. "I've dreamed about you like this for so long."

"Me too," I admit.

In one swift movement, he flips us, and my back hits the soft blanket. My heart pounds as he leans over me, his hips pressed between my thighs, shoving them apart.

It's an image stolen straight out of my deepest forbidden fantasies, and I'm *living* it.

Dark strands of hair fall across his brow as he shakes his head, his whiskey gaze trailing over my face. "I've also dreamed about you naked under me more than I should." Gliding his broad hand down the side of my body, he squeezes my hip. "I've dreamed about tasting you." He slides it down to my inner thigh. "Touching you." His knuckles coast over my center in a featherlight touch. "Sinking into you."

I whimper, and my knees widen. "Do it. All of it."

He rewards me by sweeping a finger lightly over my clit, and my hips lift greedily toward him. "Mmm," he sighs, his possessive gaze traveling over my body. "You're so sensitive for me already."

As his finger dips agonizingly slowly into my pussy, we groan in unison, and it's the most perfect sound I'll ever hear. We're unraveling simultaneously, and I've never felt anything more incredible.

"Fucking hell, Lena." He presses a kiss to my collarbone. "You're so fucking tight." My nails dig into his biceps as he pulls out and thrusts another finger in. "And so wet for me."

It's always *for me*. He says it so absentmindedly that I don't think he knows how serious it is. How it feels like every physical reaction *is* for him. Only him.

Gavin's teeth dig into his bottom lip as he watches his fingers slide in and out of me. "That's it, baby."

My eyes roll back in my head as he hits a spot that has me moaning his name. He pumps his fingers, curling them with each stroke and pressing his thumb against my clit.

Just as my hips jerk up to thrust against his hand, he pulls away with a wry grin. A strained whimper flies from my chest as I'm about to scream at him, but then he lies back on the bed.

"Come here," he orders.

My stomach clenches with delight as I straddle him, sitting right over his hardness, his towel still stopping me from seeing all of him.

To my surprise, he grabs my hips and lifts me higher onto his chest, nudging me forward until my thighs bracket his head.

"Sit on my face, little menace. I want you to ride my tongue until you come all over it."

My breath hitches as he grips my ass to hold me steady.

"Grab the headboard, baby," he commands, eyes pinned to mine as he pulls me toward his mouth.

And when his tongue drags through me slowly, I dig my nails into the wood bedframe and hold on for dear life as Gavin keeps his promise to ruin me.

Chapter 23

Gavin

I could die here, savoring the sweet taste of Lena's pussy and listening to her desperate moans echoing through these cabin walls.

She's sassy and mouthy, and I love that about her.

But then as soon as I have her aching for me, she's soft and responsive and needy.

I'm obsessed. I was right. One night was never going to be enough.

Flicking my tongue over her clit, I hold her steady against my mouth. She mutters incoherently, and little cries hiccup out of her as she rides my face exactly how I hoped she would.

My girl is dripping for me, and I want every bit of it. She bucks and gasps as I dive my tongue into her tight heat, and thank fuck I'm already lying down, because the sight and taste and feel of her is enough to bring anyone to their knees.

If I could speak right now, I'd praise her for listening to me and doing exactly as I said. She's so fucking good at it.

Abandoning the headboard, she grips my hair, and the prickly sharpness tugs at my arousal, lighting me up everywhere. Honestly, I can't believe I've lasted this long without touching my cock. I've been painfully hard since her dress dropped to the floor, and it's only gotten worse with every passing second.

"Yes. Gavin. Oh god, yes," she cries out as I thrust my tongue into her core and she pulses around it.

I hold her tight to my mouth as I suck her clit between my lips, and her body jolts as she comes, her thighs quivering around my head. She sounds so beautiful singing my name at the peak of her pleasure that I want to reward her and hear it all over again.

I keep licking and moaning at the taste of her, drawing out every bit of her orgasm until she hisses and pulls away. With a deep sigh, she collapses to the bed beside me, her body boneless and chest heaving.

God, I want to fuck those tits too. Slide right between them until I hit her throat.

One night, Gavin. You can't possibly do every single thing imaginable in one night.

Lena lifts a hand and swipes her thumb over my mouth. "Your lips are swollen."

I cast a devious grin between her legs. "So are yours."

"Gavin Moore," she scolds, choking out a laugh. She loops her fingers into the towel at my waist and tugs it open, freeing my cock. "You did *not* just say—" Her humor dies as her eyes drop to my hard length. She swallows, brows popping up. "Goddamn."

I lean toward her and chuckle against her throat, pressing a kiss to her rapid pulse. A hiss seeps from my chest as her hand wraps around my base, and I pull back to see her delicate fingers circling my flesh.

Fucking hell.

A shiver racks my body as she glides her hand up, rolling her thumb across the bead of precum gathering at the tip.

"*Fuck*. Lena. Oh, that's perfect, baby."

Her gaze dances between my face and her hand around me until I can't stay away from her anymore and seal my mouth to hers. She moans into the kiss, our tongues tangling and clashing in desperation, and it's almost enough to make me come all over her stomach.

"Fuck me. Right now," she demands, abandoning my cock to tug my hips toward her. She brackets her thighs on either side of mine as I kiss her forehead, her cheek, her neck.

"I need to get a condom out of my wallet," I tell her, sliding my tongue over her nipple.

"I have one in my purse," she says, voice dazed.

"You were ready, huh?"

"A lady can never be too prepared," she teases. "But . . ." Her voice fades out as I place my palm over her tiger tattoo.

"We don't have to keep going, Lena. If this is all, it was more than I ever dreamed would happen."

She meets my gaze, eyes clear and sure. "I want to keep going. But I don't want a condom. I want to feel *you*." Her lips keep moving, but my heart is pounding in my ears, dulling out the sound of her voice. When I focus back in, she's saying, ". . . skin to skin. I'm on birth control, and I was tested after my last partner. Everything was negative."

My chest heaves as I lean toward her and press a kiss to her lips. "I haven't been with anyone in . . . three years," I admit.

Pushing my shoulders back, she studies me critically, a crease between her brows. "Three years?" she repeats in disbelief.

I pull my lips between my teeth and shrug, hoping she doesn't ask more questions about why I haven't been with anyone in so long.

Because here she is, the woman who fills all my fantasies, naked and perfect, leaning back on her hands, beautiful tits on display as she watches *me* with intense hunger in her eyes.

How could I *ever* want anyone else?

I want to fuck her right into this bed. I want her so full of me that she can't remember any other person who's ever made her come.

I want it to just be *me*.

"Well, we better make it worth waiting three years for," she says, a coy smile on her lips.

My thumb swipes over her tattoo. "Baby, I'd wait forever for you."

The words slip out before I can stop them, and Lena's lips part as my admission floats in the space between us.

Damning. Revealing. Honest.

But I can't seem to take them back, even though the tightness in my chest begs me to.

"Come here," she whispers, a hand on my forearm as she falls back to the mattress.

As my weight settles over her, the tension in my body trickles away with her soft skin against mine, and I wish so badly that I could feel this peaceful all the time.

She reaches between us, wrapping a hand around the base of my cock. "You're huge," she whispers, gliding my crown over her clit.

It's too much. I'm too sensitive.

My fingers clench the sheet tightly as she writhes and whimpers beneath me, sliding me over her bundle of nerves again.

I drag her mouth to mine and whisper against her lips. "You can take it, little menace. Now guide me in."

Her breath hitches as she notches me at her warm entrance.

Pleasure shoots down my spine, all the way to my toes. With one hand digging into my hip, she tugs me toward her an inch. My attention stays glued between her thighs as the head of my cock disappears inside her tight, wet heat. We look so fucking perfect like this, our bodies fitting together like they were made for each other.

"More," she whimpers, canting her hips toward me. The movement draws me in another inch, and our deep moans echo through the cabin.

Her walls clench around me as I whisper, "That's perfect." I slide in one more torturously slow inch. "Fuck. That's my girl, Lena. You take me so well." Another push.

"Oh my god. I'm so full," she mumbles, digging her nails into my biceps and squirming beneath me.

That's fucking right. Full of me.

I bring my lips to hers, kissing her slowly to relax her as I push the rest of the way in with a deep thrust.

Fuck. Fuck. Fuck.

She whimpers into my mouth as I bottom out inside her. I stay right there, hips flush against her, pleasure beating through every nerve ending in my body.

Hot. Tight. Soaked. Mine.

Little moans drift from her lips to mine, and I steal every single one.

Her walls flutter as I pull back slowly, the firm tug of her pussy almost sending me over the edge. "You feel so good," she murmurs, writhing under me as her nails scrape over my scalp.

I lean back enough to watch my cock drag out of her, glistening in the dim light, and then disappear inside her again. "Look at us, Lena. See how perfectly we fit together, your pussy taking every inch of me?"

She lifts up on her elbows to watch as I pull out to the tip, then thrust back in to the base. "Gavin," she moans, falling back to the mattress, and that's when I snap.

My name on her lips, with my cock buried inside her, frays the last bit of my control.

Sweat rolls down my spine as I fall over her, pinning her down and making good on my promise to myself to fuck her into the mattress. I tug one of her knees up to push in a little farther, and thrust after thrust, she takes everything I have to give her. She's flawless beneath me, beautiful and needy and mewling at every rock of my hips, her core gripped tight around me. Our lips crash together feverishly, and her nails scrape down my back.

She's everywhere, weaving her way further into my heart. Like those creeping vines that held me in place when I first saw her are now coiling deeper and deeper into my soul, and I have no chance of ever removing them. There will always be traces of her left there permanently.

"You're killing me, little menace," I mutter against her neck.

And I mean it. She really might be.

We're both gasping for breath as I fill her to the hilt. I spread her thighs wider and fuck her like I've always wished I could. Hard and deep and loud.

"I need more," she whines as she trembles and thrashes.

Sliding my fingers to her clit, I circle the bundle of nerves, grinding harder into her, and her pussy clenches around me. "Yes, baby. That's perfect. Come for me."

Our gazes connect, bonded together as she shatters, crying out my name, body shaking and muscles fluttering. The pressure in my spine builds and tightens until I'm blinded by pleasure, jerking and pulsing into her.

We're panting and moaning and tugging each other closer,

desperate to mold our bodies together as much as possible as we ride out every wave of euphoria.

When I can't hold myself up anymore, I pull her with me as I fall to the side. My lips connect with hers as I kiss her slowly, languidly, like we have all the time in the world.

For tonight, I'm going to pretend we do. I'll spend every moment touching her. *Loving* her.

"Oh god. That was . . ." She shudders in my arms, little spasms gripping my cock as we float down from our highs.

I press a kiss to her forehead and tighten my arms around her. "Yeah. It was."

When we catch our breaths, I reluctantly pull away and head to the bathroom, bringing back a warm washcloth. I help her clean up before she goes to the bathroom, and then she returns, burrowing under the covers beside me.

Her breaths deepen and her muscles relax as I cradle her against my chest.

And for this one night, I have my entire world, my one true home, inside my arms.

Chapter 24

Lena

Gavin's soft exhalations brush my ears as I blink into consciousness. It's barely dawn when I crack my eyes open to see the faintest bit of sunlight flickering through the trees behind the cabin. A strong arm is banded around my waist and a leg is shoved between mine, holding me firmly in place, like I might try to escape.

My muscles are spent and exhausted, my hair probably looks like a pair of eagles have built a nest in it, and my eyes are sticky around the edges—likely from a few tears that might've snuck out at some point last night.

Or this morning. Or whatever time it was when I awoke to Gavin sliding down my body and making me writhe against his tongue. His possessive grip and murmured moans had me coming undone for him in minutes. Then he flipped me over, sliding between my thighs exactly how I needed him to. With whispered praise and one hand planted firmly over my tiger tattoo, he sent bursts of pleasure shooting through my veins until we collapsed together again.

It was paradise.

But the sun's morning rays dancing through the windows have shattered our one night together.

I'd love to stay in this bed, in the safety of Gavin's embrace, but my bladder has other plans. So I somehow manage to wiggle away from his arms without waking him and make it to the bathroom.

Staring back at me in the mirror is a woman I don't recognize. Hair wild, pillow creases on her cheeks, smeared mascara around her puffy eyes.

I look like a woman who got fucked good and hard last night, and I'm kind of obsessed with it, honestly.

After finger-combing my hair and washing my face, I glance down at my naked body. My gaze lands on a small hickey on my inner thigh, right where Gavin's mouth was in the hot tub.

Warmth swells in my chest. He's marked me, and I *adore* it. I wish it was permanent so I could show it off to everyone. Get a tattoo of it.

I'm Gavin's.

But the situation's devastating reality quickly steals my good mood.

One night. I made the rule, and over and over again, I repeated it to myself.

When he sank into me and the pressure was absolutely perfect.

When he kissed me ravenously as we came undone.

When he tucked me close to his chest and lulled me to sleep with his breaths.

One night.

And yet, here I am, wishing for more.

Opening the bathroom door as quietly as I can, I sneak to my side of the bed. Gavin's lips are parted, eyes shut peacefully, with his strong arms wrapped around the spot where I used to be.

I should get dressed. Call Auggie to come get me. Sever the ties to this bed and this cabin and this naked man right now.

But my heart crumples at the thought of never being with him again. Never kissing, touching, or hearing him moan my name again.

I can't do it. I can't let that be the only time ever.

I don't think I'll survive it.

One more morning together will be fine, right?

Half of me is terrified of this idea. Scared that it will push me over the edge into addiction territory. Into a world where I can't breathe without him. Can't think without him.

But the other half is screaming that I'm already there. I'm already so far gone for him that one more time won't hurt anything. It will merely give me an extra memory to hold on to when I'm failing to recreate it with my vibrator.

Lifting the covers, I scoot back into my spot, facing him this time, breathing in his masculine scent in case I never get to do it again.

"Mmm. Good morning," he sighs as I settle against him. He presses a tender kiss to my forehead. "How did you sleep?"

"Probably the best I've slept in months," I whisper against his chest.

He groans, pulling me closer. "I was sleeping so well with you pressed up against me."

"Me too," I admit as his fingers trail through the ends of my hair. "What time do you think the bridge will be clear to get back home?" I ask, trying to calculate how much time I have left in his arms.

"Probably early afternoon, once the sun can melt the ice." His hand roams down my back and over my hip.

"Okay. So we have a little time." My palm slides blindly over his fox tattoo, absorbing his warmth. "Merry Christmas Eve. I'm glad I get to spend this one with you."

"Me too," he breathes.

I lean back and meet his sleepy eyes. "What did you do last Christmas Eve?"

"Watched movies and ate too much," he says with a yawn.

"What did you watch?"

His cheeks lift in a grin. "*The Holiday, Miracle on 34th Street*, and, umm—"

A chill spreads through my chest as I wait for him to finish. But he doesn't, and deep in my gut, I already know the answer. "*Home Alone*," I whisper.

His body stills, and my breathing halts.

"Those are the exact movies Gary and Joe watched last year on Christmas Eve," I tell him as his heart accelerates beneath my palm. Thoughts swirl, race, and tangle in my mind until I pull out of his arms and sit up. "Where did you spend Christmas Eve last year?"

He lifts to lean against the headboard, heaving a deep breath and flicking his gaze around the room. Finally, he admits, "This cabin."

My brain short-circuits as I croak, "Here?"

"Yes."

Betrayal simmers in my veins as my brows pucker. "You were *here* last year?"

His throat moves on a swallow. "I stayed here for a few days the last two Christmases."

"Here, as in ten minutes away from us, and we didn't know it? Why?" Dread sinks low in my stomach.

With a sigh, he wipes a hand down his face. "Because I couldn't think of anywhere else in the world that I'd rather be for

Christmas than *this* town. The need to be near your family was so strong that I got as close as I possibly could."

Shaking my head, I cross my arms over my bare chest, hoping to shield some of the raw vulnerability pouring out of me. "Why didn't you say something? Come visit? Have a meal with us? Anything?"

His gaze tracks all over my face, his lips a flat line. "You know the answer to that."

I've been slowly putting the puzzle together to reveal why Gavin left three years ago, and this feels like another piece I've settled into place.

"Because of me?" I whisper.

He nods sadly as he tucks a loose strand of hair behind my ear, guilt written in the crease of his brow. "Because it's so hard to look your family in the eyes when I want you so much." His shoulders hunch. "I rented this cabin. Avoided everywhere you all might be. Forced Gary and Joe to keep it a secret. Drove to Fern River for groceries so no one would ask questions." He's talking so quickly that I can't even form follow-up thoughts. "And I laid in this bed and thought about you all. I wondered what you were doing and what Pen and Jack got for Christmas and if your mom needed my help in the kitchen."

My nose scrunches as I try to control the tears gathering on my lashes.

"I'm sorry, Lena."

My mind whirs through memories from last year's Christmas, trying to recalibrate them with this new information.

When we were opening gifts, he was only a few miles from us. When I was attempting to make my own lemon pie, he was right here. When we were picking out a Christmas tree, was he really only a short walk away?

My chest feels like a heavy weight is squeezing all the air out.

"Why didn't you tell me?" I wonder as a tear slips down my cheek.

"Because it's embarrassing." A ragged sigh stutters from his chest. "It's humiliating to feel like this clingy, broken, lonely guy who didn't want to be too far away. But also couldn't show his face."

All the fight leaves my body with a slow exhale. I scoot closer to him until my knee touches his thigh under the blanket. "Listen to me, Gav." Grabbing his chin so he meets my stare, I tell him, "You are *not* broken. You are *not* clingy. And most of all, you should not feel embarrassed. Of course I wish you had been at our house, but I'm still happy you found a homey feeling with Gary and Joe." His warmth envelops me as I cuddle under his arm, my hand over the fox tattooed on his heart.

"I missed you all, though," he admits softly, chest lifting with a deep breath. "I've never felt at home like I do with your family."

I've never felt at home like I do in his arms.

I swallow those words, though, and whisper, "We missed you too."

A long silence stretches between us, and in its midst, guilt trickles through my thoughts.

Who am I to make judgments about someone keeping secrets when I have my own? I haven't told anyone here about my job, and while I know these two secrets are nothing alike, I still wonder if he would care to know mine.

It doesn't change anything, though. He'll still go back to Eugene, and I'll go home to Wilhelmina.

One more day of withholding information won't make a difference. We can get through tomorrow, and before I leave on the twenty-sixth, I'll tell everyone. That way it doesn't ruin Christmas.

A deep breath of relief sweeps through my chest as I try to find a way to let him know that it's okay. To show him that I understand how hard it is to tell people things you feel ashamed about.

So I go for something lighthearted. "Last year, I tried to make my own lemon pie, but it was like soup in a leather crust," I admit, snorting a laugh.

He chuckles, his muscles loosening around me. "What else did you do? Tell me all of it. Leave nothing out."

* * *

"AND THEN PENELOPE held up the letter from Santa and said, 'Mama, his handwriting looks exactly like yours.'"

Gavin's laughter vibrates against my cheek. "Did they manage to convince her it wasn't?"

"Oh yeah. She was easily distracted when Auggie shoved a gift in her face, and nobody mentioned it again."

I sit up beside him, arching into a yawn and letting the blanket slip down my torso.

His grin turns wicked as it slides down my body. "Speaking of 'easily distracted.'"

My cheeks heat as I let him devour the sight of me. "I was thinking. You know how in hotels, you pay for a 'night,' but that really means you have until a certain time the next day?" I flutter my lashes at him.

His husky laugh warms my chest.

"Well, I was thinking our 'one night' should include until a certain time today."

"Were you, now?" His fingers glide up my arm in a light caress, his heavy gaze following the movement.

"It seems fair. I want to make sure I get my money's worth."

Gavin throws off the covers and slides down the bed, pulling me with him. Shivers dart down my spine as he runs his hand over my hip.

"You're insatiable, old man." I giggle, squirming under him.

He presses a kiss between my breasts. "I'll never be sated with you." He clamps his mouth over my nipple and moans around it, the vibration shooting straight through my core.

My thighs spread wider as he kisses my stomach, then just below my belly button, and right over my tiger tattoo.

His whiskey eyes sparkle as he smirks up at me, with his mouth poised right over where I need him. "Can I taste this pretty pussy again?"

My fingers grip his hair greedily. "Yes, please."

He drags a possessive palm over my inner thigh until he reaches the hickey he left last night. Gliding a thumb over it, he studies the bruise before pressing a soft kiss there.

"I like it," I admit.

He looks up at me, primal satisfaction seeping from his gaze. "Me too."

We let those words flash in the air like a warning flare that goes ignored. I can't think too hard about what happens next, because if I do, the emotional damage might be too heavy.

So I shove it aside. I push away all my thoughts of *after* and focus all my attention on this moment right here.

With one more gentle kiss on my thigh, he brings his attention back to my center. He slides his fingers through my arousal, coasting them over my sensitive core. And when his tongue makes a slow pass through me, I melt against the mattress.

There's no rushing; he exacts every bit of pleasure from my body with languid, lazy movements.

Like there isn't a looming deadline on this whole affair.

I try to memorize every detail. The covetous look in his eyes as he watches his fingers disappear inside me. His strong shoulders and flexing biceps. The way his lashes flutter shut as he sucks on my clit. The vibration of his groans against my flesh.

He plays with me, toys with me, like he's never touched something so special.

So fucking perfect.

Oh, you like that, don't you?

Come for me, baby.

Every word from his lips is kindling for the fire in my veins. The sensations and pressure build between my thighs until his burning stare meets mine and it snaps. It's those dark whiskey eyes, that hint of his control slipping in the best way, that makes me tumble over the edge, sparks of pleasure shooting through my body.

After he takes a few more savoring licks, he drops on his back beside me, pulling me with him.

My heavy breaths echo through the cabin walls as he guides me to straddle him. He grips my hips tightly, holding me back from sliding down his thick cock.

I drop my hands to his hard chest and kiss him.

If last night was desperate and needy, this morning, in the light of day, is slow and thorough.

Final.

Even though I don't want *final* at all.

I writhe against him as his hands touch every bit of skin they can. Like he's trying to memorize exactly how every curve of my body feels against his palms. He leans up to press kisses to my breasts, shoulders, cheek, and jaw.

And when I wrap a hand around his base and bring the tip into my wet heat, he hisses.

"Oh, *fuck*. Please." His abs vibrate under my fingertips with the pressure to hold himself still. "Please, little menace. I need you," he begs, his raspy voice echoing through the room.

Heart skittering inside my rib cage, I reward him with a swift downward plunge. His grip digs into my hips as I straighten over him and writhe against the pressure.

"That's perfect, Lena. Ride my cock, just like that." His gravelly voice is punctuated with pauses every time I thrust against him.

My breaths deepen with the effort, and sweat slicks down my spine.

Our eyes stay locked on each other as he brushes his fingers over my clit. "Yes, Gavin. Harder. Yes." The words are incoherent as pleasure rolls through me, building in my spine and curling my toes until it engulfs every nerve ending.

A tear slips down my cheek as he pulses and spills himself inside me, moaning my name like a prayer.

For the last time.

Chapter 25

Gavin

*H*ow on earth are we supposed to move on with our lives after that movie?" Lena sniffles as she sets her head on my chest and floods my senses with her peppermint-and-chocolate scent.

Gary watches us from the other couch, a knowing smirk on his lips. I shoot him a frown and a subtle headshake, trying to silently scold him for whatever thoughts are going on inside that brain of his.

Joe and Gary are the only people in the world who know about my feelings for Lena. In their nonjudgmental but thoroughly annoying way, they have teased me about it for two years. And if I'm gauging their expressions correctly, they think the two of us are adorable together.

Their mysterious cousin, Patrick, doesn't seem to exist today, but my will to question them is nonexistent after the evening I had. I couldn't care less about whatever ruse I fell for last night.

"Might be time to check the bridge and see if the ice has melted," Lena says, patting my thigh and pulling herself out from under my arm.

A lead weight sinks straight into my stomach.

Reality.

It's been haunting the back of my mind, looming there for every moment I spent with Lena, and I finally have to face it.

We're going back to her house soon, even though I sure as hell don't want to.

I spent a lot of time wishing I could be back with them. But now that I have Lena in my arms, I'm content to stay here.

She stands from the couch in Joe's navy sweatpants and a baggy sweater that says HO, HO, HO.

Fresh-faced, loose curls, pink cheeks.

She's never looked prettier.

"I'm so glad you joined us," Joe tells her at the door, kissing Lena's cheek and then mine.

"Let's make it a tradition," Lena proclaims, hugging Gary. "We meet up next year for more waffles from this guy"—she pinches my side—"and more Colin Firth movies." She waggles her eyebrows suggestively, and everyone laughs.

But in the car, as we drive to her mom's house, no one is laughing.

Instead, there's a staggering silence threatening to strangle me as we approach the bridge.

Maybe by some twist of fate, the blazing sun will have never shone on the icy bridge today. It's only early afternoon; maybe there's a chance we can't cross it.

Gliding my hand over her thigh, I splay my fingers like they belong there and imagine a world in which they do.

If the bridge is still icy, we could go back to the cabin. We can strip out of these clothes and sink back into our lust-filled haze, her perfect body against mine as we cling to each other.

But minutes later, I discover that fate is not on our side, because the bridge is clear, the road wet with melted ice.

Lena lets out a long sigh and intertwines her fingers with mine for the rest of the drive.

I pull the car safely into the empty spot in the driveway and turn it off. The air is heavy as we both try to come to terms with what happens next.

And the truth is, I have no fucking clue.

"Keeping my hands off you is going to be torture," I finally admit.

She huffs a sad laugh. "No eye-fucking each other either," she says as she unbuckles her seat belt. Her voice bubbles with sarcasm as she adds, "I know I look fantastic in these sweats, but you'll have to resist the temptation."

My palm scrapes over my stubbled cheek. "You're always a temptation, little menace." I scan over her body. "You could be in a tarp and I'd be dying to unwrap you like a present."

She swallows hard, her caramel gaze flickering with heat. But when her attention moves to the house out the windshield, her skin pales. "I don't know how to do this."

I don't either. Today, tomorrow, next Christmas. I have no idea what I'm going to do.

"I think we just have to pretend like everything is normal," I tell her, trying to keep my voice even. "We act like I slept on Gary and Joe's couch."

The corners of her lips pull down, and she shakes her head. "I don't know if I can keep pretending."

My mind races, trying to figure out what she means, but before I can solve it, she turns and opens the passenger door.

Chapter 26

Lena

We Catan Beat Finn

Lena: So . . . Gavin's dick is huge.

Lena: Like, could probably be used as a weapon.

Millie: WTF, LENA???

Lena: Don't be too jealous. I bet Finn's is huge too. He gives off that vibe.

Millie: No comment.

Micah: Lena. Explain.

Lena: We got stuck in town last night and had to stay in a cabin together 🍆

> **Lena:** So worth it, by the way. It was a "get it out of our systems" situation.

> **Millie:** And it worked? He's out of your system?

> **Lena:** No comment.

* * *

"Tɪᴀ Lᴇɴᴀ, ɪᴛ's your turn," Pen says from beside me at the kitchen table, where she's effortlessly beating me at this game of Skip-Bo.

Because I can't stop watching Gavin roll out pie crust.

Dragging my eyes away from him, I assess the cards between us. I manage to play three before my gaze drifts back toward the handsome man in the kitchen.

He has already made two batches of cinnamon rolls, delivered one to Shannon, and now he and Mama have moved on to pies.

With a kitchen towel over his shoulder and a red apron tied around his body, his bulging muscles roll and glide as he presses into the dough. A small smirk plays across his lips like he knows I'm watching.

I'm tempted to dash over and lick that flour right off those tattooed forearms and then thank him for the opportunity.

What the *fuck* is wrong with me?

I'm acting like a sex-crazed version of myself after one night with him.

Earlier, I went to change out of Joe's oversized sweats, but as I stuffed my feet into my leggings, I spotted my red dress hanging in the corner. I hadn't worn it yet, and a spark of mischief shot through me at the thought of putting that on instead. With the low-cut neckline and tight fit against my curves, I imagined what Gavin's face might look like when he saw it.

Just the thought of him growling *little menace* in my ear had me jumping into the shower, fixing my curls, and painting my lips to match my dress.

I'd show him what a menace I could be.

He looked like a nutcracker as I came back into the kitchen, jaw wide open like he couldn't get control of it.

Eat your heart out, Gavin Moore.

I dare you to *pretend everything is normal.*

Nothing is normal.

Jack nudges my arm. "Tia Lena, it's your turn."

Shaking my head, I blink back to the game and realize even a five-year-old is kicking my ass.

But I can feel Gavin's piercing stare like a hot brand on my skin. At this point, we're both guilty of eye-fucking each other every chance we get, despite our plans not to.

As I attempt to refocus on the cards, Mama pats Gavin's arm before leaving the kitchen. He brushes his flour-covered hands down his apron and heads toward the walk-in pantry.

Without thinking, I mumble, "Be right back," to my niece and nephew.

My heels click with purpose on the hardwood floors as I waltz toward the pantry. I reach the doorway as Gavin grabs a container of gluten-free flour. Shoving a hand into his chest, I nudge him until his shoulders hit the back row of shelves.

"Lena," he hisses, eyes wide.

I grab his cheeks before he can say another word and tug his lips to mine, kissing him hard. My tongue dives for his instantly, and I put every bit of pent-up frustration over the last few hours into the kiss. All the flaming desire pumping through my veins constantly because my body knows he's around.

Hopefully, by the time I'm driving home in two days, the distance will make the craving lessen. But for now? When I'm subjected to seeing these perfect arms roll out pie crust? When I'm doused in his scent every time he walks into the room? When I have to hear his husky laugh skate over my skin?

It's fucking *agony*, and I tell him that with my bruising kiss.

The container of flour lands somewhere with a *thud*, and he drags my hips to his. A low growl rumbles from his throat as he squeezes my ass firmly.

"What are you doing to me?" he mumbles against my lips, hands kneading my curves.

I loop my arms around his neck, my pulse hammering in my chest. "I don't know. You looked irresistible, and I didn't stop to think." Lips against his ear, I whisper, "Just one more."

His mouth moves to my neck, and he drags his teeth over my pulse point. "You're killing me with this dress. And the fucking lipstick. I can't take it." He peppers kisses down my collarbone and straight to the cleavage showing above the neckline.

"You like it?" I tease, arching my back to give him better access.

His finger dips into the crease between my breasts and pulls the fabric out an inch. "Fucking love it, little menace," he growls, just like I hoped he would.

"Where's your tia Lena?"

We both freeze as Mama's voice echoes from the kitchen.

I pull away, biting back a grin. Gavin's jaw clenches tight, and I swipe a thumb over the stain of lipstick on the corner of his mouth.

"You're going to get us in trouble," he grits, but there's no heat in it.

I toss him a wink before spinning to leave the pantry and screeching to a halt when Mama appears at the entrance, her brows drawn together. Her eyes scan me from head to toe, then flick over my shoulder to Gavin.

"He couldn't find the flour," I say as steadily as I can, hoping my lips don't look swollen and ravaged after only a moment of kissing.

She squints as I slip past her, and Gavin lets out a faint choking sound behind me as I scurry for the table.

I drop back into my seat, grab my cards, and try to calm my heartbeat as I refocus on the game before me.

"What's on your dress?" Pen wonders, tilting her head.

My gaze snaps down, and a strangled gasp leaves my throat.

Flour is pressed into the red fabric, perfect fingerprints bracketing my hips. And when I twist to glance at the back, two white handprints adorn my ass.

All the blood drains from my face.

* * *

"Did you really have to make this a competition?" Auggie sighs, adjusting the third and smallest snowball on top of his snowman. "I'm trying to impress my kids here."

I squat in front of my snow sculpture and prop my elbows on my knees. "It's literally three pyramids. I just packed the snow into a triangle."

"The fucking snow sphinx, Lena," he grumbles. "I look like an amateur compared to that."

"Huh, oh yeah." I shrug, pretending it isn't the most badass thing I've ever made. "Sorry your kids think I'm cooler than you."

As I go to brush invisible lint off my shoulder, Auggie collides with me, and we both fall right into the sphinx.

"*Auggie*," I scream at the top of my lungs, my gloved fists slamming into his puffy jacket and having absolutely no effect. "I didn't get a picture!"

Pen and Jack jump right on top of us, rolling back and forth, and pressing snow into my cheeks. After a few minutes in the scuffle, I manage to wiggle out of their wrestling pile and seek refuge where Zara and Gavin are building something together.

Gavin kneels beside their structure, his all-black ensemble a stark difference from the snow. His gloved hands are working diligently to construct some sort of playground, with steps to climb up and a long slide that ends in a heap of fluffy powder.

"I can't decide if this looks like a great idea or an injury waiting to happen," I tell them, brushing snow off my pants.

Zara tilts her head as she creates a snow-railing along the edge of the slide. "At least if they fall off, they've got some padding on."

Jack shoves himself by me, heading fearlessly toward the steps. When he gets to the bottom one, Gavin stands to hold his waist while he climbs up, then keeps a grip on his hand as he goes down the other side with an earsplitting squeal.

"Me next," Pen calls, running to the steps.

Looping an arm through Zara's, I lean my head on her shoulder. "Want to go on a walk with me? Leave these overgrown boys to watch the children?"

Auggie dives down the slide headfirst with a roar and crashes his face into the pile of snow at the bottom. The kids fall over laughing as Gavin attempts to yank him up.

"Don't whine to me when you're sore tomorrow morning. You're too old for that," Zara calls over her shoulder as I pull her toward the field beside Mama's house. "I don't even know if we can trust Gavin to be in charge," she murmurs to me.

We create our own path through last night's untouched snow, walking directly onto the empty lot. Following the line of trees, we stay in the open field at the front of the property, chatting about the party last night and what they did this morning while Gavin and I were gone.

As we get to the far edge of the field, she voices the question I've been equal parts dreading and hoping she would bring up.

"What did you and Gavin do?"

"Umm . . ." I bite my lips, and something she sees in my expression answers her question immediately.

She gasps and pauses her steps, hands wrapping around my wrists to turn me to face her. "Lena Santos. What happened?" The giddiness in her tone relaxes my shoulders a little.

"Can you promise you won't talk to Auggie about it?"

"Only if you promise to give me all the details."

With a breath of relief, I pour everything out to her—the tamest version I can, while also giving her all the little details she begs for in the middle. And by the end of the story, her jaw is practically in the snow.

"What happens now?" she asks, bouncing on her toes with excitement.

"Fuck if I know." I shrug. "But I think my mom might suspect something already."

"What? How?"

"I . . . might've followed him into the pantry and kissed him. But he was covered in flour, so I got it all over myself." My voice rises at the end like I'm asking a question.

Zara's loud laugh bounces around the field, likely echoing all the way into town. "Please tell me you're joking." She holds her stomach as she chuckles, completely ignoring my stern glare. "Did she say something?" she asks, wiping tears from her eyes.

"Not a single word. She could've been mad or happy or annoyed, for all I know."

Zara loops her arm through mine again, and we wander back toward the house. "Can I tell you what I think? As a happily married woman?"

"Okay," I grumble, biting the inside of my cheek at this role reversal. Normally I'm the one pushing advice on my friends, and here I am hoping someone will offer it to me.

"I've seen the way he looks at you," she says, lifting a brow in my direction. "Hell, I've seen the way you look at him. It's a wonder Auggie hasn't noticed yet."

My stomach tangles in knots. "What do you think Auggie would say if he knew?"

"I can't predict exactly what he would think, but I *can* tell you that he wants both of you to be happy. And I know deep down, even if he had a little bit of a struggle with it at first, he would come around. At least by next Christmas, for sure." She snorts a laugh as she hip-checks me. "But I'm willing to bet that this thing between you and Gavin isn't just one night. I mean, you couldn't even make it one full day without scandalizing the pantry."

Her words crawl into my ears, bouncing around my mind as we make our way back to the house.

She's right. I couldn't last one day in his presence without needing to touch him again.

But hopefully, by the time I'm driving away in two days, the distance between us will lessen the need for him.

Chapter 27

Gavin

This thing is half as tall as the tree," Auggie says in astonishment as we set the top level onto the new dollhouse.

I step back, snagging a cookie from Santa's plate on the coffee table. Gluten-free almond spritz cookies, with a buttery flavor that melts in my mouth. I've had . . . maybe this is number ten? I'm not sure. Counting Christmas cookies should be illegal.

Zara's and Lena's giggles drift from the couch, where they're snuggled together with a sleeping Noah. They've found Auggie and me struggling through this late-night dollhouse-construction project quite entertaining, judging by their snarky comments and endless laughter.

Auggie tightens the last screw and swipes his hand over the red roof. "That should do it. They're gonna love it."

I drop onto the open couch and watch as he pushes the house over a few feet and presses a big green bow to the top. He stands next to it with a proud grin, fingers tapping together as he surveys all the gifts.

When Auggie and I met as freshman roommates in college, we quickly discovered how different our personalities are. He's bubbly and open and has never met a stranger. Meanwhile, I'm quiet, closed-off, and a steadfast introvert.

But Auggie was the first person who *wanted* to be around me and who wouldn't let me drift into the shadows like I'm inclined to. When I was struggling through college, barely surviving my depression and thoughts of self-harm, he was constantly there. He managed to worm his way into my life and never let me shut him out. He has a magical ability to bring out the best in me, and I don't know how he does it.

I owe him my life.

So when he brought up moving from Eugene to Juniper to help restore their historic downtown, I agreed without a second thought. I trust him entirely.

As I snag another cookie, Auggie examines his kids' stockings. He straightens their contents and positions them perfectly for tomorrow morning.

Watching him weighs my chest down with longing.

Will that ever be me? Will there ever come a Christmas where I'm fixing stockings and preparing gifts for my own children?

Helping create that magic for Auggie and Zara's kids is fun, but I would love to do it for my own one day.

Right now, though, that reality seems impossible.

My eyes land on Lena, like thinking of having children automatically means I should look her way. Noah's cradled in her arms like it's the most natural thing in the world.

She would make a fantastic mom. Protective and fierce, loving and compassionate.

And I can't help but wonder who that lucky partner will be. She'll find someone eventually, and I'll have to meet them and pretend to like them.

Even as jealousy grips my throat.

"Ready for bed?" Auggie asks, offering a hand to Zara.

She kisses Lena's cheek and whispers something into her ear that makes a pink flush slide over Lena's face and down her throat. Then she picks up Noah, and they wish us good night as they ascend the stairs.

Lena watches me in silence while they walk to their room.

My body is an anxious, jittery live wire, electrified with the need to touch her. Like maybe one point of contact with her skin would calm my nerves and my racing heart.

I'm like a fiend. I just need *one more* hit.

One more time to hold her hand. One more time for her soft, supple lips to meet mine.

That will be all, I tell myself. I can stop after that.

When the door upstairs clicks shut, Lena shoots off the other couch like a spring, jumping around the coffee table to me like our thoughts were aligned.

As she lands on the couch beside me, I pull her toward my body, right where she fits perfectly.

My arm around her shoulders, her head on my chest, her hand over the fox on my ribs.

She's home.

Even though we swore it would be over last night, and then this morning, here we are, drawn to each other like magnets. Like it's inescapable.

As she burrows closer to me, I whisper, "I have an errand to run tomorrow. Would you like to come with me?"

Her eyes meet mine, the reflection from the tree's lights sparkling in her caramel irises. "Of course. What's the errand?"

I run a hand over her shoulder, reminding myself to only touch her arm. Nowhere else. "I want to take pizzas to Shannon's house. That was Julia's Christmas wish, and Peter's Pizza is going to make some for me to pick up."

"My Gavin is a softie," she murmurs, pressing a kiss to my jaw.

My Gavin.

I let those words nestle inside my heart.

I want to be hers. I want this cozy comfort every day. I want her presence to soothe my soul like this every night.

"Come upstairs with me," she whispers.

Dropping my lips to the top of her head, I shut my eyes and inhale her sweet, citrusy scent. "I can't."

Her little whine makes me huff a laugh. "I want another night. Just one more."

My hand betrays the Arm Rule and runs through the ends of her silky hair. "I want another night too, but you're just going to get me addicted."

She looks up at me, her gaze glassy. "What if I already am?"

When she licks her lips, I follow the movement of her tongue and have to stifle a groan.

I'm clearly addicted too. The intense pressure in my chest to simply be *closer* to her is debilitating. I don't even know if I'm even thinking straight at this point.

Putting a palm to her cheek, I press my forehead to hers. "Please go to bed, Lena. For my sanity. You're too tempting to resist when you're cuddled up beside me, all soft and sweet. It's so hard to say no."

"Then don't," she pleads, standing and tugging me to follow her.

Somehow I manage to shake my head, keeping myself rooted to the couch. "I can't." But even as I say the words, my attention drags down her body, to her hardened nipples and the flare of her hips.

When my gaze drifts back up to hers, she bites her bottom lip. "I'll be waiting for you." Then she saunters to the stairs without a second glance.

My chest aches as I watch her walk away.

Can I really stay away from her? Can I let her sleep upstairs knowing how impeccable it feels to lie with my body pressed to hers?

I already know the answer. My willpower when it comes to her is as fragile as chipped glass. It's cracking and splintering further into a spiderweb with every moment I spend in her presence.

And I'm wondering if I'll ever be able to gather up all the broken pieces after this.

Chapter 28

Lena

I thought he'd be here by now.

Maybe I should go back downstairs? What if he's waiting for me, hoping I'll surprise him and drag him into the pantry?

Do I have a thing for pantries now?

There's just something intimate about the closed space and the fear of getting caught that makes my heart pound.

Fuck, I think I have a thing for pantries.

As I'm debating pantry-based jobs I could look into, my doorknob turns with a small squeak. My breath pauses in my lungs as it opens a few inches.

Through the darkness, Gavin's broad shoulders appear in the opening, and a small whimper of excitement escapes my throat.

He puts a finger over his mouth, quickly sneaking into the room and shutting the door. "There's no lock," he hisses softly.

"It's fine." I wave him toward me as I flip the covers back on the opposite side of the mattress. "Everyone's asleep anyway."

He hesitates at the foot of the bed, his frame caressed by moonlight from the window. "I shouldn't have come," he mutters, pulling at his hair.

I roll my eyes even though he can't see it. "Get your ass over here. No one is going to come into my room, and it's not like you can sleep past five a.m. anyway. We're going to wake up early for our Christmas-morning coffee."

With a weary sigh, he crawls up the bed and drops to his back, an arm slung over his face. "This was an awful idea."

"It's an excellent idea. Best idea I've ever had." Crawling over him, I straddle his hips and shove my arms under his, curling toward him in a hug. "I missed touching you today," I admit as he strokes a hand up my spine. "You were right there, and I couldn't."

His deep, quiet moan vibrates against my ear. "That's been my life for the last ten years." When his hand makes another pass up my back, he slides his palm under my shirt, and my eyes fall shut.

"Gavin." My hips wiggle against him involuntarily, and I whisper my thoughts before I can overthink them. "Can we have one more time?"

His other hand comes to the back of my head, tangling in my slouchy bun. "I must be going straight to hell because that's all I can think about." His fingers wander along the waistband of my pajama pants. "Even though I know you're leaving, I'm still craving you like it doesn't matter."

My chest shrinks at the thought of me leaving.

Wilhelmina is my home. I have friends, jobs to apply for, a house I'm renting.

Things are tethering me there, but none of them make me feel the way *he* does.

The ache intensifies in my chest as I try to breathe in all the way. But when I do, no air comes to my rescue. All I can inhale is *Gavin*.

He's everywhere. My lungs, my heart, my head, all the way to my *bones*.

And even though it terrifies me, I need more.

I skate my lips over his neck, and when I bite down lightly, his hips shift under mine. Sliding down an inch, I leave a kiss on the hollow of his throat.

His grip tightens on my waist. "Lena, baby," he whispers as I scoot farther down his body. He tosses a hand over his face and mumbles, "What are you doing?"

I drag his shirt up his taut stomach, fingers gliding over the tattoos across his body. He's all dark lines and shadows, but I know they're there as I trace his fox tattoo. "I want to taste you. Can you be quiet?"

Warm hands cup my face until I lift my head. "No, I can't be quiet," he whisper-yells. "Especially if you keep going."

My mouth waters, heat pooling in my core. I drop a kiss right above his waistband, running my tongue along the edge of it, and his low rumbling growl resonates around the room.

"Do you want me to stop?" I whisper, letting my lips sweep over his skin.

His breath is ragged as he brushes a thumb gently over my cheek. "I *should* want you to stop. But fuck, that's the last thing I want."

Grabbing the fabric at his hips, I tug down his lounge pants and briefs together. A smile pulls at my lips as his cock springs free between us.

Goose bumps skate down my neck as his grip moves to the back of my head, fingers grazing my scalp. "I want to make you feel good, but I'm going to have to cover your mouth if you can't be quiet," I say, repeating his words from the night of our first kiss.

He huffs a dry laugh, his fingers tightening in my hair. "Will *you* be quiet, or will you be moaning while you slide those pretty lips down my cock?"

My core clenches tight. I *love* the way he talks when he's unraveling for me. I wish I could record his words and play them back for myself in the coming weeks. Months. Years.

"I'll be moaning," I admit, wrapping my hand around his base, my chest practically vibrating with anticipation. He chokes on a gasp as I lean closer and run my lips over the velvet skin, then lick the bead of precum gathered on his crown. A hum of pleasure flows from my throat.

"Oh, little menace," he whispers. "You're desperate for it, aren't you?"

His words surge over my skin like wildfire as I take him into my mouth, my lips wrapping around his head and sucking gently.

When his hips buck up and he hisses, I swirl my tongue over him.

His smooth skin glides through my wet mouth with ease as I slide down his length. Tangling his fingers deeper in my hair, he whispers, "That's perfect, baby. Just like that."

I slip him out of my mouth slowly, sucking and hollowing out my cheeks until my lips slide back to his tip.

"Oh, fuck yes." His thighs spread wider, making more room for me between them.

My low moan rolls through the room as I slide him back down my throat.

"I bet you can take me a little farther this time," he encourages, caressing his fingers down to my neck.

Pulling my hand away from his base, I relax my throat to dive deeper and swallow him as far as I can.

"That's my girl," he praises, and I preen, *wanting* to be his girl. Only his, forever.

When I flick my eyes up, his are glowing in the dim room, searing into me. I moan around him and work him faster, harder, tighter. My nails dig into his hips, and he whimpers. The bun in my hair dissolves in his grip, letting the curls fall free, but he gathers them in his fist.

"You're taking me so well," he whispers, voice strained and gravelly as his hips punch up. "Making me feel powerless to resist you, you know that?" He strokes the back of my head, cheeks, and neck with a branding touch like he's marking me. "You look so fucking beautiful like this, Lena."

Waves of pleasure zing through my muscles until I'm squirming and writhing between his thick thighs. There's an earth-shattering tension building in our bodies, his legs twitching beneath my hands and his hips pressing him up into my warm mouth.

God, I wish I could see him better, to mark every detail of the ecstasy on his face.

When his legs tighten and his hips pause their movement, I suck harder. But with a hand on my chin and one in my hair, he pulls me back until his cock slides from my mouth.

His chest heaves with deep breaths, his hands shaking. "As much as I want to come down your throat, I need to feel you squeezing my cock." He groans, pulling me up his body. "One more time," he adds, and I can't tell if he's saying it for me or himself.

He scrambles to pull my shirt over my head and tosses it to the side. Desperate kisses land on my neck and jaw as he drags my pants off and pulls me down next to him.

The mattress is shockingly quiet on the frame as he positions us on our sides, his hot chest against my back. He pulls the covers up, encasing us in their cozy protection. Then he reaches over my hip to slide his fingers between my thighs.

"Oh fuck, Lena. Is this pussy all wet for me?" he asks, swirling his touch over my clit.

Stars scatter across my vision. "Just for you. Always for you." I whimper as he shoves his other hand under my neck and around to cup my breast.

"Gavin," I whisper as softly as I can, pressing back into his hard length.

"Yes?" he asks airily, his fingers strumming over my nipple and clit in slow movements.

I writhe against his length, trying to silently convince him to give me what I want.

"Beg for it, little menace."

His touch moves harder over my bundle of nerves, and warmth pours down my spine. "Please. I need it."

"You need *me*," he growls against my throat before sinking his teeth into my neck with a playful bite.

"Yes. Please. I need *you*."

"You beg so pretty for me," he whispers as he pushes into me in one quick thrust. He grunts against my ear as he reaches the hilt, filling me more than I thought possible, and the pleasure steals my breath.

His slow, grinding cadence of thrusts wrecks me. One hand kneads my breast, and one plays with my clit while his forearm holds my hips in place for him to push against. My walls flutter as he drags himself in and out of me with perfect friction.

I'm consumed by him. Living, breathing, needing him. Wrapped in his strong arms, with his warm breaths cascading over my skin, and I feel like I could be his forever.

Every sense, every inch, every wish. He's there, stealing all of it.

"I'm going to be thinking about you like this forever," he whispers. His movements slow to a lazy pace, and I arch my back for more. "You feel perfect, baby. Like you were made for me."

The bridge of my nose burns, and my moan chokes off in a hiccup.

"Tell me you'll remember this," he breathes against my ear.

"Yes," I whisper as his touch slides over my clit. "I'll always remember this."

A tear drips from the corner of my eye, and I'm not sure why.

This is just sex. This is just the hormones and pleasure bleeding into my emotions. Right?

But when I grip his arm, his muscles bunching as he moves his hand against me, and when he thrusts deeper, grunting into my neck, and when my nerves are firing, pressure building in my core . . . I think I might be wrong.

He holds me tighter, no space between our bodies as his movements speed up. My walls clench around him, and he purrs, "My Lena."

My moans are louder than a whisper, so he steals the hand from my breast to place it over my mouth, muffling my cries as I come apart around him. I shatter into a million blinding lights, legs shaking and breaths stuttering and heart bursting.

He comes with a groaning sigh of satisfaction rattling against my ear. His grip on my mouth loosens, and he caresses me with gentle strokes as our bodies settle against each other. He whispers my name, kisses my shoulder, glides his palm along my side soothingly.

And as our bodies relax, muscles spent and breaths steadying, one thought beats like a drum in my mind.

He's not leaving my system. Instead, he's etching himself there permanently.

Chapter 29

Lena

I found them!"

Jack's scream startles me awake. My heart stops. The warm arm over my waist goes rigid.

Surely, I was just dreaming about my nephew's voice.

But when I blink open my eyes, there he is, smiling widely with his hair sticking in every direction. "Are you and Uncle Gavin having a sleepover?"

I choke on a breath, but before I can form words, Zara swoops behind him. Casting an apologetic look in my direction, she grabs him and scurries out the door, shutting it behind her.

I yank the covers over my face with a groan, thankful we were smart enough to put our pajamas back on in the middle of the night, so my nosey nephew is not scarred for life.

Gavin sits up and grumbles, "What the fuck?"

"Maybe no one heard him," I murmur, flipping to face him.

He shoots me a skeptical glare. "He was yelling."

"Maybe everyone else is outside."

"It's Christmas morning."

"Shit," I hiss, springing from the bed and scrambling to the bathroom. "We slept in!"

My heart rages in my ears as I wash my hands, slip on my house shoes, and brush my teeth. Then I attempt to tame my hair to hide the fact that I spent my night with a six-foot-four sex wizard running his hands through it while I choked on his cock.

Two braids down my shoulders is as good as it's going to get.

When I open the door, Gavin sits on the edge of the bed, his cheeks drained of color. "I never sleep this late," he blurts.

Stepping in front of his knees, I lift his chin until he meets my stare. "I think both of us sleep better when we're together." I run a hand through his silky strands, pressing down on the little cowlick on the side. He's adorably rumpled this morning, with pillow creases on his cheek and sleepy eyes blinking up at me.

As he nods, I *almost* bend down to kiss him. My lips tingle with the urge to do it.

But I remember the plan at the last moment.

I told him one more night. I promised him. And every step of the way, it has been *me* pushing for more. *Me* begging him to touch me again.

It's probably time to stop pestering him.

"We have about four seconds before someone either comes back up here or we miss opening stockings," I say, pulling him to stand. "And I need a peppermint mocha, and you're the only person who knows how to make them the way I like."

One corner of his lips kicks up in a grin as he rises to follow me out of the bedroom.

The house is eerily quiet as we descend the stairs. When I reach the bottom step and see the living room, Auggie and Zara are missing, and no one else looks our way. The kids are buzzing with anticipation as they clutch their stockings, patiently waiting for all of us to get started.

The smell of cinnamon and sugar draws us into the kitchen, alerting me to the fact that someone must've started the cinnamon rolls without Gavin. As my hand wraps around the coffee pot, angry, hushed voices filter from the laundry room.

Zara's distinctly firm tone whispers, "It's Christmas morning. If you have a problem with something, keep it to yourself until later."

I'm not trying to snoop, but stifling curiosity is not something I believe in. So I hold my breath, hoping to hear more as Gavin checks the cinnamon rolls.

There's a long beat of silence, and then Auggie grunts a *fine*. I can practically feel his scowl lasering into my back as he leaves the laundry room, and I stay frozen in place until I can't hear his stomped footsteps anymore.

Gavin lets out an unsteady sigh as he joins me at the coffee pot. He pulls my mug in front of him and grabs the peppermint and chocolate syrups from the cabinet, drizzling them into both of our cups.

My grin blooms slowly as I watch him contaminate his black coffee with the sweet additions. Then he gets the half-and-half and his homemade whipped cream from the fridge to finish them off.

He meets my gaze as we clink our festive mugs together, mine adorned in a snowy tree scene, and his decorated with elves in a workshop.

"Thank you," I whisper with a secret smile just for him.

"Anytime."

He takes a careful sip, then lowers the mug, biting back a grin. "It's pretty good."

I don't even try to hide my smug smile as we turn to join the Christmas-morning calamity. My free hand floats toward him, and I slide my pinky around his, linking them together until we get to the living room.

* * *

"Okay, we have one more gift this morning." Auggie stands by the coffee table, wrapping paper and presents littering the floor around him. "Everyone is going to have to get dressed to go outside, though." He glances at Gavin, lifting his brows in question, but there's a heat to his expression that I wish I could smack right off my brother's face.

A silent conversation takes place between them before Gavin nods. "Yeah, let's do it."

As we all layer ourselves in jackets, boots, hats, and gloves, the list of what we could possibly be doing runs through my mind like news headlines.

- *Tired father accidentally buys his ten-year-old daughter a car for Christmas.*
- *Best friends reveal they've caught the real Edward Cullen and kept him tied up in the shed.*
- *Watch this family attempt to build a sled from a seventy-foot pine tree in their backyard.*

Literally any of those could be possible when Auggie has something planned, but we blindly follow him outside anyway.

"Just a few more yards," he calls, leading us onto the property next door.

"You said that thirty yards ago," I grumble, picking my boots up higher in the fluffy snow. Luckily, Jack is on Gavin's shoulders, and Luci stayed home with Noah, so most of us are tall enough to get through it.

But I'd still give Jack a year's worth of candy to trade spots with him and let me be the one carried by Gavin.

"Okay," Auggie announces. "We're here."

I stop beside him and cross my arms. "If you're about to make us dig for some hidden treasure under the snow, I'm leaving." My gaze flicks to Zara, who has been suspiciously quiet on this five-minute trek. "Do you already know what we're doing?"

She nods, her lips folded between her teeth, and I narrow my eyes at her.

"Gavin, you want to take over?" Auggie asks, his voice laced with tension that makes this whole situation feel like it's a bubbling pot about to boil over.

And I have no idea how to prevent it.

"I think you're doing a great job," Gavin replies as Jack wiggles on his shoulders.

"Well, Mom and Lena, the rest of us have an announcement. A final Christmas gift," Auggie says, spreading his arms wide. He meets Gavin's gaze across our small circle. "Gavin and I are starting our own architecture firm, right here in Juniper. And you're all standing on the property that will hold our future homes."

A beat of silence passes before Penelope erupts into cheers. Confusion wrinkles my brows as I turn to Gavin, but he's staring at his boots.

"Really?" Mama croaks. "You're moving here?"

Auggie slings an arm over her shoulder, beaming down at her. "Yeah. We're building houses next to you."

"Like, right here?" I ask. My gaze bounces all over the place as I attempt to catch up. I'm trying to align this information with things I already know, and I'm having trouble figuring out where to file these changes.

Gavin finally looks my way with a shy grin. "I don't know if it'll be exactly where you're standing, but near this spot." He adjusts Jack on his shoulders and turns to look around the bright field.

Mama steps closer to Zara and kisses her cheek. "You're bringing my grandbabies closer?"

When Zara nods, Mama's chin quivers, and she turns to Auggie, burying her face in the front of his coat to sob with joy.

Words are impossible to find as my gaze locks with Gavin's. He merely offers me a small smile as my mind swirls with these updates. My lips part, about to say . . . *something*. I'm not even sure what, but Auggie tugs me toward him.

"What do you think, sis?"

"It's amazing," I tell him, but my eyes stay pinned to Gavin, to the way the sun casts shadows over his face.

"Our first job is fixing up downtown Juniper." Auggie keeps talking, but I tune him out as the world tilts around me.

My thoughts churn. Gavin is going to live here. In Juniper. Right next door to my mom and Luci. Right here. So close.

Jack squirms to get down, and Gavin helps him to the ground. When Jack runs to Auggie's legs, I take the distraction to sneak out from under his arm.

"What are you thinking?" Gavin asks as he steps toward me, straightening his black trench coat over his broad shoulders.

I don't know how to answer that question. I can't identify what's happening in my heart right now, but it feels similar to a pulled muscle. A sharp stretching pain that's tugging the life out of me.

"You didn't tell me." The words leave my lips as I scan his face. "You didn't say a word."

Beside us, laughter and chatter surround a group hug between everyone else. They sound like they've won the lottery, but all I can see is the betrayal turning my vision dark.

Maybe if he had told me, I could've . . . I might've . . . I don't know. Planned what my reaction would be?

His eyes crinkle on the corners as he winces, reaching to pull my hat farther down my ears. "I'm sorry I didn't tell you sooner. Auggie wanted it to be this big Christmas reveal. It's been eating me alive not to tell you."

My head shakes. "I'm mad you didn't."

A long silence stretches between us before he says, "I guess I thought it wouldn't affect you that much."

As the words hit my heart, they sink their claws into the muscle fibers.

He's right. This shouldn't affect me. It has nothing to do with me.

It shouldn't change anything.

The pain burns in my chest, and I force myself to suck in a deep breath.

My mind flashes with images of the future. Everyone here together, laughing as they clink glasses over weekly dinners. My family sprawled around the living room after a board game. Gavin and Mama cooking, music filling the kitchen.

Maybe this tugging in my heart is homesickness for something that doesn't even exist yet.

Gavin continues, unaware of my panicked thoughts. "You have your life in Wilhelmina, so I didn't think it would make a difference where I live. You have your friends and your job and—"

"I got fired." The words explode out of me way louder than I intended, and the bubbling excitement beside us dies abruptly.

Gavin's mouth is agape as he stares at me, confusion etched across his brows.

"You got *fired*?" Mama squawks, turning me to face her with the stern expression I expected. "Lena, this is not okay. You need a job."

"I *know* that. Why do you think I didn't tell you?" I meet my brother's wide eyes over her shoulder.

My chest collapses as I realize I've succeeded in doing exactly what I was trying to avoid, and on *Christmas Day*, no less. I have stolen this celebratory moment and turned it into . . . this.

"I'm applying for jobs when I get home," I tell them, crossing my arms over my red jacket in an attempt to conceal how raw my heart feels right now.

"What will you do until then?" Mama's voice is sharp with concern.

"I don't know. Use my savings?" I throw my hands into the air, my anger splashing to the surface.

She means well. I know her own life experiences have made her adamant that this is one of the most important things in the world for a woman, but it still stings for her to concentrate on that instead of wondering if I'm okay first.

"How much money do you have?" she asks, shaking her head.

I shift on my feet. "Enough. I prepared for things like this the best I could, putting money into savings every month."

Her lips are a thin line of disappointment that I can't look away from. "But what will you do—"

Gavin's hand settles on her shoulder, and her words pause. "I think we can let Lena talk about it when she's ready." His whiskey eyes meet mine, and I try to send him a silent *thank you*. "And I promised Shannon I would be there with pizza for lunch, so I need to get going."

Mama's hands wring in front of her as she assesses me. I feel like I'm being analyzed, every flaw appearing for her to see.

But I must be found worthy, because she gives a firm nod. "We should all go to Shannon's. I want to bring her a gift and some of the pie we made yesterday."

Without another word for me, she pulls Gavin back toward the house. Zara offers me a sympathetic smile and a kiss on the cheek as she passes.

Auggie loops an arm around my shoulders, and we all walk back to the house, the loaded silence punctuated by the sound of our boots crunching through the snow.

And I try not to focus on how it feels like an earthquake has just split my chest in two.

Chapter 30

Gavin

*Y*ou have to press that button right there." Aaron's finger nudges mine onto the toggle, attempting to show me how to work the remote for the car he got from Santa. Despite meeting him for the first time only a few hours ago when we got to Shannon's, he hasn't left my side since we arrived.

"Ohhh." I pretend not to know how it works, even though I spent a while testing this car at the toy store before I bought it.

He pushes my finger enough to move the car forward a few feet, and it bumps right into Lena's sock-covered toes. She squeals, dancing away animatedly, and Aaron's giggles bring a smile to my face. He uses my finger to scoot the car closer to her, and she jumps again.

My hearty laughter echoes through the small house, and Lena's gaze catches with mine. Her face is alight with pleasure, cheeks pink and eyes sparkling.

So different from her hollow expression this morning on our new property.

When she blurted out that she had gotten fired, I couldn't stop the hopeful jolt that went through me. I selfishly thought maybe she might want to stay.

But she deserves to leave. She deserves the life she wants, not one tangled with a man like me. I would stifle her. The last thing I want is to make her feel like she should shrink herself for me, for this town.

My gaze slides down her body. Her beautiful, lithe curves that I've selfishly enjoyed too much for the last few days. I've let her wrap tighter around my heart and soul every time I kissed her or touched her.

And where has that left me?

Completely ensnared while she's looking the other direction at her life in Wilhelmina.

She's leaving tomorrow, even though everything feels utterly unfinished. We swore one night, which turned directly into another, and yet it still feels incomplete.

I have to drag my attention away as Shannon enters the living room with a book in her hand.

"Who's ready for a story?" she asks, handing me a copy of the book my foster sister read to us all those years ago. I found a vintage one online and gifted it to Shannon. This is my second time reading it to her kids on Christmas, and I hope it's a tradition that never dies.

These kids have a safe, loving home with her, but that doesn't mean their lives are easy. They still deal with plenty of difficult obstacles and relationships and trauma from their lives before they got here.

So helping Shannon give them an amazing holiday, just like the Santos family has done for me, has become one of my favorite new traditions.

Even though I was devastated not to be with the Santoses for the last few years, it forced me to build a friendship with Joe, Gary, and Shannon, and forming those new connections has given me a sense of peace I wasn't expecting.

It almost feels like I'm reclaiming my childhood, in a way, by changing the future for these kids.

Penelope, Jack, and Shannon's four foster children swarm to me as I open the book, taking up spots around and behind me like little monkeys perched on every bit of space. Julia settles next to me, leaning her head on my arm, and my heart melts like ice cream on a summer day.

For a moment, I simply stare at the top of her head, unable to concentrate on anything else.

There's a tugging sensation in my chest, like an invisible connection that tells me I'm *meant* to know her—*meant* to be a part of her life. And the way she's curled up against me has me wondering if she feels that too.

A few hours later, after many stories and slices of pizza and holiday desserts, everyone gathers at the door for goodbyes.

Julia pulls on my wrist, and I kneel beside her. With a shy smile, she wraps her arms around my neck and whispers, "Thank you, Santa."

The backs of my eyes burn as she clings to me like I'm someone special. Like being here means something to her. Burying my head in her hair, I grip her tightly to me. I try as hard as I can to keep the tears from leaving my eyes, but one crashes down to my cheek.

When Julia draws back, I cup her jaw. "I hope you had an amazing day," I tell her, forcing a smile.

She lifts her small fingers to wipe my damp cheek. "Will you come back soon?"

"Of course. I can't wait to see what you've made with those new paints and brushes." I wink, and she blushes sweetly.

* * *

WHEN MY CAR comes to a stop in the Santoses' driveway, Bea leans over from the passenger seat to pat my thigh. Luci and Lena unbuckle their seat belts in the back and leave the car like there was a silent order to do so. But Bea stays, watching as they make their way inside, and my stomach turns with nerves at what she's going to say.

Finally, she looks my way. "I want you to know that I love you like you're mine." Her voice is firm and adamant, like there's no doubt in her mind. "When you weren't here, I missed you. And I need you to know that you're wanted here, no matter who you love." She gives me a soft, knowing smile.

I love you like you're mine. You're wanted here.

The leftover tears I managed to control with Julia threaten to spill over. I didn't know how badly I needed to hear those words until this moment.

My hand falls to cover hers, and she grips mine tight. "I love Lena, and it's part of my job to protect her. But I *know* in my heart that you would do the same. I trust you. And even if things don't work out, we still want you here always."

Everything in my mind is a disaster. My thoughts, my wishes, and my hopes about Lena that swarm around my heart. They all feel like a maelstrom that I can't get through.

But her words are like a blanket of calm. If nothing else, Bea loves me, regardless of my feelings for her daughter.

"Thank you," I whisper.

She grabs my shoulders to pull me toward her in a hug, and as I leave a small tear stain against her shoulder, relief washes through me.

Once we make it inside a few minutes later, the house is a buzz of activity as Zara and Luci serve the *feijoada* Bea taught me to make yesterday. When the table is set, our dinner is served into bowls with rice and *farofa*, and we commence our late-afternoon Christmas dinner.

"This is delicious," Lena says beside me, circling her spoon in her bowl while everyone else discusses sledding in the backyard tomorrow.

"Thank you." My throat aches to tell her everything on my mind, but I settle for, "How are you?"

"Fine. Distracted thinking about all the things I need to do when I get back to Wilhelmina." She takes a sip of her water, not meeting my gaze. "I have to start looking for jobs as soon as possible."

The words are on the tip of my tongue. *Look for a job here. Or I'll visit you on the weekends in Wilhelmina. We can figure it out.*

But all she's ever said is that she wanted a short-term thing.

One night, one morning, one more time. That's all she's promised me.

I may be in love with her, but she doesn't feel the same way. We're temporary in her eyes.

My entire life has been full of people leaving. My father, my mother, my grandmother, and every foster family since. Auggie is the only person who hasn't left me.

Watching people walk away is standard for me, and I've hardened my heart to it at this point. It's practically second nature.

So I can survive her leaving. I can watch her drive away tomorrow with a fake smile and a wave. I can do it for *her*.

Because it's truly what she wants, and I could never deny her anything.

Chapter 31

Lena

"Come sit with us, *amorzinho*." Mama pats the couch between her and Luci.

The tree lights and roaring fire cast a golden glow around the living room as I drop into the spot, my muscles weighed down from the day's exhaustion.

And the emotional roller coaster.

My stomach has been full of nervous flutters for the last few minutes since Auggie clapped Gavin on the shoulder after dinner and told him they should have a chat on the back porch.

And my attempt to spy on them through the window didn't result in any helpful information.

"How's my Lena?" Mama asks, wrapping her hand around mine.

"I'm . . . sad," I whisper, my voice cracking in the middle as my emotions creep to the surface.

"About your job?" Luci wonders.

I lean my head back on the couch. "Yes, but also everything."

"I'm sorry my tone was rough this morning," Mama says, rubbing the back of my hand with her thumb. "You surprised me."

My vision blurs with tears as I look her way. "I didn't want to ruin Christmas with bad news. I just wanted you to be proud of me in a few weeks when I found something new."

"Oh, sweetheart. I'm always proud of you."

Shaking my head, I admit, "I've been scared to tell you I failed. I wanted to have good news for you."

She wraps her arm around my shoulders and pulls me toward her. I barely fit next to her petite frame, but I pretend I can. "*You* are my good news. From the moment I knew you were in my belly, I wanted to protect you."

"That's true," Luci adds solemnly.

"And I still want to protect you every day. So what I said this morning is only because I worry about you. I want you to be safe and happy and *whatever* you want to be. I want to help you find what you're looking for."

I sniffle against her chest and admit, "I feel like . . . I'm floating in a giant ocean, lost out at sea, with no direction of where to land."

"Oh, Lena. You don't have to know yet." Luci soothes a hand over my thigh. "You can surround yourself with the people you care about, and they can help you figure it out. Sometimes we don't know where we're going until we get there. For now, there are only two things you need to do. You trust your gut"—her gentle hand falls to my stomach—"to tell you if something's off. But you follow your heart"—she lifts the same hand to pat my chest lovingly—"to where it wants to go."

I swallow hard. "What if it's all a jumbled mess, and I can't tell what I want?"

"Then you let the people who love you help untangle it," Mama says. "Sometimes you ask your family. Sometimes your friends. And then sometimes you trust the man you've fallen in love with to help you." Her tone is gentle but laced with meaning. My heart jumps into my throat as I pull out of her arms and stare at her, but she only gives me a knowing smirk. "You think I don't know the way you look at each other?" She laughs. "Think I didn't see that flour on your dress?"

"You think we didn't see your heartbreak the last two years?" Luci adds.

I shake my head adamantly, my breath trapped in my lungs. "I'm not in love with him."

Mama smirks again as dread seeps into my veins, burning as it spreads through my body.

I love Gavin, but there's no way I'm *in love* with him. That's why we set the one-night boundary. I know it turned into two nights, but there was still a deadline. We woke up this morning and left it all behind.

Right?

I'm *not* in love with him, and he's not in love with me.

Hell, he didn't even tell me he was moving. He doesn't see me as a part of his future like that. We're simply two people who are wildly attracted to each other.

Not in love at all.

Because if we were in love with each other, that would mean devastation when I leave here. That would mean that I—

The sudden need to move my body hits me like lightning.

Standing abruptly, I turn around to face Mama and Luci. "I have to go. I need to get home."

Mama grabs my hand, trying to lure me back to the couch. "But it's Christmas Day."

I blink a few times as I look around the room, memorizing the tree and the mantel and the warm glow from the fire. "I was here for most of the day. I need to get home." As I back away, my shoulders shake, a chill running down my spine.

Luci nods and stands to hug me. "Okay."

When I release her, Mama's hands bracket my face. "You follow your heart," she says, hugging me close.

I nod, even though I'm not sure I know how to do that. I know how to push Millie to follow her heart, and I know how to protect other people's hearts. But right now, it feels like mine is raw in my chest. Like barbed wire has been wrapped around it, and time and distance and reality are pulling it tight, pricking my lungs and forcing my breath to seep out.

I run up the stairs two at a time. Blindly grabbing every piece of clothing I can find, I shove them all in my bag and drag the zipper shut.

Is this what Gavin felt like when he was leaving that night? Frantically packing his bags and trying to escape before his emotions became too much to handle?

The full weight of this moment hits me like a north wind. The force of it rushes toward my stomach, and I hunch forward as the ache settles in.

It feels like I skipped over some very important steps in the last few days, necessary conversations we should've had. We just vaulted right over them. But instead of sturdy ground to catch me, there was only open, stomach-dropping air, with nothing below.

And who knows where my body is going to land after this tumultuous descent.

I hurry to the bathroom to gather my things and meet my reflection in the mirror. Puffy eyes and tear-stained cheeks greet me, so different from the satisfied woman I saw there this morning. My fingers grip the edge of the counter so hard that I wouldn't be surprised if my nails leave crescent-shaped indentations in the granite.

Deep breath.

In for four. *One, two, three, four.*

Out for four. *One, two, three, four.*

I need someone to point me in the right direction. I don't know how to trust my heart or my gut. They're both a strangled, knotted mess right now.

My friends. They can help me. They can guide me.

Millie, Micah, Emil, Finn, Avery, Eloise. Their faces float through my mind like a string of Polaroids.

They are the people who have kept me steady for months. For years.

When I was crying into a bowl of mint chocolate chip ice cream three years ago, Millie was the one tucking my hair out of the way and telling me Gavin would come back. When I was feeling lonely in my house, Micah and Emil took me out to dinner and made me laugh. When I lost my job, Ave and El were the ones pulling me out of my funk with homemade pizza and a marathon of Disney movies.

They are the ones I need.

And they need *me*.

Chapter 32

Gavin

So far, my conversation with Auggie has consisted of fifteen minutes of silence, the only sound between us an occasional sip of beer.

He's my best friend of twenty years, so quiet is normal for us. With how much time we spend together at work, and the number of evenings each week that I have dinner with his family, we frequently don't have much left to say.

But this silence feels different, and despite how well we know each other, it's hard to get a read on what he's thinking right now.

With a heavy sigh, he finally asks, "How long has this been going on behind my back?"

"Physically? Less than two days."

He gives me a sidelong look that says he doesn't believe me.

"Emotionally? About ten years."

His forehead wrinkles as he stares at the gas fire between us. "Ten years?"

I swallow another sip of beer before admitting, "I think I've had a crush on her since I met her."

"She was nineteen," he snaps, sharp gaze flicking up to me.

"Well, fuck, I didn't do anything about it," I groan. "I thought she was beautiful and funny and smart."

He stays silent, so I keep going. "But it wasn't until three years ago that I realized . . . it might be more than that."

A loud breath gusts from his lungs. "Is that why you left? Was all the bullshit you gave me about not feeling like you belong in our family a lie?"

"No. When I have feelings like I do for Lena, I don't think I *should* be a part of your family. You told me she wasn't going to be here this year, so I thought I could come back."

"But you agreed to move here with me." He yanks his hat off and drags a hand through his hair. "Did you think you were just going to avoid her when she came to visit?"

I shrug. "Yeah, I guess I did."

He shakes his head with an aggravated sigh. "What happened three years ago to make you leave?"

The memory of that night burns a hole through my stomach. "I saw her kissing Brandon at the Christmas party, and I was so fucking *angry*, even though I didn't have any right to be. I wanted to punch him in the face." My hands clench at the thought. "I was so close to doing it. Then you found me a few minutes later, and you were laughing and acting like everything was normal, and I couldn't fake it. I had to leave."

His throat works as he chugs the last bit of his beer. "Why didn't you say something sooner?"

My mouth feels like it's full of cotton as I say, "You all let me into your house and family, and I feel like I've betrayed you all for even thinking about her." I drop my head into my gloved hands and whisper the last part. "I didn't want to ruin the only family I've ever had."

Auggie clears his throat. "How long have we known each other?"

Lifting my head, I meet his gaze over the dancing fire. "Twenty years."

A ghost of a smirk passes over his lips before he bites it away. "And do you think I trust you? Care about you? Love you?"

A few beats pass before I admit, "Yes."

He shoves his hat back over his head and stands. "Hell yes, I do, Gavin. You're a good man. To me, to my kids, my wife, my family." His hands land on his hips, and he levels me with a glare. "And you're good to my sister."

I press my lips together to keep them from shaking. "I'm fucked up, Auggie. My life has fucked me up."

A sigh leaves his lungs as he kneels beside my chair. "That's not true. All those people who let you down were fucked up. But not you." His sharp gaze focuses on me. "You are good. And honest. And one of the kindest people I've ever met."

My nose burns, and my chin wobbles.

"Do you love her?"

My heart thumps wildly in my chest. "Yes."

"Does she love you?"

"I don't know."

His head tilts. "Have you told her you love her?"

"No."

Auggie blows out a breath. "Ah, come on, Gav." He puts a hand on my knee and jostles it. "You need to. How's she going to know if you don't tell her?"

He says it like the idea is so simple. But for someone who has kept those words from his lips for most of his life, it's not simple at all.

Sure, I love Auggie and his entire family, but it's not something

I say out loud. It's not something I can admit as freely as he always has.

My muscles ache to move, so I drop my beer bottle next to my seat and stand to pace the back porch.

Can I even say those words to her, or will they die in my throat when I try? I don't even remember the last time I told someone I loved them. I was too young, and my own self-preservation has washed it from my memories.

"I don't know how to tell her," I admit, my feet pausing on the porch before I turn to face him.

Auggie huffs a laugh. "You just say it. You'd be surprised how easy it is once you start." He grabs my shoulders firmly and pins me with a stare. "You have to tell her."

Okay. I just say it. I grab her cheeks and pull her toward me and whisper it against her lips until it's easy.

The hinges squeal as I throw the back door open, going in search of Lena. I toss my jacket on the counter in the empty kitchen.

The dining room is empty.

The living room is empty.

But the entryway is not.

Everyone but Auggie is there, gathered around the front door, where Lena stands with her bags sitting beside her and a deep crease between her brows.

My stomach drops to the hardwood floors. Every bit of enthusiasm is extinguished as quickly as someone snuffing out a flame.

Vines wrap around my feet again, holding me a few feet away as I watch her kiss her family in slow motion. I hear the hinges of the back door, and I feel the shift in the air as Auggie walks past me toward her. I faintly register the regret in her voice as she tells Penelope she has to leave early.

But I see it all as a distant bystander.

My clothes are constricting. My skin is too tight. My chest is caving in on itself.

And all I can think is, *she's leaving*.

Like my father did. Like my mother did. Like my grandmother did. Like I did.

She's leaving, and who the fuck am I to stop her? This is Lena. My independent, bright Lena, who deserves to write whatever story she wants for herself.

I can't stop her. Stifle her. Keep her for myself. I'm not worth it.

"Can you hold Noah for me?"

Zara's voice breaks through the white noise in my brain, and I reach out for him without thinking. His small frame settles in my hands, and I pull his back to my chest, soaking a bit of his warmth into my bones.

Lena hugs Zara beside me, their whispered goodbyes filtering into my ears, but I can't make it out because my brain seems to be stuck on two words.

She's leaving.

When she pulls away from Zara and stands in front of me, her wild curls framing her pink cheeks, I swallow hard. I force my brain to dig through the quicksand it's sinking into and make words.

"It's your tia Lena," I hear myself say to Noah in a low tone. "She's going to help you get in trouble one day." Lena's lips quiver as she reaches for Noah's little fist. "She's beautiful, isn't she?"

The words hit her with a small flinch of her brows, but she takes a step closer.

Everyone else fades away, a low murmur of voices in the background, until all I can see is Lena.

"I need to go home," she whispers, her chin quivering.

Disappointment floods my veins like a tsunami, making my legs unsteady.

"When are you moving?" she asks, her voice much sturdier than mine.

I hear myself mumble, "I'm staying in Juniper for a while to iron things out with the downtown plans. But I officially move in a few weeks."

"That's good." She shrugs, and for fuck's sake, I adore everyone here, but I desperately wish we were alone. Without the entire family watching this tense moment play out when I don't even know what I'm saying.

There's a small rattle in my chest as I inhale. "Can I walk you out?"

She nods, and Zara grabs Noah from my arms. Protection from the cold seems trivial at this point since my entire body is already frozen, all the way down to my heart. So I skip the jacket, grab her bag, and bring it outside.

The car beeps as she hits the button to open the trunk, and I place her suitcase inside. Silently, she waits for me to close the hatch, and then I follow her to the driver's-side door.

"You need new tires as soon as possible." My gruff words grate on my own ears, but I can't apologize for them. If something happened to her, I would never forgive myself.

Goddamn it. Why didn't I take them to get fixed the first day I noticed?

"I'll be careful. Promise. I'm stopping for gas in Juniper, then I'll be in Wilhelmina before I get too tired."

I nod slowly as we both stand before each other with no idea what to say. I have a million things I *should* say, but none of them leave my throat.

She shuffles on her feet. I swallow. She shrugs.

It's all painfully awkward for two people who were moaning each other's names last night, but I guess I have to get used to that.

This is the reality we've chosen.

Finally, with a deep sigh, she steps toward me and slides her arms around my waist.

Her sweet, citrusy scent envelops me, and an anvil drops into my chest.

She's leaving.

Lena's shoulders hitch as she sucks in a breath, and I wrap my arms around her, encasing her in the safest place in the world. Exactly where she belongs.

But she's leaving.

My emotions thrash in my chest as I raise my hands to slip my fingers through the ends of her hair.

"It's going to be okay," I whisper, even though it's not.

She's leaving and taking my heart with her.

My heart was tiny and cold after so many people took pieces of it with them. My mom, my grandmother, my foster families. I've given bits away my entire life and never gotten them back.

The only difference here is that I saw this coming. From the moment her lips touched mine, I knew it would be like this. My heart would be hers forever, but she would be leaving with it.

Cupping her cheeks, I tilt her face up until I can see her red-rimmed eyes and perfect lips.

Stay with me. Figure it out with me. Be mine somehow.

But I've begged people to stay before. Tear-stained and hiccuping, I screamed for my mom to stay. Thrashing in the arms of a social worker, I sobbed for my grandmother to stay.

It did nothing.

People who want to leave will leave. I've learned that lesson my whole life.

So instead, I press a kiss to her forehead and whisper, "Please be careful. You're precious cargo."

Then I release her. I let her go.

And as she pulls out of the driveway, I stand at the end of it, watching her taillights disappear around the corner as the first hot tear plunges down my cold cheek.

Chapter 33

Lena

*M*y hands tremble on the steering wheel as I turn onto the highway leading me away from Juniper.

I should've ripped my heart out and thrown it at his feet. That might have been easier than this. Then at least I wouldn't be able to feel this pulled muscle burning in my chest. It's a sharp pain that I can't identify, but it *aches*.

Tears blur my vision as I drive into the sunset, passing cozy homes where families and friends are gathered for the evening.

I should be doing that. I should be with my family, eating that lemon pie Gavin made me and listening to the sound of my niece and nephew's laughter.

A shaky breath rattles in my chest as I try to inhale around a sob.

Fuck, this hurts.

My body is a tug-of-war rope right now. One side is yanking me home to Wilhelmina, toward the people who make up my everyday life. The ones who cheer for me when I need it and relax with me after a long day. To my honorary nieces who say they want to be like me when they grow up. The people who treat me like their best friend and an irreplaceable part of their lives.

But the opposite side is pulling me toward the other important people in my world a few miles back up the road. Mama and Luci and their unconditional love. My brother and Zara and their beautiful kids who I wish I could see more.

It's home and family and the very things that make my soul happy.

And there's *him*.

His small grin that's reserved just for me. The way he always makes me feel safe enough to be myself. How he goes out of his way to see me happy.

He feels like relief and comfort and passion all twirling together.

As I approach the city limits of Juniper, tears stream down my cheeks, dripping from my chin.

I already miss him. Even after years without him, it didn't hurt like this. Like my chest is splitting open from the pain. The loss. The grief.

How can I miss him so much already?

I *just* left.

Guilt racks my body as that thought crashes into my stomach.

I *left* him. Drove down the road, his dark form shrinking in the rearview mirror while he watched my retreating car.

Just like all the people he has trusted in his life.

I did that to him. Add me to the list of people who let him down.

Fuck.

Sharp pain lances my lungs, and I can't breathe around it.

I have to turn around. I can't be like them.

Rubbing the back of my hand across my cheeks, I try to keep my grip steady on the wheel. I tuck my loose curls behind my ears, looking for a spot to turn back, but as I round the final curve into town, my vision falters. The tears and the blinding sunset before me make it hard to see the lines on the road, and I veer too far into the other lane on the turn.

A car horn pierces through the air. Headlights shine directly into the windshield.

I swerve back to the right, but my tires—my *fucking* bald tires—can't get traction on the slick roads, and before I can register what's happening, my little SUV makes a full circle and smashes into the snowbank beside the road.

My pulse throbs in my skull. Loud, raspy breaths fill the car as I do a mental inventory of my body. Legs, arms, back, neck, head. Everything seems okay, except my heart, but that was in pain before the wreck.

Violent sobs shake my shoulders as adrenaline floods my system.

I could've died. I could've collided with that car or spun further into something. I could've been lost in the snow for the entire night. I could've never seen anyone I care about again.

Warm air from the heater still blasts my cheeks, but I can't see anything through the windshield. It's entirely covered in snow. Turning to the passenger window, I find the warm glow from the lit sign for Bear Creek.

I've landed right at the edge of their parking lot.

Right where my life veered off course, where I spent the best night of my life in the arms of the man I—

My whining moan echoes through the car.

Is this a joke? Is this some sort of intervention from the universe telling me I'm making poor decisions?

Suddenly, I'm too hot, and I slam my hand over the knob for the heater to turn it off. My hands shake as I fumble for my phone and try to swipe it open. It takes me four tries, but I finally press the name of the person I want to talk to right now.

I put it on speaker, and the rings reverberate through the car's interior.

"Lena!" Millie's musical voice sweeps through like fresh air, and my shoulders relax a tiny bit. "How are you?"

"Um, I don't know." My voice cracks through every word.

"Oh, honey." She lowers to a soothing tone, and rustles filter over the line like she's moving to a different room.

"I'm sorry," I cry, wiping more tears as they drip down my cheeks. "It's Christmas, and I know you're with—"

"Lena, don't. You need me, and you would do the same if I needed you." A door shuts through the phone. "Okay. What's going on?"

A hiccup bursts out of me before I admit, "I got in a wreck. With a pile of snow."

Her gasp ricochets through the car. "Are you okay? Where are you? I can be in the car in two minutes." The words are a jumble as she moves around the room.

"I'm okay. I'm okay. I promise." My gaze flicks to the lit sign beside me, and the tension in my shoulders loosens a little more. "I'm right by Bear Creek, so I can go get Joe and Gary to help me in a minute." She exhales a sigh of relief. "I just wanted to hear your voice."

"Well, I always love hearing your voice, but you sound like something's very wrong."

Swallowing the lump in my throat, I whisper, "I was trying to drive home, but I was crying too hard and couldn't see clearly, and the universe yelled at me and sent me into a snowbank."

"Lena, honey. You're only giving me breadcrumbs. I don't understand. Why were you crying? Who do I need to fight?"

I try to breathe a small laugh at the idea of Millie fighting someone for me, but it just comes out as a whimper. "I left because . . .

because . . . it was only supposed to be one night, Mills. And then it turned into one more morning, and then it was the pantry and the next night. And somewhere along the way, one night turned into . . . *everything*." A tear lands on the phone in my hand with a tiny *plop*.

"Oh, Lena," she soothes. "Then why are you on your way home?"

"Because that's where my life is. That's where my home is. I miss you and the girls. And Micah and Emil. I need to start looking for jobs and try to put everything back together." I slouch into my seat before adding, "Can we bring Micah and Emil into the call? I want to hear their voices."

"Absolutely. Hold tight. I'll add them." Millie's call clicks away, and after a few moments of quiet agony, her concerned voice drifts back to my ears. "You still there?"

"Yeah." My shaky breath gives away my emotional state.

"Oh, love," Micah says in his deep timbre, and just those two words send homesickness flushing through my chest.

"While I was connecting the call, I gave them a quick rundown of updates," Millie says.

"Did she mention the orgasms?" I ask, my small, stuttered chuckle an attempt to lighten the mood.

The most beautiful chorus of laughter bursts from the phone, and for some bizarre reason, it pulls another keening sob from my throat.

"She forgot to mention that detail," Micah rumbles, and I can virtually see the wide smile on his face.

"Bummer. It's a really good part." I slide my palm over my chin to wipe the tears cascading down.

"You can fill us in on that later. For now, tell us why you were driving home instead of staying back there with your family and Gavin."

My lips flatten as I try to find the right words. It's difficult when I'm not even one hundred percent sure about the decision I've made. How do I tell them out loud when I haven't untangled the mess myself yet?

"I think I have . . . feelings for Gavin, but he's going to be living in Juniper, and I live in Wilhelmina," I start, trying to focus on facts.

"Okay," Emil says gently. "What kind of feelings are you having? Because I think that information dictates our advice."

"Ugh. Why are you hitting me with the hardest question first?" I murmur, and they wait patiently while I attempt to dissect it. "I feel . . . like I just left my heart back there in his hands. Like I'll never get it back. It's his now."

A thoughtful hum sounds between them.

"And do you trust him to take care of it?" Emil asks.

"Yes," I whisper breathlessly.

"Then why are you driving here?" Micah wonders.

"I don't know. Everything feels twisted and confusing," I admit.

"Should you try a visualization?" Millie asks, a hint of teasing in her tone.

Gasps bounce through the car before Micah says, "Millie? Asking if someone wants to visualize?"

"Oh, hush it," Millie scolds. "I'm willing to admit that it did something for me. It definitely alerted me to the fact that I had feelings for Finn and the girls."

I drop my forehead to the leather steering wheel with a groan. Crossing my arms over my stomach, I mumble an unenthusiastic, "Okay. I'll do it."

Millie hisses a triumphant *yes*.

"First, imagine what happens if you keep driving home," Emil prompts. "How will you feel in one week?"

I slowly pull in a breath and let it out through my nose, picturing TV static in my mind. And when it fades away, I see myself at home. Millie, Micah, and Emil line the couch next to me, looking between themselves sadly. The house is messier than normal. The Christmas tree is still in the corner, with only half of the ornaments it normally has since Millie took hers to her new house. I'm hugging my knees while we watch *Gilmore Girls*, and I can see the heartbreak written all over me. It's in the downward curl of my lips and in the pale tone of my skin.

But my eyes are the sharpest warning bell. They're downcast, puffy, and dull. The eyes of someone who has been crying for days.

I know exactly how *that* Lena feels. Like she isn't whole because she left a piece of herself in Juniper.

She served him her heart on a silver platter and didn't realize he'd taken the whole thing. Didn't realize how significant it had been at the time because everything about offering it to him had felt natural. It had felt like the exact right choice. The *only* right choice.

It was either *give her heart to Gavin* or *never give it to anyone*.

"You okay?" Millie asks, worry lacing her tone.

"Yes. But I looked devastated. Broken. Like the world has moved on without me, but I'm still stuck there, waiting."

Hums of acknowledgment flicker through the phone.

"Can we try the second option?" Micah asks. "Maybe you'll like that one more."

"I don't know if I can," I tell them.

"Lena." Millie's voice is firm. It's the mom voice she's been practicing, one I heard her perfect recently when Eloise tried to sneak up the stairs with an entire bag of chocolate chips under her shirt. The little chocolate gremlin froze mid-step when she heard her name in Millie's mom voice, just like this.

"Yes, Mom." My own sass brings a grin to my face.

She scoffs. "I'm going to talk to you the way you would talk to me. Okay? Are you ready?"

"Fine," I grumble, lifting my head from the steering wheel.

Millie clears her throat like she's trying to get into character. "I think everyone on this call can agree that you are a badass."

I huff a laugh. "You're saying that to a woman who has been crying in her car for twenty minutes on Christmas night."

"Badasses cry too. But you are also a badass who"—she pauses for dramatic effect, and it works, putting me on the edge of my seat with anticipation—"stands up for the people you care about. You fight for every single one of us to get the respect and the lives we deserve. You are the number one person we would want at our back for good times and bad times and in-between times."

Millie sniffles before continuing. "I'm not always the best at standing up for myself. But you showed me how to do it, and now I'm going to return the favor. You need to fight for *yourself*, for the future you want. You have to take a break from protecting us and protect *you*. Stand up for *you*. We're all behind you, cheering for you, but you have to decide which path you're going to take."

"You're giving me too much credit. My *job* is to protect the people around me. It's my main role in life. I don't know how to do it for myself." A bitter laugh tumbles from my chest. "And I'm just a stepping stone. I teach people what they can do better next time, but I'm not the kind of partner someone sticks around for."

Emil dons his professor voice as he says, "Then they don't matter. They're not your people."

Emotion strangles my throat as Micah adds with a sad lilt to his voice, "You taught us how to be brave, Lena, and now it's your turn."

"Don't think about anyone but you," Emil says. "What does

Lena Camilla Santos *want*? Not considering if other people need you or what makes sense to anyone else. What does *your* soul want?"

My heart feels as fragile as rice paper, like the slightest brush could tear it open and spill everything.

"I didn't know how much these feelings were going to hurt," I admit, squeezing my eyes shut. "It was a dull heartache for the last ten years, like a constant sore muscle that never healed." I press my palm over my heart and try to rub away the pain. "But driving away just now felt like it got ripped out."

"And what do you think that means?" Millie whispers.

The final puzzle piece I've been searching for appears before me. It's a little damaged on the edges from being tossed around and neglected for too long, but it's the perfect fit. And as I press it into place, the entire picture takes shape.

"I love him," I whisper, his solemn face from earlier clear in my mind. When he gazed down at me beside my car, his expression full of sorrow and yearning and . . . love. "I love him," I repeat a little louder this time.

The hurt, the ache, the swelling beyond its limits, and the fragile rice-paper feelings I've put my heart through. It all makes sense.

"I love him," I moan this time, setting my phone in my lap and dropping my head into my hands.

Emil and Micah let out soft laughs, and Millie cries through hers.

Hope swells like a balloon in my chest. I want to tell him. I want to shout it from the rooftops and scream it into the woods.

He's my person. He's my Gavin. He's *mine*. And I love him.

But from the highest of highs comes a shattering crash when I realize what I'm skipping over.

My friends.

"But," I start, "no one lives in the same place."

"Lena, listen to me," Millie says. It's not a mom voice this time. It's a gentle best-friend voice that reminds me of myself. This is how I sound when I'm giving her advice. "You chase your happy. You deserve it. This, right now, is your chance to be selfish. Don't think about us. Think about you."

Micah joins in, saying, "Not your house. Not your job applications. Think about your *heart's* home. Where is that?"

The answer is immediate.

With Gavin. That's where it belongs. Now and forever.

"But if I move, I'll miss you," I tell them, the tears starting anew.

"Oh, honey," Millie soothes. "We will miss you too. But you deserve this. You deserve to be selfish. You've fought for us and encouraged us, but now you're going to fight for yourself."

"But Ave and El are—"

"Going to come visit you," Millie finishes. "With their aunt Millie and uncle Finn."

A laugh hiccups out of me.

"And Uncle Micah and Uncle Emil," Micah adds.

"Those girls sure have a lot of aunts and uncles," Emil says with a laugh.

"A two-hour drive to see you is a piece of cake," Millie adds. "It takes us longer than that to get the girls ready for bed most days. Or if we want to meet halfway in Fern River, we can do that too! We're there at least once a month visiting my family, and we can loop you into that trip."

A soft smile grows over my lips as I let that idea absorb into my mind. Park trips and coffee shops and walks and visits with Millie's parents and sisters.

It could work, right?

A knock rattles the window next to me, startling a screech from my throat.

But when I turn my head, Gavin's wide, whiskey eyes greet me through the dim window. He's scanning my body quickly, his jaw tight.

My stomach flips. "Gavin's here," I hiss to my best friends.

"Oh shit," Millie squeals.

"He looks all disheveled," I tell them, surveying his wind-blown hair and flushed cheeks that give the impression he ran the ten miles into town.

He tries the door handle, but it's locked, so he presses his palm to the window, concern etched across his brow.

"Holy fuck. That's hot," Micah says with a groan.

"Take a picture," Millie whispers.

"Can I call you guys back?" I laugh as I unbuckle my seat belt.

"You fucking better," Micah says, and Emil chuckles.

"Stand up for you," Millie says. "And we love you and adore you and want pictures." Then the call ends, and the car's sudden silence fills my ears.

Chapter 34

Gavin

*I*t only took one minute for me to decide to follow her. One minute of tears streaming down my face before my body snapped into action.

This time, I'm an adult. I'm not watching the taillights again and never following. I'm doing something about it.

This time, the woman who owns my heart is driving away, and I'm not going to let her without telling her how I feel.

I love her. And I have to tell her.

Sprinting to the door, I was desperate to grab my keys before she made it much farther. But when I swung it open, Lena's family stood in the entryway, faces scrunched in sadness.

"We thought she would stay," Bea said through a sob.

"I'm going to get her back," I announced, sliding past Auggie to grab my keys and phone from the coffee table. I decided at the last minute to swing through the kitchen and snag my coat and Lena's untouched lemon pie.

Squeezing my keys so hard that the sharp points dug into my skin, I made my way back to the door and watched as their tears transformed into hopeful ones.

Luci's chin quivered as she wrapped her hands around my wrists. "Bring our girl back."

Next, Bea patted my cheek. "You love her," she said, not a question, but a confirmation.

I swallowed thickly and nodded. "I do."

Auggie dipped his chin and wrapped me in a tight hug as he said, "Tell her. She needs to know."

It was only a ten-minute drive here, but it felt like hours. With my heart in my throat and my stomach in knots, I sped toward town, desperately trying to catch her at the only gas station.

But fear strangled me when I spotted her car, the front bumper smashed into a snowbank, windshield covered in snow.

My pulse pounded like hoofbeats in my ears as I accelerated to pull up next to her.

It was her tires. I know it was those *fucking tires.*

The things I should've done will haunt me for the rest of my life. I should have taken care of her tires the moment I saw the wear on them. I should've begged her to stay. Told her the truth. Admitted that she's the only home I've ever needed.

But I didn't.

Shoving the car into park, I threw open my door and ran to hers, gripped by the terror of what I might find. But as my feet skidded to a stop by her window, a soft smile colored her lips, and the relief of it had me gasping for breath.

Now she looks at me through the window, her caramel eyes puffy and red-rimmed, but after a quick scan, the rest of her body appears to be fine.

She brushes her fingers over her cheeks as I step back for her to open the door. Then I fall to my knees in the snow beside her, cold moisture seeping into my jeans and the hard ground biting my knees, but I don't care.

"Are you okay? Does anything hurt?" I pat her thighs, her arms, her shoulders, her cheeks, searching for any sign that something's wrong.

"I'm okay." Her broken sob cracks my chest wide open.

My shoulders slump toward her, and I wrap my arms around her waist and bury my face in her neck. "Please don't leave," I murmur. "I should've asked you sooner. I should've begged you to stay." Pressing my lips into her throat, I inhale her scent and sigh against her silky skin.

Only twenty minutes, and I missed her like hell.

She turns in her seat, and after a little readjusting, her knees bracket my body, and her arms circle my shoulders. "I was coming back."

"What?" The word leaves me on a gasp. "Really?"

"Yes." She laughs softly. "But I sure like you begging on your knees for me."

I cup her face between my palms. "I'll be on my knees for you every day."

Her smile lights up my chest as I swallow my nerves, focusing on the foreign words that want to burst from my lips. Saying them to her doesn't feel nearly as frightening as I expected. It feels completely natural.

"I love you, Lena. I love your smiles and your sass, your feisty attitude and your sweet one too. I love every bit of you, and I want all of it, forever." I suck in a deep breath, and it's even easier this time as I say it again. "I love you."

Tears glisten on her cheeks as she smiles. "Really?"

I kiss her jaw gently before bringing my mouth to hers. "You brought life to my tiny, cold heart, and it's yours. It's been yours for so long, and it always will be."

The sweetest, most soul-fulfilling whisper comes from her lips. "I love you too."

Those words slot themselves inside my chest and land with a relieved *whoosh*.

I've been searching for something to fill that spot for my entire life, and it's finally *here*.

It's Lena. She was meant to fit there all along.

Reaching around her to turn off the car, I pull her out. She squeals with laughter as I grab her by the waist and sling her over my shoulder. I grip her thigh tight as I cross the parking lot and walk up the steps to Gary and Joe's cabin. The urgency in my knock rips through the air, and Lena wiggles in my grip.

I slide my hand up her thigh, resting it against the soft curve of her ass just as Gary opens the door.

His eyes flare wide as he takes in the scene. "Carolers usually sing for us," he deadpans, leaning his shoulder on the doorframe.

Lena giggles before her raspy voice starts behind me. "We wish you a merry Christmas, we wish you a merry—"

She chokes off as my palm lands with a playful smack on her ass, and I bite my lips to keep from laughing as Gary's eyebrows shoot up.

"I'm assuming the cabin is still rented under my name?" I can't help my smug smile.

"It's all yours. We thought you two might be back." Gary gives me a wink and a knowing grin.

"Perfect." I nod.

"Merry Christmas," Lena calls as I turn around. She presses

into my back to lift up as I make my way down the steps. "See you later."

Gary laughs. "Honestly, I hope not. You guys can stay there as long as you want."

"Thank you," I shout over my shoulder, grabbing a handful of her ass this time to hold her steady.

I don't even want to stop touching her long enough to rescue Lena's car from the snowbank or drive mine across the property, so I grab the pie and walk to the cabin with her over my shoulder. The strings of lights around the railing are like a beacon, calling me forward past the field of trees and the sleigh where I played Santa.

When I reach the door, my hands are full of pie and Lena's curves, so I turn and tell her the code to punch into the lock. Then we step inside our cabin, and I kick the door shut behind me. The pie is set on the kitchen counter, and I drop Lena onto her back on the bed. She lands with a sigh, her hair fanned out across the bed like a dream.

Her eyes are still puffy from crying, and I want to kiss her all night for the trouble she went through.

I kneel between her ankles, sliding my hands up her buttery-soft leggings. "This was never one night for me. It was one moment of meeting you that turned into one week with your family that turned into ten years of dreaming of you. Fuck *one night*. I want them all."

She nods as she sits up and shrugs out of her jacket, throwing it to the ground. I toss mine on top of hers and fall into her arms, exactly where I'm meant to be.

An immediate relief sweeps through my muscles when I touch her. Every time, whether it's just our pinkies or I'm buried deep inside her, the comfort and solace that washes over me is the best feeling in the world.

"It was never one night for me either," she whispers. "I knew before it even started that it wasn't possible."

We roll to our sides, facing each other, her leg thrown over my hip. Her eyes are soft, warm caramel, her lips sweet, plump cherries.

I press my mouth to hers and breathe out a sigh against them. "We can figure this out. I'll move to Wilhelmina with you. I can find a job there and—"

"No," she breathes. "You and Auggie have plans and a dream."

My fingers dive into her hair. "Fuck all that. Wreck my plans. Obliterate them. *You're* my dream. None of it matters compared to you." I coast my lips over her soft cheek. "I want to be where you are. Auggie would understand."

She glides her palm up my arm. "What if I want to move to you?"

I shake my head against hers. "You don't have to do that. I don't want you to give anything up for me."

Her hands press into my shoulders until I land on my back, and she crawls over me to straddle my waist. "Gavin Moore, you've had a life full of people not choosing you. You've fought hard for every scrap of family you've ever had." Her fierce gaze holds me captive. "But this time, *I* am choosing *you*. I'm fighting for this"—she points from my heart to hers—"because I choose you and I love you."

I slide my hands up to her hips as the bridge of my nose burns.

She *chooses* me. She *loves* me. She's fighting for *me*.

My heart aches as it expands in my chest, trying to burst from its cage.

Her shoulders lift in a small shrug. "I don't know what I want to do in my life yet. I don't know what job will make me the happiest, but I want to be here with you while I figure it out."

I nod as a tear sneaks past my lashes and runs down my temple. "Thank you for choosing me."

She catches it with her thumb. "Always."

Her lips move to mine, and she kisses me gently. It's soft and quiet, like whispered secrets between lovers. She glides her mouth against mine, and when my tongue sweeps in to touch hers, we groan in unison.

Our clothes fall to the floor like both of us instinctively know we need to touch as much skin as possible. We need our warm bodies pressed together. Promises murmured with nothing between us.

Every inch of her velvet curves glows in the lamplight as she pulls me over her body.

I let my gaze travel over all the soft little details about her that are solely mine to cherish now.

As I slide between her thighs and into her wet heat, her nails dig into my hips. She arches, dragging me closer and twining our bodies so tightly that it feels like our souls are swirling together. Soft moans and whispered *I love you*s fill the air between us as we move together until our bodies are spent.

While our breaths return to normal, Lena traces her fingers over the tattoos on my chest while I let mine drag through her hair. She murmurs to me about her conversation with her friends, and my chest aches as I tell her about what happened after she left.

And when we've kissed a new set of tears away, I leave the bed long enough to grab the pie and a spoon from the kitchen.

I lean against the headboard, and she sits beside me, legs crossed under her naked body, as she takes a bite right out of the middle of the pie.

She swallows and waves the spoon around the room. "We

should rent this cabin until your house is built. I like it here. So many good memories," she says, eyebrows dancing.

Goddamn, I love how she's skipped straight to us living together.

My gaze follows the wooden beams forming the interior of the cabin. Thoughts flicker through my mind of the two Christmases I spent inside these walls, wishing I could be somewhere else.

Those memories have been replaced now. Instead, my thoughts are full of the woman beside me. Her body against mine, her teasing grins, her bright laughter, her heartfelt words.

"Let's rent this cabin until *our* house is built." I open my mouth for her to give me a bite.

She grins as she puts the spoon to my lips, the tangy flavor hitting my tongue.

Sweet, with a little kick, just like my Lena.

"Do you think Gary and Joe would let us get a dog? I've been wanting one." Her head tilts as she brings another bite to her mouth.

I brush her curls off her shoulder. "I bet they would."

"Wow, you sure are easy to convince. A woman barely has to ask, and you're willing to please her."

I lean forward and bring my lips to hers. "It's just you, little menace. It's always been you."

Epilogue

Lena

Two Years Later

*D*o you mind if I sneak out a few minutes early?" Peeking through the studio doorframe, I catch Victoria's gaze as she glances around her easel.

"Go right ahead. You've been working all day, and you need to put your feet up."

With a loud scoff, I look down at my swollen ankles. "You put a whole armchair and ottoman behind the register for me. I've had my feet up every chance I can get." My flats beat across the studio's wood floors as I walk her way.

Her hands smooth over the knit sweater covering my swollen belly. "Yes, but you were standing for an hour during your class." She drags in a weary sigh. "I should've pulled your chair in here."

A soft laugh bubbles out of me. "Vic, those kids barely listen to me as it is. Imagine if I was trying to teach them how to paint while sprawled in an armchair with my feet propped up."

"If anyone could do it, it's Lena Santos." She stands from her stool and wraps her arms around my shoulders. "I need to channel some of that energy so I can keep them in line while you're on maternity leave."

"You think you can keep me out of here?" I quirk a brow as she pulls away. "As soon as this little one makes its appearance, I'm showing up with my baby carrier and bugging you all day again."

"Lena," she scolds playfully. "You're not coming back to work right away. And we both know that husband of yours is not letting you and this baby out of his sight for a while."

I bite back a grin at the mention of Gavin's protectiveness. I've already seen plenty of it channeled toward me for the last nine months. He hasn't even let me open my own car door since we found out I was pregnant, and when our house got finished this past summer, he wouldn't let me carry a single thing inside.

But I've loved every second of that special treatment, because watching him wait on me hand and foot is one of the hottest things I've ever seen. Forget rolling out pie crust, I want to watch him fuss over satisfying my pregnancy cravings *forever*.

My stomach rumbles at the memory of those lemon bars he made me last night. I've already demolished the entire pan, but I bet I could convince him to make another.

"Then he'll have to come with me," I tell her with a definitive nod. "He can wear the baby around, and I'll teach. Win-win."

"Sounds perfect." Vic pops a kiss to my cheek. "Now, you get out of here," she says sternly, steering my shoulders toward the doorway.

In the gallery, I pause by Victoria's self-portrait that took my breath away two years ago. It's even more beautiful to me now that I know her better and get to see her sweet, generous heart every day at work.

Now my own self-portrait rests beside hers.

Tiger stripes line every bit of visible skin, showcasing my fierce protectiveness. But my expression shows my softness. In the smooth lines of my lips and the calm glow of my eyes radiates a warm sense of self-confidence.

It's *me*, finally landing where I'm supposed to be and owning who I am.

I grab my bag from behind the counter, pull my jacket on, flip the sign on the door to *closed*, and hop into my car.

Gavin and Auggie's downtown rehab project is almost complete. The street is lined with improved storefronts, and businesses are renting every available space now, including my mom's new office and Santos Brothers Architecture on the corner.

Which makes it rather convenient for Gavin and me to grab lunch together and steal a few kisses down that alley beside his office afterward.

As I pull my car into Bear Creek, excitement crests through my chest. My tires crunch over the snow until I park beside Gavin's truck.

At the back of the property sits the little cabin where we fell in love. Where that one night turned into forever in the most beautiful way. Where we found our homes together.

We spent a year and a half in that cabin while our house was being built, and I loved every moment of that coziness. But it has been nice to spread out into our new one over the last few months.

I turn off the car and scan the tree farm for Gavin, eager for that little skip in my heartbeat when I'm near him.

And when my gaze lands on the bakery steps, my pulse skitters like I expected it to.

Black coat over broad shoulders, forest-green hat that Luci knit him over his head, and two coffee cups in his hands.

I get out of the car in a daze, and as he steps forward, his focus lands on me, and a wide smile lifts his cheeks.

My lighthouse. My love. My Gavin, with that endearing glint in his eyes.

When he reaches me, his masculine pine scent wraps around me, and like an instinctual response, my body relaxes. He presses a long, soft kiss to my lips with a sigh.

"I missed you. How are you both?" he whispers, offering me a cup. Then his free hand lands reverently on my stomach.

"We're perfect now." I grin at him as I sip my sweet peppermint coffee.

He leans down to kiss my jacket-covered belly. "Good. We've got a tree to pick."

When he wraps his arm around my shoulders, I pull his mug toward me and smell its contents. "How's that peppermint mocha?" I tease.

He winks as he guides me toward the rest of our group. "Delicious."

***

Gavin

Okay. What's your favorite number?" Lena asks, tying the cranberry-red scarf around Julia's head.

To her credit, Julia looks completely trusting as Lena blindfolds her, even though she's never seen this tradition before.

Last year was my turn. At forty years old, I let Lena wrap a scarf around my eyes, and while I tried to convince everyone that two was my favorite number, Lena made me pick ten.

Ten for the number of years it took us to realize where our hearts truly belonged.

"Nine," Julia says confidently.

"That's a good number," Penelope tells her, folding their hands together.

A smile stretches over Lena's beautiful face. She winks at me and asks, "How many times should we spin her, Gav?"

Julia giggles, squirming in her spot.

Since her adoption was finalized three months ago, she has blossomed more than I ever could've imagined. Lena and I spent a lot of time with her before the adoption, but having her home with us now is a dream come true.

Have I baked homemade cinnamon rolls every Saturday at her request? Maybe.

Have I let her become addicted to decaf peppermint mochas right along with the rest of us? Possibly.

Have I let her and Lena paint murals across her bedroom walls in our brand-new cabin? Yeah, I did that.

Do I regret any of it? Absolutely not.

She has me wrapped around her finger.

Well, they both do. And there's about to be a third family member who I can't say no to.

"Spin her ninety-seven times. Once for every day she's lived with us," I say, ruffling the top of Julia's head.

"Uncle Gavin," Pen scolds as Julia squeals, "Okay!"

Lena's raspy laugh caresses my ears as she starts spinning Julia slowly. "One, two, ninety-five . . ."

For the last two years, my heart has felt like someone's taken a defibrillator to it and jump-started *life* into the muscle fibers.

Family. Friends. Community. Laughter. All the things I had been missing for years are now surrounding me every day.

And I have one person to thank for it.

The woman who made all of this happen by choosing me. By wanting to be by my side. By fighting to hold my hand through life.

She's given me everything I ever hoped for but never actually thought I could have.

Lena steadies Julia's shoulders and positions her toward the field. "Ninth tree. Pen, are you keeping count?"

Penelope nods, and Lena releases Julia as she stumbles toward the first tree. Giggles fill the air as Pen, Jack, and little Noah follow her, Auggie hot on his heels to catch him when he inevitably falls in the snow.

Lena reaches for her cup and tucks herself under my arm as we follow the group.

And like they always do when she's near, my muscles loosen and my heart relaxes in my chest. Like she was the missing piece, and she's finally back in her spot against my body.

* * *

THE CRACKLE OF the fire fills the living room as I pick up the boxes from our evening of decorating the tree. There's finally silence upstairs, which means my girls are done giggling, and Julia is settling down for bed.

Our massive windows overlook the woods behind our house, and tonight they reflect the glow from the fire and the colorful lights from our scraggly tree.

We wanted our house right in the middle of the forest, and while Auggie and Zara's place is only a short walk away, ours isn't visible through the woods at the back of the property.

The two-story cabin has an open floor plan, porches in every direction, and, of course, a hot tub on the back deck.

It's everything I dreamed of.

But in my dreams all those years ago, it wasn't filled with the bright laughter and family that it is now.

Those are details I never could've imagined would be possible back then.

But Lena has made my life better than any dream.

Cub's nails click on the hardwood floors as he follows my wife down the stairs. Our rescue pup has barely left her side since she got pregnant, and some evenings I have to force him off the couch to get to cuddle with her.

Tonight Lena bypasses the couch, walking right to where I'm standing beside the Christmas tree and sliding her hand into mine.

I turn her around and pull her closer until her back rests against my chest. "Dance with me, Mrs. Santos?" I whisper.

"Always, Mr. Santos." She tilts her head, leaning into my body as I slide my hands over her belly.

I sweep her hair over one shoulder and bury my face in her neck. "Only a few more weeks," I murmur. "Then we get to meet this little one."

She hums as we sway our hips to the silent beat. "I can't wait to see you holding a baby again. That's part of what got me into this mess in the first place, but I'm still feral for it."

I huff a laugh, skating my lips over her pulse. "Thank you for giving me all of this. Do you know how much I love you?"

She lifts a hand and grazes her nails over my scalp, sending chills racing up my spine. "Yeah, but tell me again."

"I love you, little menace."

And they're the easiest words I've ever said.

Bonus Epilogue

Lena

Eight Months Later

I wish you were here." I sigh as I drop onto the bed, cradling the phone so I can still see Gavin's face on the screen. "It was a long day, and all I want to do is cuddle and fall asleep with you."

His lips thin as he studies me. "I wish I was right there beside you." The dim lamp light in his hotel room plays over his features, casting golden lines across his cheekbones and dark shadows around his eyes.

He looks tired. Weary. Ready to come home.

I'm pretty sure he's in Idaho right now. I think that's what he told me before he left five days ago, but I was balancing a flailing seven-month-old Bowie on my hip, trying to clean him up, as Gavin wiped up the mashed avocado Bowie had just thrown all over the kitchen. All while we were simultaneously trying to pack Julia's lunch for her first day of fourth grade.

Yeah, Idaho *seems* right, but it's too late to admit I'm not sure.

Santos Brothers Architecture is thriving, and Gavin and Auggie are frequently doing site visits to small towns all over the Pacific Northwest, helping them plan renovations to their historic buildings and downtowns.

This is their third work trip of the summer, and while I'm elated that their business is doing well, the ache of missing Gavin is sharp and constant. Between getting Julia to school, dropping Bowie off at my mom's, and working at the art studio, the last five days have somehow both flown by and moved at a glacial pace.

"How was your day?" he asks.

"Pretty good. We took our senior class outside this morning, which was adorable. A bunch of sixty- and seventy-year-olds, painting wildflowers while their sun hats flapped the breeze." I shrug. "I'm telling you, you'd fit right in with that crew. Your sprinkle of gray hair wouldn't stand out at all," I add with a laugh.

The creases around his eyes deepen with a smile. "I enjoy my *personal* painting lessons in *your* studio so much more."

His low tone arcs right through the phone and into the pit of my stomach. I feel my cheeks warm as I remember his last one-on-one painting lesson, when more paint made it onto our bodies than either of the canvases.

Gavin designed and built me a beautiful studio at the edge of the woods. It's just far enough from the house to feel like my own personal oasis, where I can concentrate on what I'm creating.

I adore my alone time out there, free of distraction.

But I adore that space even more when Gavin comes to visit.

"How's Julia?" he asks, drawing me out of the studio memories. "Has she tried the bike again?"

I shake my head. "It's still sitting by the shed. Hasn't moved an inch."

He drags a hand through his hair. "Oh, man," he sighs, shutting his eyes briefly. "I'm scared I don't know how to help her."

Julia has been trying to learn to ride a bike all summer. Penelope and Jack have ridden their bikes to the playground in our neighborhood a few times a week over the last few months, and they always invite Julia to go with them.

But Pen and Jack mastered riding their bikes years ago, and I think it hits Julia really hard that her younger cousin has figured it out, but she hasn't.

She has put on a brave face for us and tried her best, but as soon as it's time to lift her feet and balance on her own, her doubt takes over and she crumples into tears.

Gavin and I have been trying to support her and help her figure it out without adding any pressure. She just wants to master it so much, and it's heartbreaking to watch her get scared.

"I wish she believed in herself as much as we do." His eyes seem to cloud over, as though he's searching his memories for a solution. Then he blinks it away and tilts his wrist up to check his watch. "Can I talk to her? Is she still awake? It's, what, nine there?"

"She's having a sleepover with Pen tonight," I say apologetically. "So she's probably awake, but not here. Want to try calling Zara or Auggie?"

His lips twist. "That's okay. I'll be there tomorrow, and maybe she and I can work on it this weekend." His gaze travels over my face before catching on mine again. "Did you all have a good night?"

"Yeah. Zara and I organized a first-week-of-school spa night for the girls, and Auggie took Noah, Jack, and Bowie over to my mom's for a few hours." I perch my chin on my hand and turn

my face side to side. "Can you tell? We did face masks and mani-
cures and watched *The Princess Diaries*." I present my nails in
front of the phone for him to see the perfectly imperfect blue
polish.

Gavin grins. "They look fantastic. What color did Julia pick?"

"I've been sworn to secrecy until you come home to see them,"
I inform him, flashing a smug grin.

"Okay." He laughs. "Should I be frightened?"

"Let's just say, she picked out the polish thinking it might fit
your vibe to a tcc."

He nods. "Noted. Did Bowie get his nails done too?"

"No, sadly. By the time Auggie brought the boys back, Bowie
was falling apart. He was sobbing when I went to grab him, and
then the little stinker snatched a cookie right out of my hand and
shoved the whole thing in his mouth." I shake my head remembering his wide, teary eyes and full chipmunk cheeks. "I had to
pull it all out so he didn't choke on his first cookie ever."

Laughter bubbles out of Gavin. "Poor guy was *hungry*."

"He's the hungriest child I've ever known." I flick my gaze to
the ceiling, thinking through what I've fed him this week. "He's
gone through all the sweet potatoes and peas you made. And I
think we have one more serving of carrots left."

"I'll make more next time. I didn't expect him to go through all
of it." His expression softens. "Did I miss anything? Has he said
mama yet?"

I shake my head, trying to keep my expression cheerful.

Bowie says two words right now: Juju and Dada. And, yeah,
I'm a little devastated that he isn't saying *Mama* yet. But I still
love seeing Julia's and Gavin's faces light up every time he says
their names.

"Can I see him?" Gavin whispers shyly.

"Bowie?"

"Yeah. I know he's asleep, but can I just peek at him?"

I smile as I stand from the bed. "Of course."

Cub lets out a groan as he stands to follow me out of the bedroom and up the stairs to Bowie's door. I turn and whisper to him to stay right there, and he sits obediently, tilting his head to watch as I turn the handle quietly. Then I press a finger over my lips where Gavin can see, and he nods in understanding, with a wide smile brightening his face.

I click on the dim strand of star lights that hang over Bowie's dresser for late-night diaper changes, then pad over to the crib where our baby is sleeping soundly on his back. His arms are spread wide, his lips parted as he exhales heavy, steady breaths that border on snores. He has his head turned to the side, one chubby little cheek squished into the mattress.

For a moment, I consider getting into the crib to sleep beside him for the night. Julia isn't here for the normal slumber party we have when Gavin's gone, where we stay up giggling way past her bedtime.

Bowie is sleeping so soundly, though, and I'm pretty sure it's illegal to wake a baby, so I stay on my side of the crib railing.

After turning the camera, I dip the phone down into the crib so Gavin can see him.

A raw ache grips my chest when Gavin's face contorts. A crease forms between his brows and his lips press together tightly. He leans closer to the phone, his gaze bouncing all over his view of our baby.

Bowie hiccups a little sigh in his sleep and smacks his lips adorably.

"Hey, little guy. I miss you," Gavin whispers, so softly I almost don't hear it. The corners of his mouth quiver. "I'll be home tomorrow. Be sweet to your mama until then."

* * *

"Do you think they're burning?" Julia asks, nibbling at her thumb nail as she turns to me.

Kneeling beside her in front of the oven, I glide my palm between her shoulder blades and peer in the window at the cinnamon rolls she and I made. "No, sweetie, they look perfect. I think a few more minutes, and we can take them out."

She slides her hands down her thighs. "Okay. I'll stay here and wait."

"I'll stay right here with you then," I reply, kissing the top of her head.

When Julia came in the door a couple hours ago after her sleepover with Pen, she told me she wanted to surprise Gavin with cinnamon rolls. I'll admit, my first instinct was to tell her I didn't know how, that I didn't think we could do it as well as he could.

But. We're in a family quest to teach her how to believe in herself, so I smashed those thoughts immediately and gave her (and myself) a very excited pep talk.

I may have also snuck into the bathroom and called Millie for a few tips on cinnamon roll baking.

"Juju!" Bowie calls for his sister as he scoots around the kitchen island to find us on the floor.

He's mastering that pre-crawling wiggly movement and he's surprisingly quick. If his sister is going somewhere, he'll find a way to catch up with her.

Julia adjusts to sit cross-legged and pulls him into her lap. All three of us stare at the oven window.

"Juju?" he says, his voice pitching up at the end like a question. He blinks his big brown eyes up at me.

"Yes." I run my hand over his short, dark curls. "Juju made cinnamon rolls to surprise Dada."

"Dada?" he asks, turning his head to search the kitchen for him.

"No, Dada's not here yet."

"Dada," Bowie repeats, but this time it sounds more like a squeal. He flings himself out of Julia's lap and wiggle-crawls past where I'm kneeling.

Julia and I turn to follow his path and find two black dress shoes waiting at the edge of the kitchen.

We both gasp, and my stomach flips as Gavin sits on the floor. Bowie climbs into his arms and presses his face into his dad's neck, giggling and babbling as Gavin shuts his eyes. Julia crouches next to his other arm and he squeezes both of them to his chest.

Murmured words I can't make out pass between them, and my heart feels so full that I think it might burst. I want to hug him, kiss him, be in his arms. But I also want to just stand here, watching him hug our children with so much unbridled joy.

He pours his love into that hug, into their hearts. All the love no one showed him as a child, and yet he knows exactly how to show it to them. He spends every moment with them making sure they will *never* doubt their home like he did growing up.

There are plenty of times when we worry that we're not teaching the right lessons, or we don't feel confident in the words we're supposed to say. Learning to trust our abilities as parents is a daily struggle that we may never master.

But we both know the most important thing we can offer Julia and Bowie: a safe home and more love than we ever thought possible.

When Gavin's eyes drift open to find mine, his are glassy on the edges.

I crawl toward him and cup his face between my palms. His skin on mine anchors me, rejuvenates me in a way that nothing else can. With the tips of his fingers, he grips my shirt and pulls me closer until somehow all three of us are in his arms or on his lap, in one tangled, happy mess of laughter.

"It's so good to be home." He sighs against the shell of my ear.

We stay there on the floor together, catching up and talking, until the timer for the cinnamon rolls reminds me of their existence.

Gavin's chuckle follows me as I jump up to grab the hot pads and open the oven.

"Julia made them," I announce, dancing my brows as I hold the pan out for Gavin to see. "Don't they look amazing?"

He grins down at her. "Are you kidding? They look perfect," he confirms.

A pink blush creeps over her cheeks. "Thanks."

While I ice the cinnamon rolls, Julia gets herself a glass of milk and follows Gavin as he takes Bowie to the living room. I listen to the squeals of laughter that usually accompany Gavin tossing him into the air and catching him perfectly, Julia giggling and cheering them on.

As I'm sliding a cinnamon roll onto a plate, strong arms fold around me from behind and Gavin presses his lips to the side of my neck. "Hey, little menace," he murmurs. "I missed you."

Julia and Bowie's playful cries echo from the living room. I set the spatula down and grip his forearms, leaning my head back against his chest. "I missed you too."

When I turn my head to stare into his whiskey eyes, his warm hand slides to my jaw. He brings his lips to mine and kisses me in a way that says a million things all at once. Slow and thorough and soft.

I want you. I need you. Thank you for keeping everything together when I'm gone. You're everything to me.

A content sigh drifts out of me as he deepens the kiss, and I turn in his embrace. His fingers thread into my hair, his other hand spanning my lower back, pressing me close. My body arches until we're flush together, my arms winding around his neck and my heart thrumming wildly.

I wonder if there's time for me to tug him into the extra-large pantry he designed for us. We've stolen many fierce kisses behind those doors over the years, and it's even more thrilling every time.

But before I can steer us in that direction, he draws back, his eyes brimming with heat. "We'll continue that later," he whispers, brushing one more lingering kiss over my lips.

"Ewww," Julia groans as she walks into the kitchen.

Gavin laughs against my mouth. "Tonight, you're mine," he promises, just for me to hear, before grabbing the plates to bring them to the table.

And my heart skips right after him.

* * *

IF THERE'S ONE thing I've learned about myself since the Christmas I fell in love with Gavin, it's that I have a thing for watching him cuddle babies. That December, I got to see him with Noah every day, and it prompted a reaction in my heart and brain that I didn't know was possible.

But now? It's *so much worse.*

Now, it's *our* baby he's holding, and I'm pretty sure it's the hottest thing I've ever seen.

And then, combine Gavin-holding-a-baby with literally any other activity?

I'm a goner. I'm done. My ovaries are mush.

Right now, Bowie is taking his afternoon nap strapped to his dad's chest, while Gavin sweeps the back porch. He has also done some hot tub maintenance, fixed a broken hinge on the shed door, vacuumed and mopped the entire kitchen, and sat patiently on the patio while Julia painted his nails black, to match hers.

I'm supposed to be using this time to relax, read, or take a bath, as Gavin instructed. But instead, I've just let my brain melt, sipping an iced coffee and watching his every move out the back window.

If I wasn't already on board to try for another baby, this would do it.

Gavin finishes sweeping and walks to the shed to put away the broom. When he reemerges, he stares down at the bright orange bike leaning against the wall. His gaze flicks to Julia, who is on the porch, painting in her watercolor book.

He calls something in her direction, and she looks over her shoulder at him. Nodding toward the bike, his mouth moves again, but I can't hear what he says from inside the house.

Julia's paintbrush twirls in her grip as she seems to weigh her options. When she calls something back in his direction, a grin breaks out over his face.

Nerves flutter through my stomach as I watch her close her watercolors and walk toward Gavin, Cub trotting along behind her. Gavin places a hand on the back of Bowie's head as he leans over to steer the bike toward the edge of the paved driveway.

I chug the last few sips of my coffee before shoving my feet into my sandals and hurrying out the back door to meet them.

Julia clips a helmet on, casting an unsure glare toward the bicycle. "It's too loose," she tells Gavin, sliding the helmet back and forth to show him.

"Okay. I'll fix it." Gavin kneels in front of her to tighten the strap under her chin, his striking black nails standing out against Julia's blond hair.

Bowie babbles as he tries to shove his fingers in his dad's mouth.

"Hey, Bow." I laugh as I approach and pull his fingers away. "Personal space, dude." Then I ask Gavin, "Want me to take him? Might make this easier."

Gavin kisses the top of his son's head before unbuckling the strap at his shoulders and passing him to me. I lean Bowie's back against my front so he can see what's happening and step to the edge of the driveway.

With the baby carrier still hanging from his waist, Gavin crouches back down beside Julia and looks up at her. "Okay, can you tell me what part makes you nervous?" he asks, holding her hands.

Her lips twist to the side and she blinks a few times. "I don't know. Falling? Getting hurt?"

Something in my chest tugs at me to walk over and comfort her, but I keep myself in place. Gavin can do it. I know he can.

He strokes his thumb over the back of her hand. "I get that." He nods. "But see, I've learned something about you."

"What?"

"You are one of the most resilient people I know."

Her shoulders lift in a shrug. "What does *resilient* mean?"

His throat shifts. "It means you've gotten hurt before. More than you should've," he says softly, tucking a strand of hair behind her shoulder. "But you fought back. You are strong and fierce"— he blinks toward me with a small grin—"like your mom. And I *know* that even if you fall, you'll be okay, because we're right here to help you. That's what family is for. When you stumble or you feel unsure, we're right there for you. We can pick you back up and brush off your knees and cheer for you when you're ready to try again. And we'll be there as many times as you need." His voice cracks as he continues, "You're not alone anymore if you get hurt, okay? We'll always be right here."

My body surges forward, all the emotions crashing into me at once. I can't stay away anymore. I physically have to get closer to them. My heart demands it.

Bowie calls, "Juju juju," until we reach his sister. Her lashes are damp as I lean forward to let him leave a slobbery, open-mouth kiss on her cheek.

"Thanks, Bow." She laughs, wiping it off on her shoulder before taking a deep, steadying breath.

I bend to meet her eyes. "You've got this, sweetie. I believe in you."

Gavin stands and plants a kiss on Bowie's head and then mine before we walk back to the edge of the driveway. He helps Julia get into position on the bike. She stares down the driveway, a mixture of confidence and anxiety pulling at her features, but when Gavin murmurs something to her, she nods quickly.

I pull my phone out of my pocket and start taking a video, holding it just out of Bowie's reach when he tries to snatch it from me.

Gavin counts her down, keeping one hand on the back of her seat and one on the handlebars. And then she lifts her feet and he's jogging and she's pedaling, and Bowie is squealing like he understands it all while my heart jumps into my throat.

"Okay," Julia shouts, a quiver in her voice.

Gavin's hand drops away and he slows to a stop. Julia wobbles, the bike trembles. Her foot slips off one pedal, and she topples to the ground, skidding on her thigh.

I'm running before she even fully comes to stop, Bowie bouncing in my arms and my hair whipping my cheeks.

Gavin reaches her first, tugging the bike away from her body and helping her off the ground.

Cub reaches her second. He licks at her cheeks and nuzzles at her hand.

By the time I crouch before her, tears are drifting down her pink cheeks, and she's trying so hard to be brave, despite her fall.

"It's okay. It's okay," Gavin murmurs as his hands trace over her shoulders, arms, ribs.

Julia's lashes flutter as she looks between the four of us. Gavin kneeling in front of her, Cub sniffing all over her, Bowie stretching his arms out for her, and me wiping her tears from her cheeks.

She swallows hard and reaches out for her brother's hand. Her mouth curves into a small smile before she says, "Well, that was the farthest I've ever gone."

A surprised spark of laughter bursts from me and Gavin.

His wide eyes meet mine for a beat before he looks back to Julia. "See? Resilient."

"You did amazing," I confirm, blinking back tears.

Gavin's smile is luminous. "You had it for a few seconds there. I bet you can do it again."

"I can probably do it even longer this time," she says, straightening her shoulders.

Is it physically possible for my heart to burst at the seams? That's what it feels like is happening right now. I've never been prouder in my life than this moment, watching our daughter find confidence in herself.

She reaches for the bike, and Gavin helps her get situated again, casting me shocked glances every few seconds.

When she's in position, we all kiss her again, and then Bowie and I back away to give them some room. I point the camera toward her and she gives Gavin a definitive nod before she pushes off with her feet.

They hit the pedals exactly right. Gavin nudges her forward with a hand on the seat, running to give her the momentum she needs to keep her balance. The pedals turn as she coasts down the driveway.

"I got it," Julia shouts. "Let go."

Gavin keeps a hand on the back of her seat, still running alongside her.

"Let go," she repeats with a laugh, and he finally releases his grip.

He keeps running beside the bike, arms swinging at his sides, his laughter bouncing down the driveway for me to hear. "You're doing it!" He slows to a stop, letting her keep riding as he looks back at me. "She's doing it!"

She cackles with glee as she pedals down the driveway, steady and solid.

"You got this!" I yell, my voice cracking.

As she reaches the loop in our driveway, she turns smoothly, keeping her balance. She circles around the pavement until I can see her face.

Her proud, surprised expression shines brighter than the sun.

Gavin jogs his way back to me and Bowie with flushed cheeks and damp lashes. "She did it," he breathes. "Goddamn, she did it."

As I lower the phone, he kisses us both. He loops an arm over my shoulders as we watch Julia start another loop around.

"Next step, driving lessons," I say, leaning my head into the crook of his shoulder.

He groans. "Nope. I can't handle that."

"Dadadada," Bowie chants, squirming in my arms to reach out for him.

Gavin rubs his nose against Bowie's before wrapping his hands around his son's ribs and pulling him into his chest. "You want me? You're already sick of Mama?" he asks, flashing me a taunting grin.

He flips Bowie around to face me, and their matching eyes look my way.

Then Bowie reaches for me and says, "Mama mamama."

Gavin's lips part on a gasp. "You heard that right?"

"Did you say mama?" I ask in disbelief, pulling him back into my arms.

"Mama mama," he repeats with his gummy little smile.

Tears burn behind my eyes as I hold Bowie up in the air. He giggles and kicks his feet. "That's right, Bow, I'm your mama!"

I squeeze him to my chest and Gavin steps behind me, wrapping his arms around us, and curving his head over my shoulder. We watch Julia make another loop around the driveway, a bit faster this time.

"Feels good to have you home," I say, leaning my head against his.

"Home," he sighs, turning his lips to my cheek. "There isn't a better feeling in the world."

Acknowledgments

𝓕rom the bottom of my heart, thank you for reading Lena and Gavin's story. Dear readers, it is because of you that my books get to reach new heights, and I couldn't be more thankful. You all have made my dreams come true and I wish I could hug every one of you!

I want to thank my husband for helping keep our family sane when I was hidden in an editing cave and forgetting the rest of the world. Thank you for forcing me to go outside when I needed a break. I appreciate you more than you'll ever know.

To my girls, who are my biggest cheerleaders. I couldn't have accomplished this without your help. You all believe in me harder than anyone else in the world, and it's such a privilege to watch you grow.

To Priyanka and the entire team at Avon and HarperCollins, thank you for welcoming me with open arms and helping me find a home with you all. I'm still pinching myself over the fact that I have such a dream team of people to work with, and I can't wait to see where this wild ride takes us together. Thank you endlessly for all that you do and all the fantastic things to come!

Lauren, my agent and superhero, I couldn't have made it here without your enthusiasm and encouragement. Thank you for your guidance through this process and your patience when I had a million questions and for letting me borrow a little of your assuredness when my brain was spiraling.

Mom, I hope you listened to me about the increased spice level and didn't read this book. But in case you did, thank you for always being proud of me, even when I write books with sex in them. Hopefully, that continues to be true after this particular one.

Brooklyn, thank you for all your hard work transforming my messy draft into this complete story! I couldn't have done it without your guidance and friendship. I'm so sorry about those things you had to Google while editing this book. Hopefully, you've cleared your browser history so no one asks questions.

A very extra-special thank-you goes to Ada. This book wouldn't be where it is without your friendship, encouragement, and emotional support. You make me feel less alone in the world, and I'm so grateful this little corner of the internet brought us together. Thank you for listening to many hours' worth of unhinged voice memos about everything from mugs that suddenly go missing in a scene to how to make Gavin's dirty talk the hottest. Drafting Daddy™ is yours, and also, you're stuck with me forever.

Wren, thank you for loving my books from day one. I feel lucky every day that you believed in me so early in my writing career. I'm so fortunate to have you in corner, sharing about your love of my books and helping me turn this story into the best version it could possibly be. I promise to keep shoving all your favorite microtropes into books forever.

Cristina, thank you so much for sharing your Brazilian culture with me. All the little touches you helped me add to this story made Lena's family feel so authentic, and I appreciate all your personal details that I've gotten to put into the Santos clan. You are such a fantastic friend and support system, and I can never thank you enough.

Kristen, thank you for reading my book in its early stages and making sure everything was accurate and fact-checked. I appreciate you so much.

To my beta readers, Erin, Tabitha, Lauren Brooke, Heidi, and Kae, thank you to the moon and back. I'm so grateful you took the time to read my book and leave me comments and make me laugh. You are all wonderful humans, and I can't wait to meet you in real life one day and hug you!

Finally, to you, dear reader, thank you a million times. I appreciate you believing in me and reading my stories and sharing them with the world. It's completely surreal that I get to write love stories for a living, and you all make it possible. Thank you forever and ever.

Read on for a preview of Jillian Meadows's next romance . . .

GIVE ME BUTTERFLIES

Chapter 1

Millie

I'm a generous person who made a dreadful mistake, and that old man in the white Skechers is making me pay for it.

I held the door for him as he walked into Maggie's Bakery because, apparently, I have a weakness in my heart for the sweet-grandpa type. But he betrayed me by ordering the last almond croissant from one spot in front of me in line, and I've never had such horrendous thoughts in my life.

There are two things I require to have a successful first day of the week: any form of caffeinated coffee and an almond croissant.

Both of those things were essential today because impostor syndrome is a real bitch, and caffeine and an almond croissant would have given me the sugar rush I need to distract me from it.

The living fossil across the coffee shop takes a bite of that buttery, flaky croissant, and I want to fight him for it.

Put us in an arena to battle for the last one. I bet I could beat him.

Or maybe not. He has a hint of muscle under that brown sweater vest.

"We have to learn to make croissants at home," I mutter

around a bite of my consolation blueberry muffin, my eyes laser-focused on the Croissant Crook. "I can't live like this."

Lena waves her rainbow-tipped nails in front of me, pulling my attention back to her caramel eyes. "Stop staring daggers at that poor man." She grabs my face and squeezes my cheeks until my lips pucker out. "Eat your muffin. Raise your blood sugar a little so you can bring back nice Millie."

The grinder whirs behind the counter, refreshing the espresso aroma around us as I reluctantly nibble at the muffin. My leg bounces under the table, giving away the anxiety that's been running through my veins all morning.

Lena notices, and her foot nudges mine until I meet her gaze. "Don't worry about your week. You're going to walk in there with your head high and show them you deserve the department director position."

I resist the urge to roll my eyes. Anyone with anxiety knows that someone telling you not to worry is about as helpful as a hangnail.

Today is my first chance to participate in a meeting that Calvin, my freshly retired boss and previous head of the entomology department, would normally attend. While he's off vacationing with his wife, enjoying the life of a man without job obligations, I will be attending the meeting with the heads of every department at the Wilhelmina Natural Science Museum.

And then tomorrow, I have an interview for Calvin's position.

My leg twitches restlessly again under the table just thinking about it.

"I wish I could put you in my pocket and bring you with me," I tell Lena, taking a sip of my Americano. "You can coach me through the day and remind me how amazing I am."

"You've got this. You don't need me, although being your personal Polly Pocket sounds like a blast." She purses her bright red lips and perches her chin on her fist. "Can you get me the beach house with the dolphin and sea turtle? I've always wanted that one."

"Of course." I take another bite of my muffin, hoping it will settle my whirling stomach.

"Will it be the back pocket or the front? Because your cute ass would be way more comfortable."

I can't help but laugh. "Definitely the back. You'll need the bigger pockets for all those accessories you're requesting."

* * *

MY FLATS SQUEAK on the buffed floors as I walk into the Wilhelmina Natural Science Museum, trying my best not to spill the rest of my Americano while I readjust the large bag on my shoulder. The skies are gracing us with a cloudless summer day in Washington, and the bright entryway sparkles in the sunlight streaming through the large windows. Octavius, our massive fossilized *Quetzalcoatlus*, hangs from the ceiling, its broad wings and sharp teeth suspended over the museum's visitors as they enter.

Eleanor waves from her circular reception desk, her round cheeks lifted in a grin. "Good morning, Millie. Love your dress today. Looks like something I would've worn in the seventies," she says, standing to look over the counter.

"Thank you." I set my coffee on her desk and turn in a slow circle, letting her scan the vintage dress with small butterflies on the collar. "Lena and I took a break from our *Gilmore Girls* marathon this weekend to visit one of our favorite resale shops," I tell her as I come to a stop. "I found it hidden behind a thick rack of old jeans."

Eleanor nods as she sits back down. "That sounds like a wonderful weekend."

"It was," I say with a smile. "How was yours?"

"Honey, I don't think I've told you about my new book boy-friend," she whispers with a mischievous glint in her eyes.

I taught her the term "book boyfriend" a few weeks ago when she was gushing about the hero in her historical romance. She has a book club with some other widows in her neighborhood, and I love to get recommendations from them. Their standards of men are top-tier.

She launches into her weekend read and has me laughing about the audacity of the brooding duke and his love affair with a scullery maid until she suddenly stops.

Her eyes flare behind her glasses.

"Well, you better get to your meeting. I don't want you to be late." She's a little too eager as she nudges my coffee cup toward me. "Don't worry, I'll tell you all about the duke next time. You've got places to be."

"Okay." My gaze narrows as she waves her hands in my direction, clearly shooing me away. When I have everything balanced again, I spin toward my office.

But I smack right into a wall of muscle, and the scent of sage and soap invades my senses.

Two big hands wrap around my arms to steady me, and my coffee cup is crushed between our bodies before it splatters to the ground.

"Oh, dear . . ." Eleanor squeaks behind me, but there's a satis-fied lilt to it.

A sigh of defeat leaves my lungs, and I drop my forehead to the crisp white shirt before me. *A moment of silence for the spilled coffee at my feet.* My sanity will be hanging by a thread without that Americano.

Liquid seeps through my dress and into my bra, snapping me back to the reality. I pull away and find a dark stain covering the top of my dress. So much for making a good impression this morning.

My eyes are reluctantly drawn to the gray tie in front of me. Planets run down the line of fabric, and a little splash of coffee stains the blue of Neptune.

Shit. Pins and needles creep up my spine in recognition. I know for a fact that this tie belongs to a man with a gorgeous face, but his permanent scowl ruins the appeal for me.

I swallow, trying to wet my dry throat. There's no hiding from this run-in, so I plaster on my brightest smile and muster the courage to look up.

Past the tie, up the strong column of throat, over the short, trimmed beard, and into . . . stormy blue eyes behind black-rimmed glasses.

My stomach drops at the crease between his dark brows and the tense line of his mouth.

Dr. Finn Ashford has glowered at me every time we've made eye contact, but this time is the most severe.

All the air seems to vanish from the museum as I realize how wrong I was. The scowl doesn't ruin the appeal for me at all. The director of the astronomy department is still more attractive than should be legal for a man with his general demeanor.

Our lives are a wealth of opposites. My job delves into small, up-close discoveries right under our feet, while his focuses on enormous, faraway things humans may never reach.

We are microscopes versus telescopes. Smiles versus scowls. Warm versus frigid.

Was there ever a chance for us to find common ground?

Goose bumps skitter up my neck as his breath moves the hairs that have escaped my braid.

He seems to remember his hands are around my arms and

quickly drops them, making me stumble back a step. He spreads his fingers wide, flexing them by his sides before shoving them in his pockets.

The distance allows me to take a deep breath and let the replenished oxygen fill my lungs. "Sorry," I mutter, looking at the coffee on his tie.

"Yeah." He lowers his head and rubs his fingers over Neptune like he can brush away the stain.

His clipped tone makes me grind my teeth together.

The nerve of this guy. The *audacity*.

"This isn't *all* my fault," I say, my pulse quickening with irritation. "You're the one hovering so close. You should have given me a back massage while you were there."

His scowl remains, but his gaze jumps to my hair, my cheeks, and then my mouth before it snaps back to my eyes as he clears his throat. "Shouldn't you be working instead of chatting with Eleanor about dukes and secret affairs?"

That raises my hackles, and my usual conflict avoidance turns to dust in the wind as I spit the first thing that comes to mind. "Shouldn't you be rewatching *Star Trek* so you have something educated to say at work today?"

A ghost of a smirk flashes across Finn's mouth before he can contain it. It's the most positive reaction I've ever gotten from him.

I think it would be a point in my column if we were keeping score.

His jaw works as he narrows his gaze. "I'm more of a *Star Wars* guy, actually."

My laugh turns to a very unladylike snort when I try to stifle it. That would be a point for him. Damn it.

Finn crosses his arms like he's preparing for battle. "I need to speak with Eleanor. I could already be done with that if I hadn't had to wait for you two to finish talking."

I fold my arms over my chest to match him and meet his eyes. Having to crane my neck to look at him probably makes me less intimidating than I'd hoped, but I mirror his facial expression and body language anyway. "Oh, please. Do forgive us *women* for being *friendly* to each other and asking about our weekends. Not everyone can barge through the doors like Kylo Ren, with a cape floating behind them, and glower at every person who crosses their path."

This time, he has to bite his lips to hide his amusement, but I still get a peek at it. "Have you been watching me walk in every morning?" He tilts his head and arches an eyebrow.

I choke on my breath, and I hate that this is another point for him in a battle he's unaware of.

A few people shuffle past us to start their workday, quiet murmurs echoing through the wide halls of the museum, but our eyes stay pinned on each other. We are two opposing officers waiting for surrender or blood.

His gaze drops to my mouth for one small blip before it snaps back up. "May I speak to Eleanor now, or do you all need to continue analyzing how handsome the duke is?"

I guess it's blood, then.

A growl sneaks out of me, and I clench my fists like a toddler, feeling no shame in it. I don't know who pissed in his Cheerios this morning, but he should be taking it out on them instead of me.

"Absolutely. Be my guest," I grind out through clenched teeth, waving him forward.

He bends to grab my coffee cup and gives me a crisp nod before stepping past me to Eleanor's desk.

* * *

THIS HAND DRYER is no help. My green dress still has a dark stain running over it.

Anxiety fills my stomach with a familiar queasiness, dissolving the courage I had built up for this meeting. Can I be taken seriously looking like a barista's hand towel?

The minimal confidence I'd had is now in a puddle of coffee on the floor.

I look back at my reflection and groan at the sight of my cheeks, which are still pink from my run-in with Finn.

Every time I have been in the vicinity of that man, I've left wondering what the hell I did to deserve the looks he directed my way. During my first week at the museum, I held the elevator for him while he stalked toward it looking at his phone. When he finally glanced up, his navy eyes searched my face and the empty elevator behind me.

He stepped back with a scowl and mumbled, "I'll get the next one."

A few weeks later, Calvin and I were in his office going through plant orders for the butterfly vivarium, when in walked Dr. Black Hole with another scowl. He adjusted his glasses and glared my way. "I need to speak with Calvin privately," he said, his attention dropping to his phone while I picked up my things. I had to turn sideways to slide past him in the doorway while he stood there like a statue unable to move out of my way.

As the memories flood my mind, I have the sudden urge to curse him. He deserves some retaliation for the way he's made me feel.

May *his* coffee spill all over him today. May his socks get wet the next time it rains. May his window never roll all the way up, so it makes an annoying whistling sound as he drives for all eternity.

The soft knit sleeves of my sweater brush over my arms as I

tug it on and button it up to cover the coffee stain. Then I inhale a deep breath and watch my cheeks deflate in the mirror.

Mustering pep talks for myself is not my strong suit. Lena is much better at finding the right words. But when I try to channel her confidence, my mind is a blank sheet of paper, with no hint of inspiration for what to fill the page with.

My phone dings with a text, and I pull it out of my bag. I click to open the message and find a crooked selfie of my mom holding a black-and-white duck in our family group chat.

Oaks Folks

Mom: Alfred says good duck today, Millie!

Mom: *It's a pun on the word "luck." Not an autocorrect.

Tess: That's so ducking sweet.

Fabes: Dad is snickering from the kitchen while he reads his texts.

Fabes: He's been writing a response for five ducking minutes.

Dad: Haha. Ducking cute.

Mom: Millie, are you there? Alfred is waiting for a ducking answer.

About the Author

JILLIAN MEADOWS writes cozy love stories that make you swoon, smile, and squeal. She lives thirty miles past The Middle of Nowhere, Texas, with her husband, four wild daughters, two unruly dogs, and her sparkling water addiction. When she's not writing, you can find her devouring a romance novel, playing board games, or enjoying the outdoors with her family.

If you want to learn more about Jillian and her books, please visit jillianmeadowswrites.com or find her on Instagram @jillianmeadowswrites.

LOOK OUT FOR MORE BY
JILLIAN MEADOWS

Coming January 2025, the first book in the Oaks Sisters series

A swoony, steamy STEM romance in which two curators at
a science museum—a handsome but grumpy astronomer and
an anxious but sunshine-y entomologist—realize they are
the perfect match. Equal parts nerdy banter and fiery tension,
it's perfect for fans of Ali Hazelwood and Tessa Bailey.